*BEL* B̴RIDE

...ds of dignity, thoughtfulness, and grace. With admi...... ...rical detail, Shannon McNear has given us a story of quiet deter........... ...........oring of war. Lovers of Civil War–era novel....... ................ ........character explored within these pages."

–Jocelyn Green, author of the Heroines Behind the Lines Civil War series

"Shannon McNear has once again pierced through history, bringing the Civil War to life with accuracy and authenticity. The story of Pearl and Josh will haunt you like a melody carrying through time. You'll find yourself cheering not for one side or the other in the conflict that tore our country apart, but for a Rebel girl and a wounded Yankee soldier to find not only common ground but a foundation for love."

–Denise Weimer, historical romance editor and author of The Georgia Gold Series, The Restoration Trilogy, and *The Witness Tree*

"War is never easy, and sometimes neither is love. *The Rebel Bride* is a poignant peek into the harsh and complicated realities of the Civil War that will sometimes have you weeping and other times leave you with a smile. Either way, you will be touched. Another winner for author Shannon McNear."

–Michelle Griep, Christy Award-winning author of the Once Upon a Dickens Christmas series

"Don't miss *The Rebel Bride*! Through her wonderful lyric prose, Shannon McNear vividly paints the pain and conflict of the Civil War—and the abilit......... .........spirit to overcome heartache and adversity with deep and ......

.......hlarik, author of *Sand Creek Serenade*

"Shannon McNear's *The Rebel Bride* riveted me from the first page. The vividly drawn setting and complex, authentic characters on opposite sides of the Civil War drew me right into the story and gripped me until its end. In the aftermath of the Battle of Chickamauga, the Confederate Mac-Farlanes find themselves forced to house, feed, and nurse wounded enemy soldiers regardless of the loss of three sons in battle against Union forces. The wounded soldiers face an equal dilemma as they have no choice but to depend for their survival on their reluctant hosts' kindness and care. Each side believes that their cause is right and that their opponents are not only in the wrong, but evil. But Pearl MacFarlane and one of the Union soldiers, Joshua Wheeler, find themselves rethinking their prejudices as they begin to understand the other's beliefs and reasons for their actions.

I love *The Rebel Bride*'s emphasis on obeying Jesus' teaching to do good to your enemy no matter what the circumstances. And I love how McNear develops the growing attraction between Pearl and Josh, drawn together by mutual need and a shared faith. Their relationship is at first tentative, then tender, and finally one of heartfelt love and devotion. Throughout the story, McNear powerfully illustrates how deeply complicated the issues were that led to a war that tore apart not only our country but also many families and resulted in hundreds of thousands of deaths. And she answers the far-reaching question of whose side God is on in the conflicts of this fallen world in a profound way that readers will ponder long after finishing *The Rebel Bride*."

–J. M. Hochstetler, author of the American Patriot Series and coauthor with Bob Hostetler of the Northkill Amish Series

# *The Rebel Bride*

*The*
Daughters
*of the*
Mayflower

## SHANNON McNEAR

BARBOUR BOOKS
An Imprint of Barbour Publishing, Inc.

©2019 by Shannon McNear

Print ISBN 978-1-64352-240-1

eBook Editions:
Adobe Digital Edition (.epub) 978-1-64352-239-5
Kindle and MobiPocket Edition (.prc) 978-1-64352-238-8

All scripture quotations are taken from the King James Version of the Bible.

This book is a work of fiction. Names, characters, places, and incidents are either products of the author's imagination or used fictitiously. Any similarity to actual people, organizations, and/or events is purely coincidental.

Cover Photo: Robin MacMillan / Trevillion Images

Published by Barbour Books, an imprint of Barbour Publishing, Inc., 1810 Barbour Drive, Uhrichsville, Ohio 44683, www.barbourbooks.com

*Our mission is to inspire the world with the life-changing message of the Bible.*

 Member of the
Evangelical Christian
Publishers Association

Printed in the United States of America.

# Daughters of the Mayflower

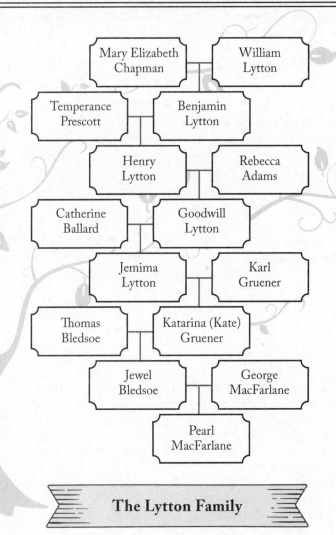

**The Lytton Family**

William Lytton married Mary Elizabeth Chapman (Plymouth 1621)
Parents of 13 children, including Benjamin
Benjamin Lytton married Temperance Prescott (Massachusetts 1668)
Henry Lytton married Rebecca Adams (New York 1712)
Goodwill Lytton married Catherine Ballard (New York 1737)
Jemima Lytton who married Karl Gruener (New Jersey 1777)
Katarina (Kate) Gruener married Thomas Bledsoe (Kentucky 1794)
Jewel Bledsoe married George MacFarlane (Tennessee 1836)
Their children included Jeremiah, Jefferson, Gideon, Pearl, and Clem MacFarlane

# Dedication

For the Blue and the Gray. . .for those who fought,
who bled and died, and for those who waged their own
private wars on the home front. . .indeed, for all
who served for the sake of conscience.
And for living historians everywhere, whose passion
for seeing history remembered is sometimes
perilously misunderstood.

Dear Reader,

I never wanted to write a story set during the Civil War. After years of living in the South—first Virginia, then Mississippi, and finally South Carolina, the very cradle of Secession—I learned too well how complicated the issues really were, how much we still bear the imprint of the conflict, and it was far from my interests or ability to try to touch anything that sensitive. I found Revolutionary War history far more fascinating—and safe.

But one does not breathe the air of Charleston (really, any of the South) and not absorb some of that history. So when God popped open the door and nudged me through, I had to be obedient.

I knew, however, that I didn't want to write just another Civil War novel. With so many authors who do this era very well (Jocelyn Green, wow!), I hoped to spin a story that would complement rather than compete with what's already in print. It helped that my editor initially encouraged me not to write a "plantation story" but to choose more of a middle-class setting, specifically from those who were not slaveholders—because non-slaveholders comprised, honestly, the vast majority of Southern society. In serving up, then, a little more obscure sliver of history, and a much more obscure social strata, I hope I have done them justice.

It was still enormously difficult. How could I show the plight of enslaved people? Explore the issue of abolition? Again, so many stories already give such an excellent treatment of these issues. Doubtless many will find fault because they are not the main focus, here.

You may also find it much different than my other stories, set during the colonial and early Federal eras. A bit of that is due to my attempt to write within period voice. Historical voices of any time have tended to be far more wordy than we moderns are used to, but primary sources from the Civil War era seem particularly so. Because of this, I took some liberty in turns of phrase and descriptions, and a more generous use of adverbs than I otherwise might.

A note about period terms and political thought. In the North, this conflict was referred to as the War of the Rebellion, while the South regarded it as hostility and invasion on the part of the North, whatever view individuals held on the issue of slavery. Militarily, Federal and Confederate are the proper terms for the respective armies, while the colloquial terms were Yankees and Rebels. Political leanings were described as Unionist and Secessionist. Both sides emphasized that slavery was at best a side issue, and I will not belabor that point here, although many who are much more intelligent and articulate than I have argued otherwise. Because I've always been a proponent of examining an issue from both, or all, sides, my intent is to portray the people of this time with as much accuracy—and yes, sympathy—as I can.

There are particular racial terms I avoid, simply because they are too inflammatory and, like the use of other language, largely unnecessary to get one's point across. I do use the term *Negro*, which simply means "black" in Spanish and was a common term for those of African descent during the time, and *darky*, which was often used as a self-identifier.

No other time period evokes such visceral reactions, even now—or especially now. This would be the greatest reason why I approached this story with trepidation. Grown men and women still argue the politics of the period online. And even as I write this note, preparing to turn in my finished story to my editor, a heated discussion takes place on a well-known writers' forum on the subject of underrepresentation of diverse cultures and ethnicities within the publishing industry, which then expands to debate over race relations and whether "whites" can ever really understand the plight of other ethnicities. One might extend that line of questioning to other areas. Can I, as a woman, ever presume to know what goes on in the mind of a man? Or as a middle-class modern myself, can I even begin to know what it was like to live in other time periods? It is the studied practice of novelists, however, to write about things we do not know. One might say that our stories are at best educated guesses at the experiences of others—does that make our stories any less valid?

Let us not forget that the cause of abolition in our country, and some could argue the Civil War itself, was fueled by the fictional work of one white woman presuming to write about the experiences of enslaved blacks. Yes...*Uncle Tom's Cabin* by Harriet Beecher Stowe. I am not arguing on behalf of "white privilege" or anything like it—just pointing out the powerful nature of story.

If you find my story enjoyable, thank you. If you find it lacking, I still thank you—because regardless, I appreciate the time and effort given to reading my work.

Blessings!
Shannon

*Judge me, O God, and plead my cause against an ungodly nation:*
*O deliver me from the deceitful and unjust man. For thou art the God*
*of my strength: why dost thou cast me off? why go I mourning*
*because of the oppression of the enemy?*
PSALM 43:1–2


Both read the same Bible, and pray to the same God; and each invokes His aid against the other. It may seem strange that any men should dare to ask a just God's assistance in wringing their bread from the sweat of other men's faces; but let us judge not that we be not judged. The prayers of both could not be answered; that of neither has been answered fully.

–Abraham Lincoln's second inaugural address, March 4, 1865

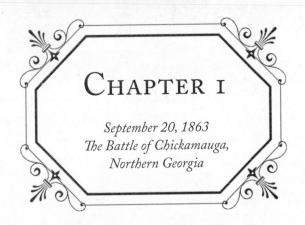

# CHAPTER I

*September 20, 1863
The Battle of Chickamauga,
Northern Georgia*

H*old the line!* For the love of God, hold it!"

Not for the first time, Joshua Wheeler wondered if he'd descended into hell. The sun blazing fierce enough to make his head ache even through a cap. The flash of fire from his own rifle as well as those to his right and left. Answering fire from across the forested, rock-strewn gully. The burn of gun smoke in his nostrils, and the screams of men above the continuous concussion of shots, both rifle and artillery, pounding through his chest.

*Oh God, save us. . .*

Fire, reload, fire again. Over and over.

*God. . .if You do love us. . .*

Cursing, frantic. "*Hold—the—line!*"

There was no holding. The return fire was too hot, the Rebels pressing hard, and those on both sides of Josh either falling back or—falling. A curse was on his own tongue as he reloaded just one more time—

Something struck him, but he barely felt it. Stared in shock at his shredded sleeve, the forearm dangling above the wrist. Tried to make his hand move, but—nothing.

The pitch of the cries around him changed to a warble, the distress of his fellow Union soldiers and the unholy glee of the Rebels alike fading as the ground rushed up to meet him. . . .

Hell took on a different face when he awoke. Darkness wrapped him about with lingering heat. A low moan rumbled from his left, while a whimpering came from his right. And somewhere not far away, the rasp as of a saw and the unmistakable scream of a man in mortal agony.

Pretty sure that had been him, not long ago.

He tried to move—but fire lit through that left arm, coursing up and into his shoulder and the rest of his body. A yelp escaped his throat before he could stop it.

*God. . .oh God. . .*

His mama's voice. *"Don't you be takin' the name of our Lord in vain, now!"*

His breath came ragged. "I didn't mean to, Mama."

A slow, deep voice rolled out of the dark. "I reckon I ain't your mama, but can I get you anything, soldier?"

He startled at both the nearness and cadence. "I—water. Please."

A hand behind his neck and tin cup brought to his lips. Trying not to whimper again, but then the blessed coolness of water on his lips, into his mouth.

Maybe this wasn't hell after all.

As he gratefully took another gulp, approaching voices overlaid the moaning around him.

"Local boy, and we're gonna have to go tell his family."

"While you're at it, see if they have room for some of our prisoners to convalesce. Perhaps those less likely to survive the train journey to Richmond. Our own boys need attention, here, and there are more yet on the field." The cultured accent of a Virginia native paused, giving way to the brief sound of boots shifting on the floor. "Portius, can any of these men be made ready to transport soon?"

"Yes, sir," came the voice of his attendant. Tennessee, if Josh didn't miss his guess. "This one's awake. Not sure for how long, though."

His pulse stuttered. Wait. Was he then a prisoner? Or—

Josh swallowed. "Sir." He cleared his throat, tried again. "Where am I, sir?"

"And who do I have the honor of being addressed by?"

His shoulder and arm were on fire again. "Sergeant Joshua Wheeler, First Ohio, Army of the Cumberland, sir."

A huff answered him, which might have been a sardonic laugh or something else entirely. "Well, Sergeant, you are now in the company of the Army of Tennessee." A definite short laugh, now. "Welcome to the Confederacy, son. You may consider yourself a prisoner at this time."

*September 21, Southern Tennessee*

The guns were silent now, over on West Chickamauga Creek and across the mountains. But as quiet fell, sullen and smoky under the moonlight, Pearl MacFarlane's tears would not cease.

She never knew a body could cry so many tears.

All three of her older brothers gone now. First Jeremiah at Shiloh, then Jefferson at Fishing Creek, and now Gideon—here. In the very hills they'd run as children.

Pearl drew her shawl more tightly around her shoulders and let her body sag against the porch post. Clem's sniffling still carried across the yard, likely from around the corner and behind the woodpile out back. Pa had taken himself straight to bed. If Mama were still here—well, it would kill Mama all over again.

Instead, all three of them had gone ahead to greet Mama in heaven. Wouldn't she be glad.

A fresh, hot stream poured down her cheeks at the thought.

*Lucky.*

Word was that the Confederacy had driven the Federals back this day through Rossville Gap and maybe even as far as Chattanooga. General Longstreet, all the way from Virginia, had swept in to help. But what good was victory if the blood of their finest lay spilled into the ground?

Never mind that her brothers had only cared about defending that ground and were only too glad to go into the fight.

All three lay in the very earth they'd fallen upon, if one counted

Gideon's being laid to rest today beside Mama. Pearl wished all three could be buried there, but they hadn't the means to find and bring the other two home. With only her and Clem left of the MacFarlane clan, and Pa being nearly an invalid, they'd barely enough resources to scratch out a living, much less go trying to find family who were long since in the grave.

Pearl buried her face in a corner of the shawl—a beautiful Oriental weave of cream and tan and brown, presented to Mama from Pa as a courting gift years before. Mama's scent was long gone, but Pearl inhaled anyway, out of habit.

No, she wouldn't wish Mama back, not in the midst of such trouble.

A slight rumble broke the quiet from somewhere down the road, growing louder by the moment. Pearl stiffened. Why would a wagon be coming this late?

The rumble resolved into a rattle, and through scraggly brush lining the road, the shape of a pair of horses and wagon could be seen, the canvas cover a white blur in the dark. As the rig turned into their yard, Pearl patted the weight of the old flintlock pistol in her skirt pocket, then stepped out from under the shadow of the porch.

Two men sat on the wagon seat, one driving and the other cradling a rifle. Both tipped their hats to her as the wagon rolled to a stop below the porch. "Evenin', miss," the driver said.

She bobbed a nod, gaze straying to the man riding shotgun.

"Pearl," said that one.

"Travis," she replied, trying to keep her voice level.

"It's been a long time."

"Indeed it has." Her weary mind scrolled back through the months—years? Yes, nearly two—since she'd last seen her cousin. In this moment, however, she could not even summon gladness for it. Nothing but a faint surprise.

"I was most regretful to hear about your brothers," he said, his voice still subdued.

She swallowed, then nodded again, harder this time. Neither man got down, but the driver fidgeted, scratching his beard and fiddling with the reins. "Miss," he said finally, "reckon we got to impose upon your hospitality for a short time. There's a couple of wounded Yankees in the back of the wagon what needs nursing care. We'll be bringing more tomorrow."

"We don't have room. Or the wherewithal."

"Well, we was thinking you'd be saying that. Captain has authorized us to help with victuals. You just need to give 'em floor space."

For a moment the night tilted around Pearl, and a hot, heavy wave of nausea overtook her. Then she pulled a long, slow breath, and the world righted itself again.

Mostly.

"Why aren't you asking me to come down and help with nursing, there?"

Travis shot her a glance from under his hat brim, visible even in the dark. "Didn't figure you'd agree."

She huffed a laugh. "You'd be right. And I will not open my home to the likes of these either."

"You ain't being given a choice," Travis said. "Every house in the area is prevailed upon to host the wounded or prisoners. We have hundreds of wounded, Pearl. Maybe more like thousands."

An ugly word came to her tongue, but she bit it back. Why were only men allowed to curse?

A heavy step and scrape heralded the open door behind her. "We'll take them," came Pa's voice from over her shoulder, steady and mild.

"Pa," she whispered, but his hand came down on her shoulder.

"Shh. Good Book tells us to be kind to our enemies."

There'd be no arguing with him, but her throat burned. That kindness would be required directly of her hand, not of Pa's, whose every step was a trial and had been for many a year.

But she'd not dare complain.

# CHAPTER 2

Morning sun slanted through a window, falling across his face and adding to the general agony in his body. Josh grimaced, instantly sorry for even the small motion that came with sudden wakefulness.

So he'd survived the night.

Was he supposed to be thankful for that turn of events?

With sunlight still stabbing his eyes, he squinted, trying to see where he was. The quiet confirmed that what he recalled of a nighttime wagon ride must not have been a dream—and the absence of men's screams and groans was a decided relief, for sure—but where exactly had they brought him?

A plain room inside a cabin or house, looked like. A single curtain at the window, lifting and falling with a faint breeze. A straight-backed chair, a narrow bed—where someone else lay, a man's hand outflung over the edge, still grimy and bloodied—and a small washstand. A blue dress hanging from a hook near the corner, and another small table behind the door holding a hairbrush and various female accoutrements.

Bits and pieces of impressions, too fragmented to even be called memory, filed through his thoughts. Lamplight, the twang of Tennessee mountain voices, first of a man, then the sharper accent of a woman. The comfort of a blanket covering a hard floor that blessedly did not jostle and bounce beneath him.

*"Prisoners?"* He remembered one voice, the woman's.

*"No fear. They ain't in any shape to try an escape. . .die trying."*

At this point, Josh would rather try, and die.

His pa's voice came swift on the heels of that thought. *"That's the easy way out, the coward's way, Son. And you ain't a coward.*"

Josh rolled his head back and forth but slowly. Could it be there were some things even Pa didn't know?

The hardness of the floor finally forced him to move—that, and an ever-increasing baser need. He had to get up, find a privy—

Agony stabbed through his arm and up into his shoulder, drawing a gasp from his throat and pinning him down. He lay still, breathing hard for a moment, then lifted his head to look. His chest and shoulders, bare. Bandages swathing his elbow and downward, but—

Wait, something there wasn't right.

He tried lifting his arm, flexing his hand. Thought he flexed his hand. But—the bandages ended several inches below the elbow. And where the rest of his forearm and hand should have been—had been—only empty air.

*Great God in heaven! Gracious God. . .no! Please no. . .*

A crushing wave of blackness rushed over him, and he fell gladly into it.

Pearl could delay no longer the unhappy task of looking in on the men taking up space in her bedroom.

She'd heard a rustling, and knowing a little of what to expect, fetched a pitcher of water, a towel, and a tin cup before setting her jaw and heading for the room with firm steps.

Heart pounding—without account, that, except—*they're Yankees, for the love of all that's holy*—she nudged the door open and peeked around it. No movement. The man they'd laid out on the floor over to the side lay sprawled as if he'd been in a fight and lost, with the one in her bed in much the same position. She peered closer to make sure both were breathing.

The one in her bed had a round but strong face, fair hair sticking at odd angles, and a short beard curling in a manner that appeared half-boyish, half-rakish, but mostly foolish with how his mouth hung open. He definitely still breathed.

The one on the floor. . .Pearl tiptoed closer. Auburn hair of a shade just missing fiery red fell in an untidy wave over his forehead. Beard of a more vivid hue covering a jaw also hanging slack.

And he too was definitely still breathing.

The waxy pallor of the man's face, with fresh-looking beads of sweat, made her frown and peer closer. Long, dark lashes lying against sharp cheekbones and a scattering of freckles standing out against his pale skin gave the similar impression of boyishness.

Both men so young, so ordinary-looking in sleep, she could not help but be reminded of her brothers.

Gritting her teeth, she slammed the door on that thought, then peered closer at the one on the floor. Fresh blood seeped through the bandages at the end of his arm. Travis had told her last night that all she needed was to change the bandages when she could, and keep the wound clean, but...

"Miss?"

Pearl flinched toward the owner of that voice, rusty from sleep, and found herself staring into the wide blue eyes of the man on the bed—her bed, but she wouldn't think about that either. He seemed as startled as she, though, and gaped for a moment before adding, "Could I—do you have any water, miss?"

She jerked a nod, then with the barest glance at the man still sprawled at her feet, stepped toward the washstand and unburdened her arms. This was, after all, why she'd brought the cup and pitcher.

She filled the cup about half-full and approached the bed, as the man there levered himself up a little, grimacing. At least he was still properly clothed, unlike the bare-chested man on the floor. But she supposed they'd had to remove his shirt because of the amputation.

He took the cup from her and gulped down its contents, then held it out to her. "More, please?"

Her throat burned at the plaintive note in his voice. With another nod, she refilled the cup then brought it back. He was only slightly less desperate the second time.

"Please," he said again, as she filled the cup a third time, "where am I?"

Pearl pressed her lips together. "In Tennessee."

Doubt filled his blue eyes, as if he wanted to consider that the foolery she half meant it to be. She exhaled, set her fist on her hip, and went on.

"We are the MacFarlane family. We live just a little southeast of Chattanooga, about as far south as you can get and not be in Georgia yet. And—we've been charged with taking care of y'all."

The blue eyes flickered. Was that—fear? Dismay at the least? "Well. I thank you, Miss MacFarlane. Or is that *Missus*?"

He pronounced his words strangely, and *thank* came out as *tank*.

"Miss," she answered firmly.

His head bobbed, and he sank back against the quilt. "I am—"

A sudden gasp from the floor startled them both, and Pearl whirled aside, clutching her skirts.

The man there lay breathing hard, eyes wide and dark, teeth bared in a grimace. One hand clutched the blanket beneath him and the other—oh, the other *arm*—clamped across his middle. His gaze was riveted to her, an echo of the fear, pain, and inquiry she'd seen in the other, but far more fervently.

"Who are you?" he whispered. "And where am I?"

Flippant answers would not serve this one. Pearl scooted toward the washstand and refilled the cup she'd taken from the other man, then sank to her knees on the floor beside him. "Here," she said, keeping her voice soft, "I expect you'll also need some of this."

He gaped at her as if she'd just spoken some foreign tongue, and she held the cup a little closer.

His hand released the blanket and came out in a movement that could only be described as flailing, slapping hard against the floor, palm down. The muscles in his arm corded as he pushed himself upright, groaning, and rolled to a half-sitting position, where he stayed, gasping again for breath. "Good—Lord—in heaven," he panted, then groped for the cup.

"Yes, He is," she murmured without thought, putting the cup in his hand, awkwardly sliding closer to help brace him as he swayed.

Predictably, he gulped the water. She took the cup and refilled it before he could ask. He downed the second one similarly, then the cup went tumbling as he flailed again to remain sitting.

"Easy now," she soothed, again without thinking.

"I need—up," he gasped. "To—the privy."

"Hold on," she said. "Let me get help. Can you sit more to this side?

There, like that. Yes."

Travis had anticipated and instructed her on this need as well. Ignoring the heat blooming across her face, Pearl helped him situate himself on his other hip, bracing this time against the good arm and hand, then scrambled to her feet and beat a hasty retreat from the room. "Clem!" she bellowed in the direction of the upstairs. "Get down here, now!"

She stood there, the morning light falling across her like a glory beam in a painting he'd once seen. Angelic, despite a gray calico dress with simple, practical skirts, brown hair escaping a sober knot, and eyes somehow severe and pitying at the same time.

He did not want her pity. He did not want her help, or anyone else's. He simply wanted to be able to get up and walk outside on his own.

And after that, return to his regiment and the war and everything else he'd signed up for. Because this house, snug as it seemed, was not that.

A scrawny, gangly boy somewhere in his midteens entered the room, found a chamber pot, and with the woman gone from the room, helped him use it. After, she returned, offered him another drink, then once he was settled again, lifted his arm to inspect the bandage. He took the moment to study her.

Plain, up close. Tendrils of hair curling wildly about her face, eyes shadowed, mouth pressed in a line. High cheekbones and slightly hollowed cheeks.

Then her gaze snapped to his, green as the leaves on the trees. Shimmering like deep water. As startled as they were startling.

Her expression closed, and she looked away. "I'll need to change this later today. Try to keep still for now. And if you want for anything else, just holler."

She rose from her knees and made to leave.

"Wait." He could hardly get the word out.

She hesitated, skirts swaying.

"Thank"—he coughed, tried again—"thank you, Miss—"

"MacFarlane," she said after a slight hesitation, softly, and was gone.

# CHAPTER 3

Standing at the top of the porch steps, Pearl clenched her hands inside her wadded-up apron and glared at her cousin, who faced her from beside the wagon holding more wounded soldiers. "And I'm telling you, Travis. These men need beds, and we haven't enough."

Travis pulled off his hat, raked a hand through sweat-dampened brown hair, and narrowed his pale blue eyes. "Blast it, Pearl. We need help. There are too many, and even our own men are mostly lying outdoors on the ground. Beds are the least of my worries, here."

"I won't just put them on the floor, I don't care who they are." She chewed her lip. "We do have extra beds upstairs. If. . .if I had help moving them to the sitting room. . ."

He huffed. "Fine, then. I can do that." He gestured to his driver to climb down before turning back to Pearl. "Where's Clem?"

"Out wandering, hunting relics of battle, I'm sure."

But amazingly enough, the boy emerged from the barn. Obviously he'd seen the wagon coming and hung around out of curiosity.

He peered inside the conveyance as he walked past, then at Travis, shaggy locks of dark hair falling over his blue eyes. "More Yankees?"

"Yep," their cousin said before Pearl could reply.

He stopped, looking from one to the other. "Why?"

"Everyone hereabouts is being asked to take them in," Travis said. "Like I told you last night, you'll help Pearl and make no complaints about it."

Clem rolled his eyes but made no further comment. He might be tall as Travis now but didn't yet outweigh him and doubtless knew their cousin could still whup him in a fair fight. Pearl bit back a smile. It was rare enough these days that she had the upper hand with her younger brother. "Take Travis and Mister Jones up to the attic and help them bring down the extra beds."

While the men accomplished that, Pearl set herself to rearranging the sitting room, clearing space. Her brothers' beds, they'd been. One wide enough for two men, but the others more narrow, as they'd fought and kicked and determined they needed less space as they grew in stature, and Pa had directed them in building their own.

The ticks were dusty but would do. Linens might be more of a problem. They'd given so much to the war effort already. . . .

They got the larger bed and two smaller ones set up in the sitting room, and one bed frame remained. Pearl directed the men to set it up in her own bedroom and to put the man with the amputated arm into that one. The man winced and groaned at being moved but did not open his eyes.

His companion, however, gave her the barest smile and nod, the boyish look once more wrenching at her heart.

She hardened herself to such frivolous feelings and went to see about the others getting settled.

They'd jammed four men in that wagon bed—four, with wounds varying from ordinary gunshots—if there was such a thing—to the loss of another limb, this time a leg. And there was one sack of beans. One.

As Travis and his driver, Mr. Jones, went out to the wagon the last time, Pearl stomped after them. "How am I supposed to feed all these men on one sack of beans?"

Her cousin's mouth thinned. "It was all we could spare right now. I'll bring you more."

"More like you expect Clem to hunt, even with all the game chased out of the woods."

Travis didn't bother denying it. Pearl caught his quick grimace as he turned and climbed up onto the wagon. He retrieved his rifle from the floorboard and flashed her a rueful glance.

With a quick dip of his head, Mr. Jones shook out the reins and clucked to the horses.

"I won't forget this, Travis Bledsoe!" she yelled after, as the wagon rattled away.

No answer. As she knew there wouldn't be. She turned and stomped back up onto the porch then stopped. Leaned on the post beside the steps. Made herself breathe in, breathe out.

*Lord God in heaven, help me. I can't do this.*

*I cannot.*

Another breath in and out.

*"Be not forgetful to entertain strangers: for thereby some have entertained angels unawares."*

The words floated through her mind, echoing deep in her heart, bringing an ache to her throat.

*"If thine enemy hunger, feed him; if he thirst, give him drink: for in so doing thou shalt heap coals of fire on his head."*

Well. That she could live with.

Though it was the hardest thing she felt she'd ever done, she put one foot in front of the other and went back into the house.

"I should have given you my bed," Pa said, watching her bustle around the living room.

"Nonsense," Pearl said.

She'd come back in to find him settled in his favorite chair, which she'd tucked against the wall next to the hearth, situated between the kitchen and the rest of the main room. He leaned on his cane, looking at the array of beds in what was formerly his sitting area.

Pa could no more climb the stairs to the attic, which once belonged to all her brothers but she now occupied, than they could fly to the moon. And he knew it. So where else was he expecting to sleep?

"It's all right, Pa," she said, more softly. "Truly."

His gaze strayed toward her, and back across the room. Most of the men had fallen asleep, obviously grateful for a real bed and exhausted by the wagon ride here. And Pearl had been so busy making sure everything was set up that she hadn't even asked who the men were.

Their injuries, now—the man in the nearest bed had sustained gunshot wounds in three different areas of his body. The next one over had lost most of a leg. Another was gutshot and not expected to live. When Pearl had asked Travis why they'd bothered to bring him, he'd just shrugged and not replied. The fourth man's head was wrapped about with a bloody bandage, and he hadn't awoken even when they carried him in.

Pearl quailed at the thought of having to tend that one. Brothers she'd had, including the younger, whose swaddling she'd helped changed, but grown men, and strangers, were another thing entirely.

*Lord God. . .help. . .*

She tucked the thought, and the prayer, to the back of her mind. So much still needed to be done. Water fetched, food prepared—oh, the food! How was she to feed them all? That alone nearly buckled her knees.

*One meal at a time.*

Very well, then. They had the sack of beans and some freshly smoked hog hidden high in the barn rafters. She'd work with that tonight, and think about tomorrow when tomorrow came.

On her way past her room, she peered inside. The man in her own bed shifted, but the other, who'd lost his hand, hadn't moved from where Travis and Clem had settled him earlier. Heart dropping, she leaned closer until she caught the movement of his chest, rising and falling.

But, oh so shallowly.

Deep shadows lay beneath the long, dark lashes, stark against the paleness of his skin.

She forced herself to turn away and go to start supper.

Gauging how much to cook this first night proved nearly more than her mind could sort, and in the end, she fell back on preparing what would have fed the family had her brothers been present. In the process she could ignore who she was actually doing the cooking for and pretend—if even for mere snatches of time—that the meal was indeed for her brothers and not for these motley and uninvited guests who lay, occasionally moaning and tossing, in beds across their sitting room.

Pa sat and watched them, making no comment. Pearl almost wished he'd chatter, as he sometimes did after the spell that left him weakened on one side not long after the war had begun. But silent he remained, before heaving himself to his feet and shuffling toward her bedroom, where the other two men lay.

Pearl scooped handfuls of cornmeal into a bowl. What on earth was he doing? As she broke two of their precious store of eggs into the meal, Pa emerged and shuffled toward her, his tall, lean form now stooped and slightly doughy in the middle. Slightly curling gray hair and beard, both thinner than they once were, graced his mild face.

She sent him a questioning look.

"I was praying," he said.

She nodded shortly and stirred the mixture with the worn wooden spoon. He watched her for a moment.

"If your enemy hungers, feed him."

Pearl glanced up again. "And so heap coals of fire on his head," she responded, without thought.

Pa smiled, his creased face lighting up. "I reckon you wouldn't mind heaping a little fire on a Yankee's head, now would you?"

Pearl coughed a laugh. Sometimes Pa surprised her so, though he had always been fond of sliding a rebuke toward her in such a sly way. "I surely wouldn't."

His blue eyes went grave in an instant. "Then care for them, Pearl, as you would your brothers. They are someone's sons. Brothers, and husbands as well, some of them."

Her jaw ached before she realized she was gritting her teeth. And she'd stirred the corn bread batter too long. "I—am trying." Leaving the spoon in the batter, she set both hands flat against the table, one on either side of the bowl. "Am I not feeding them?"

He nodded slowly. "But they need more than food for the body. More than water for their physical thirst. They need"—his gaze wandered as his mind searched for the words, and Pearl waited—"they have. . .hearts and souls that need to be fed."

She sniffed and reached for the baking pan. Lifted the bowl and poured the batter, scraping the sides with a little too much force. "We are nothing to them, Pa. Rebels. You know it's true—they think themselves the only ones with a just cause."

But Pa's gaze held steady. "Even so. Coals of fire, my girl. Coals of fire."

And with that, he shuffled away and resettled himself in his chair.

# CHAPTER 4

When those who were going to eat had been fed, with Clem's help and even a little of Pa's, Pearl started the process of making sure all were made comfortable for the night. She'd some idea of how to do this—nursing Mama through her last illness and Pa through the worst of his spells—but having half-a-dozen men at one time presented a daunting task.

Whether it would have been better to simply go help at a field hospital, she could not say.

The gathering dark outside finally forced her to light a pair of lamps. A knock came at the door, startling her, but Pa was on his feet and shuffling to answer it before she could get there.

"Sir? How can I help you?" Pa said.

"I reckon you could allow me to help y'all," a deep, resonant voice responded. "My name is Portius. Mister Travis sent me, thinking you might need an extra pair of hands."

"We surely do." Pa scooted back to allow the man entrance.

Portius stepped across the threshold, a tall, sturdy sort with close-clipped hair and skin so ebony he could have been formed of midnight itself. He surveyed the room until his gaze landed on her, and he gave a slow, deep nod. "At your service, ma'am."

She nodded back. "Thank you for coming." She could not deny the relief of an able-bodied man to assist, but—did they not need him worse, elsewhere? "We have but half-a-dozen men here."

He nodded again. "So they told me. Mister Travis was right

concerned for you, though."

When his gaze became searching—and not a little speculating—Pearl turned away, her cheeks heating. "That's very kind of him. But as I told him, we've little enough to offer here. He'd have done as well to keep these men at the field hospital."

"I 'spect he had his reasons," Portius responded, his slow, deep voice remaining even. "And I 'spect these men have as good a chance at surviving here. Better, more like."

"Yes. Well." Pearl cast him another glance. Did Portius belong to Travis, or was he a freeman? Her own parents had not held with owning slaves, but others in the family did, whether for economic expediency or other reasons, and while Pearl thought she knew everyone in their households, it was possible in a time of war that one such as Portius had changed hands. He did not behave as though he were familiar with her or her family. "I trust that Travis made sure your papers were in order, so you could get here safely? The Home Guard is very zealous hereabouts."

He cracked the barest smile. "Thank you, ma'am. My papers are just fine, and I had not a bit of trouble."

"I am glad of it." Pearl turned this way and that. "Let me show you about, then."

They went to each of the beds in the sitting room, with Pearl relating what she knew about the men, and Portius nodding and making the occasional comment. She took him next to her bedroom, where the man in her own bed had fallen asleep after being fed supper, but the man with the missing hand had not awakened to eat.

Portius leaned closer then laid a hand across the second man's forehead. "I remember this one. Reckon he's having a rough time of it, mebbe rougher than others who've lost a hand or foot."

How could such a thing not be rough? Pearl held the words back.

"He'll bear watching a bit extra, the next few days," the black man added, softly. He stepped back and rubbed his palms together. "If you could show me where to find water—?"

She called Clem in from the barn and tasked him with taking Portius about, then climbed the narrow stairs to the attic. She and Clem had already agreed that because they'd had to put wounded prisoners in her room downstairs, he would move to the barn—at least for the time being—and she'd take the attic as her own.

She turned a little circle in the middle of the floor and blew out a breath. Simple, narrow frame bed with a straw tick in one corner—that was all she needed, really, and at least she had this much.

Rather than undress completely, she merely lay down on the bed and, despite the pressure and pinch of her corset, pulled the worn quilt up over herself. It amounted more to hiding from the horror that lay downstairs than taking proper rest, but she could not bring herself to do more, in this moment.

Much later, she awoke to quiet voices downstairs. She stiffened, listening, clutching the quilt. What—oh yes, the wounded prisoners. Throwing back the cover, she pushed herself to her feet and padded across the floor to the top of the stairs.

The unmistakable deep tone of Portius alternated with Pa's slightly higher twang, then Clem's still-reedy voice. Pearl lifted her shawl from the chest against the wall then tiptoed down the stairs.

The three men clustered around the bed on the far right of the sitting area but turned at her approach. "Is something wrong?" she said.

Clem and Pa just looked at each other, but Portius straightened a little. "This one has expired, Miss Pearl. I was about to get Clem here to help me carry him out for buryin'."

Her insides congealed, and her heart stuttered then regained its beat, hard and painful. *Lord, have mercy.* Her hands came up to cover her mouth, and then she dropped them and looked closer at the still form on the bed.

"We'll take him out straightaway, miss," Portius said.

She drew a deep, unsteady breath, ignoring the stench that hung in the air. "It's all right. I'm no shrinking violet. I've tended the sick before."

And if she'd be tending these wounded men, she'd best toughen up even more.

Portius nodded gravely. "The others might need a bit of watching, before we get back from buryin' this one. Especially the one in the other room who lost a hand."

She bobbed a quick nod of her own. "Thank you," she said, after a moment, and a brief smile creased the dark face before he turned back to the bed and directed Clem in helping wrap the body.

She went to each of the other beds in the room. Two men were fast asleep, another lay awake watching the proceedings with the man who'd expired. Nothing seemed amiss with any of them.

Aided by the sheet they'd wrapped around him, Clem and Portius heaved the dead man up from the bed and headed toward the door. Pearl went to open it for them, shut it after, then crossed the floor to where Pa still stood, leaning on his cane. "Go to bed. I'll sit up with them now."

He nodded distractedly, gaze flitting everywhere before finally landing on her face, then shuffled toward the tiny room that was his.

At least he could spend the rest of the night in comfort.

Waiting until he stepped inside and shut his own door, she gave one last glance to the men in the sitting area. "Might I bring you some water?" she asked the one who was still awake.

Eagerness lifted his expression, visible even in lamplight. "That would be mighty welcome, miss."

Fetching water was easy enough. *"If thine enemy thirst, give him drink."* She filled the cup, helped the man hold it, accepted his whispered thanks, and withdrew.

Now to the other room. She couldn't even think of it as her own anymore. And why did the thought of looking in on those two fill her with dread?

Feet dragging, she had to force herself to the doorway. Stopped to listen. One set of breaths, deep, slow, normal-sounding except for the occasional catch, came from the left. But to the right, the man's breathing was labored, uneven. Troubling just in its cadence.

She fetched a lamp and returned, setting it on the nightstand. Peered at the man who, yes, slept, but not peacefully at the least. Even in slumber he seemed to be in battle.

What had he witnessed, that his very sleep was troubled? What had all these men seen?

Just as quick, she hardened herself. Her older brothers, lying cold in the earth by now, all three of them. Put there by the likes of these.

*"If thine enemy hunger, feed him; if he thirst, give him drink: for in so doing thou shalt heap coals of fire on his head."*

She bent a little closer, still listening to the heaving rattle, and held one hand near but not quite touching his forehead. Heat radiated from his skin, even with an inch between them. This one didn't need any more coals heaped on his head—he was already on fire.

Even the Samaritan took pity on a man who was his enemy, though, and tended his wounds. Pearl suppressed a huff, and this time went to fetch a basin, clean water, and a cloth. Setting the basin beside the lamp, she pulled up a chair, wrung out the cloth, and with the barest hesitation, stroked it across the man's burning forehead.

This way, and that. Turn the cloth over, and do it again, until the cloth itself was too warm to be of comfort, and then she dipped it back in the water and wrung it out again.

This time not just his forehead, but his cheeks too. Neck below the beard, and upper shoulders, which were both wide and strong, the skin there pale but freckled as well.

Why was she taking note of such details, at such a time?

She wrung out the cloth, started over at his face.

*"They are someone's sons. Brothers, and husbands as well, some of them."*

She gritted her teeth at Pa's voice.

*Lord God, I do not want to be reminded of that. I do not want them here. But if this is the burden You've laid upon us for this time—help me to bear it. . . .*

*Lord, help me.*

She didn't even want to be praying that prayer.

But his breathing had slowed, and he was less restless than before.

Others were feverish, when she took a break to make the rounds, but none seemed as in distress. Still, she took a few minutes to change out her water and mop brows as she had the first man, then returned to sit at his bedside. He was tossing again and muttering.

She freshened her water then started in again. And just like before, he calmed under the cool of her damp rag.

Once, he twitched, knocking the bandaged arm about, and winced in his sleep. Pearl considered the limb. What must it be like to wake and find part of your own body missing? How would this unknown man fare once he knew—if he didn't already—that he'd now have to live and work with only one hand?

Some had much worse, she knew. And what if this were one of her brothers? How would they fare with a similar limitation?

Her eyes burned, and she blinked to clear them. Useless, maundering thoughts. She'd do what was necessary to care for these men, and then they'd be taken away to a prison camp. Their lives were not her concern, beyond fulfilling the duty of the moment.

How long it was before Clem and Portius came back, she didn't know. The night wore away under the tedium of tending the wounded, and it was with something like astonishment that Pearl finally glanced out the window to see the sky becoming lighter.

She rose and stretched then carried her bowl and rag out to be dumped. Portius was still up, tending to a bandage on one of the men, while Clem lay stretched on the floor, arm across his face, apparently asleep.

Pearl set the bowl by the door and tiptoed over to watch the Negro as he worked. His head lifted. "How much do you know about tending wounds, miss?"

She thought before answering. "I've tended hurt critters. Horses and cows, mostly, and dogs or cats that have gotten in a scrap. And I had older brothers."

A smile lightened his face for a moment. "Come and give me a hand, and I'll show you a thing or two."

She edged closer, steeling herself for whatever she might see. But worse than the sight—bad enough that, of torn flesh and crusted blood and whatnot—was the stench that hit Pearl like a visible, noxious cloud.

"Now, this poor man was gutshot." Portius's voice remained low and even. "Made worse by them moving him, if that smell is anything to go by. Best we can do, I expect, is keep him clean and comfortable. And pray."

She nodded belatedly and swallowed. Portius leaned closer to inspect the ragged, oozing hole in the man's abdomen, then covered it again. The man moaned but didn't waken, and Portius moved to the next bed. "Morning, sir," he murmured to the man lying there, who opened his eyes briefly, then drew back the edge of the wool blanket to reveal the bandaged stump of his right leg. Pearl held herself still as he loosened the wrapping and unwound it. "Have you more bandages?" he asked. "We'll want to wash these soon."

She offered another stiff nod. "Not near enough, but a few."

"We'll make do, then."

For all the horror of a man's leg ending just above the knee, Pearl found herself oddly fascinated at how neatly muscle and skin were wrapped over the end of the stump, even rudimentarily stitched. Portius bound it up again and gave the man a drink of water. "We'll find some breakfast soon, sir," he said to the man's raspy inquiry about food.

Pearl's stomach rolled. "I—could go see to the meal."

"First we finish making rounds," Portius answered, steady but firm.

The wounds sustained by the man lying in her bed were even more horrific than those of the man who'd been gutshot—his thigh was near to shredded by shrapnel—but without the stench. Pearl could not deny the relief of that simple fact alone. This time she leaned in, attentive, as Portius pointed out various aspects of the wound and what could be done to treat it.

The man himself lay quietly, watching and listening. Portius finished, gave him a nod, and turned to the other bed. "Still feverish, I see. You sat with him half the night, didn't you?"

"I did. He seemed better when I bathed his brow, at least for a while."

Portius gingerly lifted the bandaged limb and unwound the cloth. Pearl felt a bit more prepared this time, especially after seeing the amputation wound of the other man's leg, but still her gut clenched as the stump was exposed. Purplish and oozing. The same folding and wrapping of the tissues yet somehow different from the wound in the other room.

"Is that—infection?" she whispered, afraid to say the word.

"Hmm." Portius's face was grave. "Beginnings of it, yes." He cut her a glance. "Did Mister Travis leave you any medicines?"

She shook her head slowly. "I reckon he either knew they'd all die, or. . ." She hesitated, chewing her lip, thinking through her precious store of remedies. Some left over from when Mama was alive. "I've goldenseal. No idea if we can even find more. But it might be enough to give him a chance. . . ."

Portius considered then gave her a nod. "Might at that. If you have any to spare."

"I'll go look."

Pearl darted from the room, dashed into the kitchen, and knelt beside the pantry to pull out a tin stowed far in the corner of the bottommost shelf. After carefully pulling open the top and peeking inside to confirm contents and amount, she replaced the lid and scrambled to her feet again.

"Here," she said, a little breathless, handing it to Portius back at the man's bedside.

He took a pinch of the precious greenish-yellow powder, sprinkled it into the bandage, and wrapped it again. "We'll gather what fresh bandaging we have, then change those who needs it worst, this afternoon."

Next came breakfast. There was no coffee, of course, and only enough chicory for Pa—not that Pearl minded, since only he seemed to have acquired a taste for it. Pearl stifled a sigh and got to work boiling water and mixing up biscuits. At least the ones who could eat would have something in their bellies.

She thought of the man who was gutshot. The one missing a leg. The one whose leg lay in tatters—the fact that they hadn't amputated it amazed her. And the man missing a hand.

She didn't even know their names. Who were they? Where were they from, and what families had they left behind on this cause they felt was so important that they must go make war on those who had formerly been fellow countrymen?

Her hands stilled in the dough. *Fellow countrymen.* What had they done that was so terrible, that these men would come down from the North, invade someone else's home? Some said it was because of slavery, but—she knew very few who could afford even one slave. Most folk of her acquaintance worked their farms with their own hands and were proud of it.

But this was their land. These, their homes. And the bluecoats had invaded, plain and simple.

She slapped the dough into a thick mass on the table. Likely the biscuits would be tough, now. She didn't care.

# CHAPTER 5

With breakfast accomplished, Pearl set herself to find bandaging. The last of her simmering resentment had leaked away under the gratitude of those awake enough to eat what she offered, but her chest still ached, and her head was beginning to, with the weight of all there was yet to do before she could go steal a few hours of sleep.

Stacked in neat rolls on the bottom shelf of the pantry, next to where she'd found the goldenseal, remained far fewer cloths than they needed. She blew out a hard breath, thinking. Did she risk a trip into Chattanooga to see if any cloth could be found? She couldn't imagine such a venture being successful in the aftermath of a battle. Not with the Confederate army quartered there for so long, and the Union army occupying it now. Surely anything that might still be available in the mercantile had long since disappeared.

Perhaps her neighbors. . .or there was Lydia. Pearl sat back on her heels. Yes. . .she would do that.

She rose, went for her shawl and carrying basket, and let Pa know she'd be back soon. After a moment's hesitation, she found Portius and informed him of the same. He stopped what he was doing and fixed her with a grave look.

"What is it?" she asked.

"I'd like to accompany you, Miss Pearl."

"That—that isn't necessary."

"It might be," he maintained in that even voice, which somehow for all its mildness brooked absolutely no refusal. "It would, however, be on me if you met with any harm."

She held his dark gaze, momentarily mesmerized by the flecks of gold there, then let her breath out in a rush and dropped her head. "Very well. But you must be discreet about anything you might see."

"Silent as the grave, Miss Pearl," he rumbled, and she choked a laugh, despite herself.

She stepped outside. Sunlight and fresh air were a shock, nearly an insult, after being indoors with only lamplight for hours. Pearl lingered for a moment on the porch, nearly gulping her breaths, before tightening her shawl about her and hurrying down the steps and across the yard. She gave the barest glance back to make sure Portius followed.

Skirting the high, tree-covered ridge that rose along the western edge of their farm, she followed the edge of their nearest field, bare now. Her path took her across a narrow, rocky stream, barely a trickle with the dry spell they'd had, then between neighbors' fields, past a stand of corn nearly ready to harvest. How the soldiers had missed that, she didn't know, but she sped on at the edge of the field and pushed on up over the next hill.

At the crest she stopped, the breath knocked from her lungs. Not from the climb, but the view that lay before her. What was formerly a lovely vista with brushy pasture, bordered at the far edge by graceful trees arching over the winding banks of West Chickamauga Creek, now lay torn and devastated. The earth itself lay shredded like the flesh of the men being sheltered in her house, with bushes and trees likewise naked and ripped to pieces, punctuated by the occasional granite outcropping.

Pearl went forward, but slowly. It wasn't just the ground and vegetation. Evidences of battle lay everywhere—the wreckage of a cart, several bloated forms that she realized must be horses or mules. Bits of clothing, a broken musket there, a pistol here—

Without thinking, Pearl stooped, picked up the gun and slipped it into the pocket of her dress. She'd not gone another half-a-dozen steps when her gaze snagged on a mounded something that for a moment appeared only to be a small dead animal, except it had no hair—

She stopped again, gorge climbing into her throat. It was part of an arm, or had been—a man's arm, mangled and gray and black with blood, swarming with flies.

*God—oh God—how could You allow this horror?*

A living arm, warm and strong, came around her shoulders and tugged her on. "Come, Miss Pearl. This way. Just keep moving."

The air scraped her throat as her lungs worked to take in breaths, her feet numb as she stumbled along beside Portius.

"Which way, Miss Pearl?" he asked, halfway across the terrible field.

She shook her head, gaze still skimming the landscape, hardly registering where they were. She lifted a hand and pointed in what her mind finally admitted was the right direction. "Over there. Down the creek. There is—was? A footbridge."

The sights were no less horrible as they went, but somehow her feet found their way, her body kept breathing, and by the time they made it down to the edge of the creek, rational thought was beginning to return.

The bridge, already a rude affair with rough planks, lay in shambles. Portius set to work repairing it as best as he could with fallen limbs, and finally they were able to cross over.

Would Lydia even be there? Or had the tide of battle overwhelmed her house? Pearl realized suddenly how fortunate her family was to have been spared such direct devastation.

Through a stand of timber that seemed a little less shattered than down by the creek and up another hill, Pearl led, without Portius's help this time. Her legs still trembled, but she climbed with more strength, following the barest path up through the rocks and brush. And though she was winded from the steepness of the hillside, by the time she reached the top, her heart had steadied somewhat with the prospect of seeing her friend.

She slowed on the path down into the hollow, picking her way more carefully. Portius still followed hard after.

About halfway down, the cabin came into view through the trees. Pearl stopped, listening to the faint sounds of life floating upward, then gathered her breath. "Halloo the house!" she called out.

A shadow at the window, and a flash of blue, then the piping of small voices and an older, hushing them. Pearl waited, folding her hands around her basket. At last a figure emerged, tall, slender, but buxom. Dark hair pulled severely back but still escaping to frame a face that was the shade of coffee with but a touch of cream. Beautiful, slanting cheekbones with a full mouth set in equally severe lines.

Pearl came forward so Lydia could recognize her. Her expression transformed, and a glad cry burst from her lips as she ran forward to throw her arms around Pearl. "Oh, you're all right! I was worried, so worried, after that terrible long battle."

Pearl embraced the other woman long and hard, then stepped back to look for her self-appointed guard. He too came forward, and alarm flashed in Lydia's golden eyes. "Have no fear, Lydia. This is Portius. The Confederate army has insisted I help quarter a few wounded Yankee soldiers, and they sent Portius along to help. I'm most indebted to him these last several hours."

Lydia considered the tall black man. After he offered a quick nod and rumbled the word *ma'am*, Portius stood still and bore Lydia's regard with calmness.

At last she sniffed and turned back to Pearl. "Well then. And have you come just to visit?"

Pearl blew out a breath. "I need bandaging material, Lydia. We've used all the sheets and worn-out clothing we can spare."

Lydia stood, arms folded, head tilted. Her gaze strayed to Portius again. A shriek from the house broke the silence, but she did not move until the child responsible for the sound came tearing outside—a tiny girl with brown braids, in a threadbare but neatly mended dress of faded yellow, who threw herself into Lydia's skirts. Her hand went to the girl's curly head. "Child, I told you to stay in the house."

She peeked out and giggled. "Auntie Pearl!"

No greeting was offered Portius, though the man smiled back at her. Pearl could not resist a chuckle of her own. "Now, Sally, what have I told you about listening to your mama?"

A boy of four, in a likewise much-patched short trousers and shirt, ran across the space to Lydia's other side and peered solemnly at Portius. "Hello, young man," the Negro said.

"This is Jem and Sally," Pearl said. "Lydia's little ones."

The boy only hid his face.

"I think I might be able to help," Lydia said, with a sigh.

The return trip was easier. Pearl could brace herself against the sights and did not need Portius to steady her as they crossed the field. Portius did, in fact, have his arms full with a bolt of fabric as he walked alongside her.

She knew she could count on Lydia for having squirreled away something useful. She felt enormously guilty for having asked. Even more for accepting the woman's offering.

But they needed bandages.

"Who is that woman to you?" Portius asked, his voice very quiet.

Pearl thought through all the ways to reply to that. "My very dear neighbor, of course," she said, more lightly than she felt.

He gave a soft snort. "I heard the little one call you *Auntie.*"

Pearl smiled, but without humor. "And she couldn't do so merely as a term of affection?" She felt the black man's eyes on her. "Why do you ask?"

"I just wanna know who I'm protectin', here."

They were nearly to the foot of the ridge.

"Is she your sister? Or are those babies your sister and brother?"

Pearl sucked in a breath. "My father is not that kind of man, and our immediate family has never owned another soul."

With one exception. . .

Portius only smiled patiently.

"She is"—Pearl stumbled a little, came to a halt, and swung toward him—"Lydia is my sister-in-law," she whispered. "My brother Jeremiah's wife. He—was on a trip to Savannah, met her, and fell stupid in love, as my father was fond of saying. Saved the money and bought her, then brought her here and emancipated her. So those babies are his. Yes—before you ask—our family considers her his wife in truth, though it isn't recognized by law. I don't know where they found a preacher willing to marry them, but they swore that they did, and I believe them." She blew out a breath. "Officially, folk around here refer to her as his Creole housekeeper. And so far, to my knowledge, no one's troubled either of them over it."

The Negro did not move for a long minute, only searched Pearl's eyes. At last he smiled, sweet and slow. "Very well, then."

And he led on, up the ridge.

By the time they made it back to the house, Pearl was wilting. Portius nodded toward the stairs. "Go get some sleep."

"But there's more to be done—"

"Sleep, Miss Pearl. You're no good to anyone if you faint from exhaustion."

She didn't argue further. Up the stairs she went, brushing off Pa's inquiry, falling once more into the bed.

But this time, she dreamed. She stood again on the lower slope on the other side of the ridge as a column of men and horses marched on, kicking up clouds of dust that billowed to the sky until the sun hung a sullen red in the west, drenching everything in what looked like blood. The men's coats dripped with it, and the horses splashed through puddles of it. As they passed, many of the soldiers turned and waved at her, laughing—and suddenly her own brothers were among them, with ghastly, skeletal grins. Among them was a man wearing, not the blue coat he'd been brought in with, but gray, like her brothers, his hair glowing like fire in the light of the setting sun. He too gave her a jaunty smile—

She saw then that ahead of them yawned a vast cavern in the side of the mountain, of such complete darkness that there remained no trace of light or sound. The column of men kept marching, marching, disappearing into that dark, as if entering the maw of some vast monster. And Pearl could only stand and watch, as the dust now rose up and choked her, and even her limbs were too heavy to lift—

She woke, tangled in her quilt. With a gasp—oh, blessed air, and light!—she shoved herself free and sat up.

Outside, afternoon light fell across the ridge. Yellow-and-white wildflowers waved at the edges of the field, with maples and sourwoods just beginning to redden on the far hillside. In all, an ordinary-seeming day, not tinged with either dust or blood.

She rose, straightening her dress, and went downstairs to find Clem stirring a pot of beans over the stove and Portius making rounds while Pa slept. He gave her an assessing look then beckoned her near.

He'd taken some of the fabric already and torn it into strips for bandages. Pearl assisted as instructed, holding limbs or bits of bandaging, or setting the soiled aside for washing, and somehow it was easier this time. She still couldn't bring herself to look at the men's faces, however, or ask their names.

But full-blown panic beat in her throat—or something like it—when they entered her bedroom to tend the men there. Pearl forced a deep breath, and her dread changed to alarm and concern at finding the one with the amputated hand still feverish and unconscious. Even Portius frowned and hmmed over the wound, dusting it generously with the goldenseal before he rebandaged it. The man flailed, and Portius caught the limb before the man knocked it on the wall or furniture. "I'm gonna need you to bind it back up, Miss Pearl, while I hold him down."

Pearl gritted her teeth but took the cloth in both hands. She would do this. An image flashed in her mind of the forgotten arm lying in that field they'd walked through—and then of the dream she'd just awoken from. All that dust. . .all that blood. She swallowed hard and, not looking at either man, did her best to mimic how she'd seen the Negro rewrapping the limb, before.

*Just like wrapping a ham for smoking.* She didn't know whether to be amused or scandalized at the thought.

By the time she finished, the other man was awake and needing water. Finding his needs so much simpler—at the least, he hadn't figured in her dream—Pearl helped Portius tend him, tucking all unruly thoughts back into the dark where they belonged.

But it became difficult once more when Clem brought bowls of the thin bean soup and she had to help the men eat. The one with the amputated leg wedged himself into enough of a sitting position to hold his bowl and spoon, but the one with gunshot wounds still needed assistance. Behind her, when Portius went to feed the man who was gutshot, he met with argument. "I'm a gonna die anyway," the man said. "Don't waste good vittles on me."

"You don't know that," Portius said in his most soothing tone. " 'Taint a waste."

"It is, and you know it." The man's voice cracked.

The sound tore at Pearl's heart. She twitched toward the man, almost without thinking. "Hush now, and eat that soup."

His eyes snapped to hers, wide and dark in sockets already hollow from the battle that raged on inside his body. The pale mouth went slack, doubtless with desperation and a good bit of shock.

Pearl found herself trembling. "You will take nourishment and water until the good Lord decides you're done here with us. You hear?"

He gave the barest nod, then turned and obediently opened his mouth for the spoon at Portius's hand.

# Chapter 6

"We need to get some water down that fellow with the missing hand," the Negro said, when they were finished feeding everyone supper. He peered at Pearl.

She blinked at him. "I need to wash those bandages."

"Clem can haul the water and get started washing."

Why her? "I—I suppose I can then."

But she knew if she walked back in that room, she'd feel compelled to do more than just dribble water in the man's mouth. With a muted huff, she set off to find her basin and rag from before, and fresh water for both drinking and bathing the man's face.

Inside the room, with everything laid out within reach, and the window open for light and freshness of air, Pearl settled again at the man's bedside. Why did Portius insist she take this task? And why did it tie her own insides up in such knots? She wrung out the rag and smoothed it across the unconscious man's face. He did not move in any way.

The other man, with the fair hair, lay asleep as well, but even to the casual eye his was a more healing slumber.

Pearl set the rag back in the basin and blew out a breath. "I'm told I have to make you drink some water," she whispered. "Been a long time since I've done such a thing, so you'll have to bear with me. But I really don't want you dying on me, here." Unaccountably, her eyes prickled. "Please don't die. We've already had one man here expire. And one more likely going to." *Not to mention my brothers...*

She swallowed. Leaned forward a little, forced herself to keep talking.

"But you. You have as good a chance as anyone to keep on living."

No response. Not that she expected—or wanted—one. She picked up the cup and, tipping it just a little, spooned out some water. Slipped her hand under the man's neck—oh, he was burning up—and tilted it so she could spoon the water into his mouth. It went inside his parched lips then dribbled out the side of his mouth.

"Come on, you ornery cuss," she muttered. "Drink this."

The second spoonful likewise poured down into the man's beard. She set the spoon down, wiped his cheek on her apron, shifted her angle, tried again.

The water went in. Didn't come out. Pearl waited.

His throat moved, once, then again. Hesitantly, Pearl slipped in another spoonful. He swallowed that one too.

Her eyes stung even more. "That's it. Just a little more. . ."

She fed him water until the cup was half-empty and she had to tip the vessel with one hand just to get a good spoonful. About that time, his swallowing seemed to slow, so she set his head back down and wrung out her rag again. She couldn't see any change, but then—she'd known with Mama how even little things made a difference, whether or not they showed.

She leaned close again as she bathed the man's face and neck. "You just keep fighting. I told the man in the other room who's gutshot and expecting to die that he's not allowed to give up until God Himself says it's time, and you're not allowed to give up either. So there."

Not a flicker of his eyelids. She smiled thinly. "Who are you, I wonder. Seems kind of silly to keep thinking of you as *that man*."

Or any of the others, for that matter.

Something inside her crumbled.

The night wore away as she made rounds in both rooms. While his other two companions slept, the gutshot man moved restlessly, his eyes cracking open at Pearl's approach. "What time is it?" he whispered.

"Long about midnight, I reckon." Pa owned the only watch in the house, and she'd not disturb him to go look. They'd long since sold the timepiece on the mantel for kerosene and other necessities.

He shuddered a little. "Could I—might I trouble you for water?"

"Of course."

She answered without thinking, but after she'd provided the drink, helped tip his head up as she had the man in the other room, Pearl looked at him for a moment. Truly *looked* at him. The shadows in his face were deeper, his color more gray.

If he were really not long for this world, then what harm could it do for her to show at least a little compassion? Even beyond providing a simple sip of water.

"What's your name, soldier?" she asked.

He blinked at her, slow and heavy. "S–Simon Murphy, miss. Of the Eighty-Second Indiana."

A burn kindled under her breastbone. *God, help me.* She drew a long breath. "Well, Simon Murphy. I am most regretful that you had the misfortune of landing here with us."

The ghost of a smile lightened the shadows. "A man could do a lot worse than to have something as pretty as you to look upon in his final hours."

An unexpected bubble of laughter hiccupped from her. "You, sir, are a flatterer, for I am not pretty."

The smile deepened. "Are so. As beautiful as—an angel. . ."

And with a sigh, he closed his eyes and turned his head.

Fear clutched her throat. Was he—but no, his chest rose and fell with definite if unsteady breaths. Apparently the exchange had merely drained the last of his meager strength.

She rose, brushing dark hair off the man's brow with her fingertips. *Bless him, Lord in heaven. Let him make his way to Your throne, where I know all things will be reconciled at last.*

She made to turn away, but the wide-open eyes of the next soldier over caught her attention.

"Bring some of that sugar this way, would you?"

For another moment, she could neither move nor think, then heat rushed through her and with it, equally hot words to her lips. "And that, sir, is why we call y'all *filthy Yankees*."

He only laughed, and she wheeled about and fled the room, not caring that he called after her and might wake the others. Better to sit at a fevered man's bedside all night.

Voices echoed through shifting dreams that made no sense. Sometimes he thought he could make out the words, but other times it was just garbled sound that grated on his already raw nerves.

And through it all, intense pain. And cold. So cold. He could not get warm.

*Oh God, have mercy. Take me soon. . .*

Then there was her voice, husky and rich, like warmed honey dripping through the edges of the pain. *Don't die,* she said. *Don't you dare die.*

For a moment, he was warm, almost. He wanted to reach out to that voice. Argue with her. *And why ever not?* It would be easy, so easy, to slip out into the darkness. To escape the fury of sound and fire.

The woman's voice dropped to a whisper. *Please don't die. Please.*

Who was she, and why was it so important to her that he live?

The howling winds of pain and nightmares returned. And all he could do was howl along with them.

A warmth covered him. The woman's voice came again, shushing. Coolness passed across his forehead and cheeks, and he shivered. Liquid passed between his lips, and he swallowed obediently.

*More?* he wanted to ask, but the word wouldn't form on his tongue.

She was speaking again, softly, but not to him, this time.

Hours of the night whiled away, and still Pearl could not sleep.

At some point, the object of her watching began to shiver, and she went to her trunk for a quilt. Pearl spread it over the man, pulling it up over his shoulders, then settled herself to mop his still-burning face and offer him water again. He swallowed with less hesitation than before.

"Trink please?" came a rusty voice behind her.

The man with the shredded leg and strange accent was awake.

"Certainly," she murmured and poured from the pitcher on the stand.

He gulped an entire cup without stopping, sighed, and frowned a little, focusing on her. "It is still night?"

She nodded. "I've been tending your companion there."

His frown deepened. "He is—not companion. I am of the Fifteenth Wisconsin. He—" A single shake of the head. "I do not know where he comes from."

"I see." Pearl glanced behind her. Was it her imagination, or did he rest more easily at the moment than he had before? "I only meant that in reference to the two of you being in the same room."

The explanation felt silly as soon as she said it, but the man's face relaxed as if with relief. "Ah. And you said you are Miss Mac—Far—lane?"

He struggled through the syllables as if simple English—or in this case, Scottish—names were foreign to him.

Come to think, perhaps they were. "Yes. And you are?"

Another flicker of an attempted smile. "Berndt Thorsson."

Her turn to struggle. "What, now? Burnt Toors-son?"

His chapped lips parted in a grin. "Na, na." He said the name again then mimed writing. "You have—something with which to draw?"

She rummaged for the old school slate and pencil she still kept in her trunk. He took it, and with a firmer hand than she expected, wrote it out.

*Berndt Thorsson.*

"What on earth kind of name is that?" she said, then clapped a hand to her mouth.

The grin returned. "I am born in Norway. Family come to America, fight now to preserve the Union." He said the words as if rehearsed.

"There is no Union if some states can't mind their own business instead of nosing around in that of other states'," she muttered. The blue eyes continued to regard her steadily, and she pulled in a long breath. "I am most sorry that you find yourself in this predicament, Mister Thorsson, as to be wounded and under my care. But I promise I won't let you die by intention."

The Norwegian sobered and gave a nod, his eyes cutting to the other man. "You worry that he will die?"

"Yes. He has been feverish. Taken no nourishment, and very little water."

Mr. Thorsson's brow furrowed again. "I will pray he lives."

Pearl stared at him for a minute. "Thank you," she said finally, for lack of anything better to say.

Why had it never occurred to her that even Yankees could be men of faith?

The Norwegian's blue eyes sparkled back at her as if amused at the idea. . .but it was absurd to think he knew what she thought. She turned and plunked herself back in the chair next to the unconscious man.

"So what of your family?" Pearl tossed the soft question over her shoulder as she reached for the rag and wrung it out again.

Mr. Thorsson took a minute to reply. "I have two sisters and three brothers. Two of the brothers also are fighting. My father tends the farm back in Wisconsin. My mother is in heaven now."

For the hundredth time, Pearl smoothed the cloth over the fevered forehead and cheeks. Was it her imagination, or did the man beneath the covers twitch? "Mine as well."

"I am sorry for your loss."

She nodded. "And I, for yours."

They kept the quiet dialogue going until Pearl looked up and saw the horizon beginning to color with the dawn. She excused herself and went to change out the basin of water—and take a moment to linger watching the sunrise. Though bone weary, the growing wash of vivid rose and orange across the sky soothed her spirit.

With a sigh, she turned at last to go in. The sitting room was quiet. Blessedly so, because it meant that vile man in the middle would not be awake—

But wait, it was almost too quiet. She set the basin down on a sideboard and tiptoed closer to the bed of the man who'd been gutshot.

*Simon Murphy,* she corrected herself.

He lay still. Perfectly so. No lift to his chest.

Her own heart pounding, she crept nearer. Hesitantly put a hand to his brow.

Cold and smooth, like carved ivory.

He too had flown away to heaven.

# CHAPTER 7

Somehow, Pearl accomplished cooking breakfast and seeing to Pa and their four remaining charges while Portius and Clem carried Simon Murphy's body out to be buried. The man with the missing leg, the same one who had harassed her during the night, awoke enough to take his bowl and give her an oily smirk in return, but thankfully, he said nothing.

Maybe he knew to mind his manners at least while Pa was present. Pearl turned away from him and went to help the other man eat.

She thought of the Norwegian in the other room and blew out a breath. "What's your name, sir?" she asked, waiting until the man had swallowed the bite she'd just given him.

He blinked. Apparently he'd no more expected kindness from a Confederate family than she had faith from a Yankee. "Toby Jackson, ma'am. Of the Eleventh Michigan."

She nodded as if that meant anything to her. "Mister Jackson. I sincerely hope you recover and return to your own lands to plague us no longer."

That earned a weak grin, and she fed him another bite.

"And I be Abner Shaw of the Thirty-Eighth Indiana," came the voice of the other man, with just enough smugness in his tone to turn her stomach.

Pearl gave him a glance and a nod.

"Welcome, regardless," Pa piped, from across the room.

She winced. That was laying it on a bit too thick—or was Pa wandering a bit, in his mind? The others cast him uncertain glances, as if they too were unsure how to interpret his cheery pronouncement, but no one said a word.

Pearl finished her task, gathered the bowls, and went to check on Thorsson. He too had finished, and after setting his bowl on the floor, he was asleep again.

It had been a long night, after all. Strangely, she wasn't yet sleepy enough to retire, herself. Weary to the bone, for certain, but sleepy? Most emphatically not.

With a little sigh, she turned to the other man. Sagged into the chair at his bedside. She'd forgotten her basin of water and rag. Was it even making a difference? With only the barest hesitation this time, she laid her hand over his forehead. Still warm but—was that sweat beneath her palm?

Her heart leaped. Sweat would be a good sign.

As before, however, he didn't move. She sighed. "Please don't die."

She slumped against the wall and closed her eyes. Just a few minutes and then she'd go see about washing dishes.

The few minutes apparently became a few hours. Pearl woke to rustling beside her and a terrible crick in her neck.

"Miss Pearl," came the deep voice of Portius, "if you don't mind giving me a hand with these bandages, you could go lie down awhile."

She drew a deep breath and stretched her neck one way, then the other. "Of course," she answered without thinking and reached for the bundle of cloth he handed her.

Portius had hardly touched the man's arm before the limb flailed, and the wounded soldier exploded in a shouting fury. Pearl scrambled backward, out of her chair and to the middle of the room. The Negro kept a low murmur and, getting a grasp on the man's upper arm, set his other forearm across the man's chest to press him back to the bed.

The unknown patient wasn't even awake, but he subsided at last under the Negro's superior strength and lay gasping.

"That's it," Portius said. "Just settle down. All we're doing here is trying to tend your arm." He angled a glance at Pearl. "Go ahead. I'll hold him down."

She gave a quick nod and stepped forward. Obviously the arm pained him greatly. Could she remove the old bandage without setting him off? She had to try, regardless.

When her fingertips brushed his arm, the man twitched, hard, but Portius held him firm and nodded for her to keep going. She plucked at the edge of the bandage, tentatively at first, then with more purpose, until the end came free. Even then it was a bit of an ordeal to completely unwind, since the wound had seeped through and hardened the outer layers. The man beneath Portius's hold whimpered as she sought to work the worst of it free.

"Pour a little of that water over the cloth," the Negro murmured, "and let it soak for a minute."

She scooped with her palm and poured, and indeed, that loosened some of the crust, at least around the edges. At last the bandage came off, and she used the relatively clean and dry section to wash around the amputation wound itself.

"It looks a little less angry," she said.

"Mm, maybe. Be generous with that goldenseal, now."

She did as he directed and then began to rewrap the limb. The wounded man's breath caught, but he lay otherwise limp now.

*Lord in heaven, please let him not die.*

Pearl's throat closed. She almost couldn't help the prayer.

As she finished up, Portius eased his hold on the man. "Go on and take a rest now, Miss Pearl."

With a stiff nod, she rose and gathered up the soiled bandaging.

In the other room, Pa sat and read from the great volume of the Bible laid out in his lap, his voice a steady, soothing rhythm.

" 'Save me, O God; for the waters are come in unto my soul. I sink in deep mire, where there is no standing: I am come into deep waters, where the floods overflow me. I am weary of my crying: my throat is dried: mine eyes fail while I wait for my God.' "

Pearl had surely become weary of her own crying.

" 'They that hate me without a cause are more than the hairs of mine head...'"

She shot a glance at the two men remaining in the sitting room. *Toby Jackson. Abner Shaw.* The former lay listening quietly, while the latter's eyes were shut tightly as if he were in pain.

" 'O God, thou knowest my foolishness; and my sins are not hid from thee.'"

Perhaps, under the convicting power of God's Word, he was in pain. Pearl fervently wished so, at least, after the way the man had spoken to her.

Upstairs, she stretched out on the bed and let the distant murmur of Pa's voice wash over her. She could no longer make out the words, but the sound of it lulled her back to sleep.

" 'But as for me, my prayer is unto thee, O Lord.... Let not the waterflood overflow me, neither let the deep swallow me up, and let not the pit shut her mouth upon me.'"

The floodwaters had indeed swept over him. Still held him prisoner.

" 'Hear me, O Lord; for thy lovingkindness is good: turn unto me according to the multitude of thy tender mercies.'"

He cast about for words to match the plea of his heart. *Oh God, save me, indeed. Please. I am drowning....*

He felt, as it were, his body rising from the depths, floating toward the light. The pressure gradually lifted from his chest, and the fire in his lungs dissipated, trickling down from his chest into his left forearm. The burning there lingered despite the chill in the rest of his body, but at least now he could breathe.

After what seemed an unreasonably long time, he realized his eyes were open, and he could look about the room. It seemed to be dusk—was that the ending of a day, or the beginning? He had no way of knowing except to wait and see if it grew more dark or more light.

Blinking, he rolled his head to the side. A small room, with two beds—he thought he remembered seeing it before—and another man in the other bed, asleep, or at least with his eyes closed.

He scoured his memory but came up with nothing that would provide the least clue to his location or how long it had been since—yes, he recalled a battle, and the name Chickamauga, but nearly nothing apart from that. The ache in his arm demanded his attention, but something about it caused him to swallow heavily before hazarding a look.

Because he just might have dreamed the horror he thought he remembered.

But no, the bandages ended smoothly below the elbow. Just as he recalled.

*Oh. . .God.* He felt the sudden need to puke.

It wasn't that others hadn't lost more. He knew this. And to wake up and find himself in what was obviously someone's home—and a tidy one at that, by all appearances—rather than the battlefield or a prison camp was nothing short of a mercy. Except that this would undoubtedly be some Rebel's home.

Or had he also dreamed the declaration that he was now a prisoner of war?

The slender figure of a woman swept inside the room and stopped, clutching a basin. Her eyes widened. "Oh! You're—awake!"

"Not sure I'd go that far," he whispered. It hurt to speak.

She set her basin down beside the bed then whisked to the washstand, where she poured a cup of water before perching on the chair at his bedside. "You'll want this, I expect," she murmured.

He levered painfully to his good elbow before remembering he had no way to take the cup from her. But she seemed to anticipate the need and, lifting it to his mouth, helped him drink.

When he was done, she sat back while he wiped his mouth against his upper arm. "Thank you, ma'am." The wispy dark hair escaping her sober knot and the equally sober green eyes he definitely remembered. Likewise the dark gray calico of her full-sleeved dress, covered in a clean but well-worn apron. Her skirts full but limp—no hoops, then. A practical choice, that.

But what was it he'd felt the need to ask? Suddenly he could no longer find his tongue.

"Who are you, then?" the woman said, more a statement than a question. "I've learned the name of every man here, but yours."

Why could he only blink at her? Maybe because there was a steel in those eyes that brooked no nonsense.

"Sergeant Joshua Wheeler of the First Ohio, at your service, ma'am."

The corner of her mouth lifted in the slightest of smiles, and then she sniffed. "You won't be at anyone's service for a fair bit yet, I reckon. But I'm glad to see you awake." Her expression settled into grave lines once again. "I thank you for not dying."

Another memory of a voice that matched hers flitted through his mind. So it was she who'd offered those fevered pleas? "I feel I can take no credit for that."

A definite curve to her lips this time. "Likely not. I'll be thanking Providence as well."

"And I'll try not to give you cause to regret it." A muted sound, like a stifled chuckle, came from her throat, and he offered a weak grin in response, then lay back and closed his eyes for a moment. At her continued silence, he cracked an eyelid open again. "You have me at a disadvantage, ma'am. I'm aware I must be your prisoner, but I do not recall your name. Or where the location might be."

Another soft snort. "I am Pearl MacFarlane. And it's *miss*. You find yourself in Tennessee, nearly Georgia, just southeast of Chattanooga."

She winced as if she'd said too much.

"What news of the lines?"

"I've not been paying attention," she said. All steel, once more.

# CHAPTER 8

What a very different thing to tend him while asleep than to face him now, awake and talking. His hair lay askew, and deep shadows encircled his eyes, but there was an intentness to his gaze that kept her pinned to the chair even while she longed to flee. Especially when he asked after news of the recent battle.

Regardless, he remained a fair example of a wretched Yankee. And here he was, awake but still lying in what had been her bedroom.

"How long was I asleep?" he asked.

She thought back. The days and nights had seemed endless. "The better part of three days."

He blinked and frowned. "Three. . .days. . ."

"You were awake once or twice at the beginning. Then you went insensible with fever for two solid days. Which I'm not sure I count as sleep."

The frown deepened.

"Would you like something to eat?" she suddenly remembered to ask.

His eyes brightened. "I would be most appreciative, miss."

His manners were pretty at least. . .nearly as pretty as a Southern boy's. Pearl sniffed. For whatever that mattered, because there was always Travis, who presumed on their hospitality without so much as a by-your-leave.

"Very well. I'll be back in a moment." She rose from the chair.

"Wait. Miss?" His expression went apologetic. "If you could, ah. . .I need the necessary."

"Of course." She should have thought of that as well.

The rest of the house was lit at either end by two lamps. Something else they'd have to think about—finding kerosene. Papa was nowhere to be found. He'd been reading the Bible earlier—sometimes he could read and sometimes not, although daytimes were certainly better than night—but he must have retired to bed already. Clem of course would be off doing—whatever. But Portius was nowhere in sight, either.

*Oh Lord, please help.* The very thought of simply helping the man walk to the necessary, or use a chamber pot, completely terrified her.

She ran to the front door and outside, her lungs tight. The last light of day rimmed the ridge, and above its crest, a nearly full moon hung among a sprinkling of stars. The cool air washed over her, sweet and calming, and she stepped to the edge of the porch and clutched the post.

"Miss Pearl? Is something wrong?"

She swung toward Portius's voice, so deep and soothing, and took another gulp of the night air. "I—yes. Our last sleeping soldier is awake. Needs help to the necessary."

"Ahh." The man's breath escaped in a low hum. "Well, that's good news, at least."

She bobbed a nod but didn't release her hold on the porch post. "It is."

Portius came to the bottom of the steps and looked at her gravely. "P'raps you should stay out here and take a bit of the evening air."

"I—" She shook her head. "I told him I'd get him something to eat."

He dipped his own in acknowledgment then moved past her.

She waited until he'd gone in, caught a last deep breath, and finally felt her heartbeat settling to a more normal pace.

Maybe she could face the rest of this night, after all.

"I'm weak as a kitten," Josh muttered, as the massive black man helped him to his feet.

"I reckon so," the man responded evenly.

Doggone it all, but everything hurt. His arm was merely the worst of it. And the room spun each time he moved. Being on his feet, though, felt like either the best or the worst thing he'd ever experienced, and no journey had ever been so long as the one across the house where he was quartered, out to the porch, and through the yard. A light wind greeted him, and a moon and stars in an almost-black sky.

So it had indeed been sunset when he'd awakened.

His escort brought him back and steered him toward the kitchen, where lamplight revealed the woman—Miss MacFarlane, that is—bustling about with the briefest glance in his direction. Settled in a chair at a table that looked to be oak, its uneven surface rubbed shiny by years of use, he nodded at the black man. "My thanks."

The man smiled a little and offered a blanket to wrap about his bare shoulders. Josh tucked it around himself, awkwardly, the aching stump of his forearm pressed to his belly beneath the cloth, as Miss MacFarlane set a bowl and spoon in front of him. "This was tonight's supper, though it's cold now."

She followed it with a stoneware mug of what looked like water. Josh reached for it and was rewarded with the blanket slipping off that shoulder.

What must this Rebel girl think of a half-naked, one-handed Yankee at her table?

Her expression seemed curiously blank at the moment, unlike earlier when he thought he could trace a dozen emotions as they flitted across her features. But maybe that was simply the lingering effect of being unconscious for too long.

Regardless, he'd no call to be thinking about this young woman's state of mind. He'd best be seeing to how to be the least burden to her as possible.

He curled his hand around the cup and lifted it to his mouth. Water. Sweet, cold. The most refreshing thing he'd ever tasted in his life.

Likewise the thin bean soup in the bowl before him, once he set down the water and reached for the spoon. He wanted to weep, it tasted so good. Instead he curled himself around the bowl so not a drop would be wasted.

*Thank You, Lord God, that I'm not in a prison camp. Yet, at least.*

That could change at any moment, he knew. Although why the

Rebels had brought him here instead of packing him aboard a train for Richmond, he'd no idea.

He glanced up. The black man stood at the end of the table, arms folded across his chest forbiddingly, and quite in contrast with the mild set of that one's bearded features. "How many days ago was the battle?" Josh asked, his voice still rough with disuse.

Hardly a flicker in the dark eyes. "Four days since the Federals give up and run back to Chattanooga."

He let the spoon sink back into the bowl. The Union troops had given up? After months of striving over Middle Tennessee, and slogging through mud and dust to get to Chattanooga? Not to be wondered at, some would doubtless say, given what some saw as the indecision of Rosecrans. Old Rosey hesitated often enough before, much to the frustration of Josh's more immediate superiors. The battle itself had been one long frustration for his regiment—what he recalled of it, anyway.

But now, to have expended so much effort—so much blood—to simply give up? Josh could scarce take it in.

Would Rosecrans even be able to hold Chattanooga?

"Do you know when I was taken prisoner?" he asked.

"About then," the black man responded evenly.

Josh thought about the timbre and rhythm of the man's speech. "I believe I remember you. The hospital tent. After—" He shrugged his left shoulder. "After this occurred."

The Negro gave a long, slow nod. "You may call me Portius."

Josh lifted his spoon once more. Curious, the Negro's reserve toward him. Though the Proclamation had gone out at the first of the year, giving Negro slaves their freedom wherever the Union army occupied, depending upon the state, it wouldn't be the first time he'd encountered such coolness from Southern blacks, or loyalty to the Rebel cause. In some cases, Negroes actually preferred the perceived security of a white master to their own freedom. Was Portius one of those? Or did his apparent service to the Confederacy serve some other purpose?

It could hurt nothing to ask. But probably not here and now.

He looked around. Two beds stood against the far wall of the open sitting room. "You have four of us quartered here? Or are there more?"

"There were six," Miss MacFarlane answered. "Two died."

*Please don't die*, echoed the words from his fevered dreams.

" 'Tain't all from the same regiment, if you're wondering," Portius supplied, next. "And none of you is fit to escape, so don't give that any thought."

Josh lowered his gaze to the bowl, regretfully empty now. Of course the man knew he'd have to try.

Eventually, that is.

"Do you want more?" Miss MacFarlane's voice interrupted his thoughts.

"Is there more?"

"A little." She whisked his bowl away and brought it back half-full.

He hesitated before digging in again. "Thank you."

*There* was the tiny flare of emotion across those stern features. Then she dipped her head and turned away.

Supper finished, Josh allowed Portius to shepherd him, arm aching so fiercely he could barely shuffle along, outside again and then back to his bed. Once there, he nearly stumbled over the basin of water still sitting on the floor next to the foot of the narrow bedstead. He peered at it, trying to divine its specific purpose.

"It's water. For washing," Portius said, before Josh asked.

"Washing what?"

The black man helped him get seated at the edge of the bed, then bent to move the basin from floor to chair seat before fixing Josh with a stern look. "I reckon Miss Pearl was in here nearly every waking hour while you was out of your head with fever, trying to keep you alive and halfway comfortable by bathing your face. Since 'tain't needed for that anymore, I suggest you use it to wash yourself."

And with that, he wrung out the rag and handed it off to Josh then retreated to the door.

For lack of anything better to do, Josh wiped his face, neck, and the wounded arm. Tried not to think of that plain, severe girl out there ministering to him in the way Portius described.

How foolish of him to think he could simply sail through an entire war and never—never be hit. He'd just never expected it to be like this.

There had always been a certain amount of romance attached to going to war, even to the idea of being wounded and then tended by some pretty nurse. Only with their first battle, experiencing the noise and smoke and the horror of what real killing felt like and afterward helping move the wounded, did his conjured images of clean, sunny hospitals blow completely away.

The fact that this tiny room, which he shared with only one other man, was such a contrast to the chaos and filth of a field hospital made it seem all the more unreal.

He stopped and looked at his bandaged half arm. This, however, was real enough.

*God. . .why? For what purpose did You deem it necessary to allow this to happen? How am I to make a living—provide for a wife and family?*

*Or even go back to soldiering?*

He'd known of men who'd lost limbs and still served.

He'd known of many men who lost limbs, in fact, and some of those losses were arguably unnecessary. Camp was rife with stories of cold, hurried surgeons lopping off arms and legs because they didn't have the patience to see to care for the long haul.

"Do you happen to recall," he asked the black man, "just how bad the injury to my arm was?"

Portius swung toward him. "The surgeon said it looked like damage from a minié ball. Your wrist was well-nigh gone." He regarded Josh impassively for a moment. "Taking off the hand was necessary, if that's what you're asking. Gangrene would have set in, otherwise."

Josh stopped, clutching the rag, then gave a quick nod. "Thank you kindly." It was precisely what he wished to know.

He realized with a jolt that he still had his one good arm to wash and—no way to hold the rag from the other side. He stared at the cloth for a moment then raised his eyes to the Negro, still regarding him impassively.

"Do you mind—that is—" He swallowed. "I can't reach this arm."

The ghost of a smile crossed Portius's face, but not an unkindly one. He stepped forward, took the rag, and accomplished the task with an ease that bespoke having done it many a time before.

"How did you come to be—here?" Josh asked.

"You mean, with the Confederacy?" Portius's voice held a slightly mocking note.

He blew out a breath. "Yes."

The other man chuckled. "Don't make sense to most, I own." He held up the basin so Josh could swish his hand in the water, then swiped it with the rag. "Don't even make sense to me, some days. But I can assure you"—his gaze sharpened again—"you Yankees who think you got a corner on having the right cause? Most of y'all care nothing for the black man. It's all politics. They call it 'Black Republicanism,' but—" He shook his head. "I just know I'm supposed to be where I am. Serving a man who flat saved my life, and whoever else the good Lord puts in my path. Which at the moment happens to be you."

With another smile, he set the cloth back in the basin and rose.

"Thank you," Josh said, holding his gaze.

The black man nodded and left the room.

So much to think about. Too much. Josh dragged his fingers through his hair and beard, and with a sigh, he maneuvered himself to a prone position. A bed had never felt so good.

And when had they moved him to a bed?

It was his last waking thought.

# CHAPTER 9

"Is it customary for a man sick and feverish just hours before to be up on his feet so quickly?"

Pearl found a moment to murmur the question to Portius, after the man had finally returned to bed and fallen asleep.

No, not *the man*. He had a name now. Joshua Wheeler.

The side of Portius's mouth hitched. "Hard to say. If he was in good health before the hand was taken off—but the way he was completely unconscious for two days tells me his body took it plenty hard."

She nodded distractedly. "Does anyone else show signs of infection?"

The Negro cast a glance toward her bedroom. "I confess I fear for the other man in there, Mister Thorsson. That leg is so tore up—"

He shook his head, leaving the thought unfinished. Pearl couldn't help but agree at the horrifying nature of the wound, but she'd little enough experience to be able to say if the man could even recover.

Portius leveled her a look. "Miss Pearl, I'll sit watch for part of tonight, but I'll be needing to return to camp tomorrow."

The now-familiar panic beat inside her chest, but she pushed it down and nodded. "Of course. You have—obligations, I'm sure."

And then she realized. Eight months ago and more was the Proclamation that had come down from President Lincoln, essentially declaring that all Negro slaves were to go free. Tennessee did not fall under the jurisdiction of that, however.

But why was Portius still serving the Confederate army?

He must have caught the alarmed glance she gave him, because he hesitated. "Is something wrong, Miss Pearl?"

"I"—she swallowed—"I am simply wondering. . ."

His face did not alter from its kindly expression. "Why I am going back?"

She let out her breath in a rush. "Yes."

A tired smile creased his face. "Some loyalties go deeper than the skin."

She failed to divine his meaning. "Which is to say?"

The smile widened. "Some things more important than color, Miss Pearl."

She lay awake long after she should have easily fallen asleep. The Negro man's coming had been such a relief—could she manage the four wounded Yankees who remained, with only Clem and Pa to help? It had been difficult enough to manage the farm with Pa not able to do the heavy work of planting or harvest and with her older brothers gone. They'd really only gotten enough planted to feed themselves and their stock, or what remained after the predations of the Confederate army, anyway. They still had apples, sweet potatoes, and some corn hidden away—and wild hogs roamed the hills—but Pearl was truly afraid they'd starve come winter. And now with the game chased off, or mostly so, by the battle and continued presence of two armies. . .

*Oh God, help us.*

What was Travis even thinking, dragging these men here? Wouldn't it have served just as well to load them on a train and send them to Richmond, to prison?

She should insist he take them back. Even offer to go help nurse the wounded elsewhere, in exchange.

But. . .she couldn't bear the thought of leaving Pa with just Clem to care for him. And she couldn't just take Pa along.

Daylight poured through the window, stabbing Josh's eyelids with a ferocity that rivaled the ache in his arm. He lifted the limb to block the sun's assault and was instantly sorry, as he thumped it against the wall and sent waves of agony echoing throughout his body.

Groaning, he rolled to the side and found himself at the edge of the bed.

A narrow bed, but a bed nevertheless. In a house owned by Rebels. Where he was prisoner.

But a house here and not Richmond. Not Libby Prison or any other. He had to remember that.

Prying his eyes open, he drew a deep breath. Opposite him, a mere pace or two away, the other man still lay, asleep again—or was that asleep still? Concern stirred, but the overwhelming throb in his arm silenced nearly all else.

Need pulsed through him as well—the need to be up, on his own feet, and out of the bed, more than anything else. He swung his legs over the edge, pushing himself up with his good elbow. Sat for a moment, simply drawing the air in and out of his lungs.

He shivered and glanced about. Where was his shirt—a coat—anything? There—a pair of blue coats, one short and one long, hung on pegs where he thought he remembered a woman's dress before. No shirt in sight, though two knapsacks lay on the floor beneath the coats, but the coat would do, for now. He hadn't the patience to rummage through a knapsack.

Getting to his feet was less difficult than before, and the dizziness passed in moments. Josh shuffled over to the wall and reached for the coat hanging nearest to his bed, the long one with two blue chevrons adorning each sleeve. Whoever put them there must have puzzled out whose was whose—

His gaze snagged on the bloodstained, tattered remains of the left sleeve. *Oh.* A shock went through him, as if he were back on the battlefield, among the noise and screams, and hit afresh.

*Oh God. Why would You allow this?*

Driven once again by bodily need, he gingerly tugged the garment around his shoulders.

A low murmur reached his ears from the other room. He stepped through the doorway and stopped, one hand on the lintel. The conversation came from the two men in the beds across the sitting room. "Didn't want no darky looking after us anyway," said one.

"Ah, they're all right, I reckon. Leastways this one was." To which the response was a snort.

No one else was in sight. Josh started across the floor, and both men looked up with surprise and interest. "Well, lookee! Good morning to ya," said the second man.

"Morning," Josh answered, then cleared his throat. He kept moving.

"Headed to the necessary? Lucky you, goin' outside."

Josh offered a nod. He'd stop for pleasantries on the way back.

One foot in front of the other. He gained the door and stepped out, where the severity of sunlight was lessened by the porch roof.

A pretty little farmyard greeted his sight, with a modest barn across the way and three or four elegant trees shading both the house and a hitching rail. A split-rail fence marked off a pen or paddock, and to the right stood a stone-encircled well. A bit beyond that, half-a-dozen fruit trees—apple, if he didn't miss his guess, although they were all picked clean.

The outhouse would be away to the left, as he recalled.

He went down the steps and across the yard, more slowly now. Beyond the barn lay a stretch of field and a mountain ridge rising above, the forest lit by the midmorning sun behind him. Turning, he stood for a moment scanning the steep hillside, still green except for the occasional tree turning red or yellow. All was quiet except for a rhythmic pounding interspersed with splashing, coming from the direction of the outhouse. He continued his amble in that direction.

Miss MacFarlane knelt in the tree-edged backyard near a clothesline strung between two tall posts, scrubbing a wad of cloth over a washtub and board. Josh made a beeline for the outhouse. No need to disturb her, yet.

He stepped inside and secured the latch, then hung his coat on a hook placed helpfully on the wall. Seeing to things took far longer than he expected even under the circumstances, and refastening his trousers was a painful and frustrating ordeal. By the time Josh finished, he was sweating, swearing under his breath, and entirely too shaky for comfort.

But now he had to make it back to the house.

He unlatched the door, reached for his coat, and in the process of trying to sling the garment back around his shoulders and step outside, slammed his confounded arm—no, *stump*—against the doorway of the outhouse. A strangled cry broke from his throat, and the agony buckled his knees. He only barely caught himself from pitching on his face.

"Mister Wheeler!"

The feminine voice, breathless with shock, and the sound of rustling skirts and running footsteps filled his ears.

"What on earth are you doing out here, alone?" she murmured, and small but capable hands took hold of his shoulders. "Come, let me help you up."

Heat swept through him, causing the sweat to break out afresh. He'd be doggoned if he needed a slip of a woman to assist him from the privy. "I—can manage it."

"Of course you can," she said, a slight edge to her voice. "But I'd rather not have to drag you back into the house by your suspenders, if you please. Not that you're wearing any," she added in a mutter.

"Very well," he gasped. "Give me—a moment."

He focused on taking the next breath, and another, until the throb in his arm eased enough for him to think clearly. The girl's hand remained on his shoulder.

At last he straightened, still swaying a little on his knees. He peeked at the girl and found her startlingly close, mouth pressed firm but green eyes wide.

Plain she might be, but she was still young and female and—oh, how he needed a good scrubbing.

"I might be able to get up, now," he muttered.

She shifted back and stood, then reached a hand out to brace him while he did the same. The strength of her grip surprised him, as did her lack of hesitation in setting her shoulder beneath his and an arm around his waist, before leading him toward the house.

"Can't blame you for trying, I suppose," she said as they went. "Portius returned to camp this morning, and I'm a bit shorthanded. My pa isn't able to help, not in this way at least, and my brother Clem is always running off."

"I'd rather not be a bother, regardless," Josh said.

They'd made it nearly back to the front steps, and he was only slightly out of breath. A true achievement.

"Like I said," Miss MacFarlane said evenly, "I'd rather not be dragging you back inside."

They gained the porch, and she stopped to let him rest a moment.

"Speaking of suspenders," he said. "Do I still have such a thing as a shirt?"

Her lips curved a little. "I've wondered that myself."

The chatter in the sitting room fell to silence as they entered, and then a low whistle came from one of the beds. Miss MacFarlane stiffened against his side but would apparently have kept going. Josh's feet stumbled to a halt, and his head came up.

The man in the leftmost bed wore a look of chagrin, slanting glances between Josh and the man in the other bed, but that one only gazed back at Josh with a smug expression.

For several long, painful heartbeats, Josh held his eyes until the man's smile flagged and he looked away. Only then did he let Miss MacFarlane urge him across the room and to his own bed.

# CHAPTER 10

Before Pearl could help any further, Mr. Wheeler shucked his coat at the bedside and collapsed on its edge. Shadows rimmed his eyes even more deeply than before, and his pale forehead and cheeks glistened with the effort he'd just expended, the freckles standing out in relief.

Without asking, she poured another cup of water and handed it to him, then a second once he drained that. "Thank you," he gasped, wiping his mouth with the back of his hand.

She nodded soberly then turned to check on Mr. Thorsson while Mr. Wheeler settled himself. He moved slightly but didn't wake when she laid her hand across his scorching forehead.

An ache gripped her throat. Not another. Not again.

Yet these men were the enemy. What did she care if they perished here or on the battlefield somewhere?

Because they had been placed under her care, her conscience was quick to retort. Whether by chance or no, they were here, and it was her duty to feed them.

*"If thine enemy thirst. . ."*

She gritted her teeth and went to fetch her basin. But then she remembered she'd left laundry in the side yard. A snicker interrupted her thoughts as she crossed the sitting room. She spared the obnoxious one not a glance but hurried back out to finish the one task so she could see to another.

It was a kind attempt on Mr. Wheeler's part to even think to stop and confront that other man, but what could he have done?

For that matter, what was she going to do if the man's harassment became worse?

In the side yard, she plunged her hands back into the water, not caring that she splashed her apron and skirt, and seized the entire wad of bandages she'd been scrubbing. Bandages she needed in order to dress the wounds of the men inside her house, again.

She collapsed against the side of the washtub, breast heaving, throat clogged with sobs she dared not give vent to—but could not deny. Three brothers in the grave because of men like the ones inside her house. And Pa half-insensible at times because of the strain and worry of it all.

Where was Pa, anyway?

She shoved upright, glancing around, her lungs working like a bellows and heart pounding for a completely different reason now. But perhaps there was no reason to panic. Pa had been known to sleep overlong before or wander a bit far on a walk.

But the urgency thudding through her veins demanded action.

She scrambled to her feet and ran back into the house. Mr. Shaw and Mr. Jackson perked up when she skidded to a stop in the sitting room. "Have either of you seen my pa?"

Hopeful looks faded to confusion and blankness. "Nah," Mr. Shaw said.

"I ain't seen him since breakfast," Mr. Jackson chimed.

She ran the rest of the way across to Pa's room, but he wasn't there.

Of course.

Flying through the rest of the house—even the upstairs although there was no rational way he could have gotten up the steps—did not uncover his whereabouts. Thankfully, both the men in her bedroom were asleep, which gave her a bit more time before she'd be needed again.

But where—*where?*—could Pa have gotten off to? Out through the back door, turning in circles to scan the yard and fields as far as she could see. The privy stood open, so—not there. Around to the barn and inside. The few chickens they still managed to keep scattered, squawking, then trailed her, hoping for a few scraps or choice grains.

"Pa?" Her voice echoed in the empty barn. Only the chickens answered.

Her breaths came tight and fast once more. She could not give in to the weeping, here. She had no time to waste if he was out there wandering.

And obviously he was out there wandering if he could not be found around the house or outbuildings.

"God," she panted, "oh God, please help me!"

Outside, she strode to the fence and turned again in a slow circle, scanning every bit of exposed pasture, field, or hillside. Down the road. Nothing. She made a circuit of the barnyard, looking for footprints accompanied by the telltale marks of Pa's walking stick. Still nothing.

*Lord God. I am begging. Please help.*

She closed her eyes, drew a long, deep breath. Held it. Let it out again.

*"I will lift up mine eyes unto the hills. . ."*

She did just that, setting her gaze on the ridge overlooking their farm, which she'd traversed just two days before on her way to Lydia's. A compulsion she could not explain drew her around, through the gate, and across the field, up the slope.

Halfway up, she stopped and called out again. And again, only silence. She kept going.

She crested the ridge, headed down toward the cleared region that had become a battlefield. And there—in the middle of the field, occasionally tamping his stick, turning this way and that, staring about himself—was Pa.

Heedless of the damage or debris, she ran, crying out for him. He responded but slowly, at last pivoting toward her and raising his head.

As she drew closer, the frown creasing his weathered features, and the moisture swimming in his eyes, became more visible. His gaze fixed on her but a moment then wandered again across the landscape.

"Jewel. What have they done to my mountain?"

Pearl's heart squeezed. He'd called her by Mama's name only a handful of times, mostly when his spells were the worst. She slowed and trotted to a halt at his side. Her lungs burned and her side ached. "I know, Pa. Isn't it dreadful?"

"I—I can't find my mountain." His voice was plaintive, like a child's. "They've torn it all to pieces."

*Oh Pa.* She took his good arm. "Come. Let's go back to the house."

He hiccupped, almost a sob, then sighed. "But—my mountain."

"It–it'll be back," she murmured. "I need you, though. Clem needs you. Come back home."

"Home." He sighed, once more. "Is supper ready, Jewel?"

Pearl suppressed a wince. "Not yet. But you can help me get it started."

She tugged again at his arm, and with another *tap, tap* of his stick, he took a few steps in the desired direction. "You know I don't help with the cooking. That's why I married you."

A long breath escaped her as they made their way back toward the timbered ridge. "Pa. I'm not Jewel. I'm Pearl."

He snorted. "Of course you are." Then, "Hmm. 'Pearl of great price. . .'"

She smiled. It was his favorite scripture reference, where her name was concerned. "Fine. If you won't help cook, you can read the Bible to our houseguests while I prepare the meal."

A decisive nod was his response, and he stepped more firmly now. "That I can most certainly do. 'Preach the word; be instant in season, out of season.'"

A bubble of laughter escaped her, a little more high pitched than usual, at the quote from 2 Timothy. She swallowed past the lump in her throat—Pa was found, no need to cry now—and continued guiding him up the hill.

Back at the house, she installed Pa in a chair with the Bible in his lap—much less mischief he could get into that way—made the rounds, and promised those who were awake that she'd return after finishing the washing. She winced over Mr. Thorsson, still burning with fever and a little restless, lingered a moment too long over the slumbering Mr. Wheeler because of his eerie stillness, and whisked back outdoors to attend the laundry. Clem was nowhere in sight, nor did he respond when she called. Likely enough he'd been the one to go up over the hill first, and Pa had seen him and thought to follow but had been left behind. She sniffed. She'd best keep a closer eye on him.

It was a distressing thought that Pa was becoming more childlike, or that his mind was dwelling further in the past—and for longer.

What was she to do with him if he continued to fail? Or rather when, since that was probably closer to the truth of what was to come.

Once again she gripped the edge of the washtub and set her forehead on her hands.

*Oh Lord God. . .*

She wasn't sure she had any prayers left. Not at the moment. Even though God had apparently answered one in a mighty way, allowing her to find Pa.

*And I do thank You for that. Oh, and for keeping Mister Wheeler from dying. Now please, Lord, don't let that Mister Thorsson die. Help me continue looking after Papa. And keep Clem safe wherever he is.*

*It might not hurt if You could bring Portius back, as well. Or at least give me enough strength and wit to deal with all these menfolk You've entrusted to my care.*

Apparently she had prayers left, after all. Wearily, she finished the washing and hung the bandages to dry. Next to fetch fresh water and inside.

Pa still sat in his chair, not reading at the moment, but just staring at the open pages of the Bible in his lap. Both men in the bed were asleep, or pretending to be. She'd bet the latter, especially in the case of Mr. Shaw, but she'd take the quiet and not complain.

Except that Pa didn't even look up when she passed through the sitting room.

The sound of intermittently trickling water was what pulled him out of slumber this time, and a soft sigh that might have been a prayer.

Although she wasn't yet murmuring, *Please don't die.*

Another catch of breath did sound like weeping. Josh cracked an eyelid and turned his head slowly enough to not make a sound, and sure enough, there she was, sitting at the other man's bedside this time, bent toward him as she bathed his face and neck.

Just as she had for him, by Portius's account.

From this angle, the graceful lines of her back and arms, clothed in that same gray calico she'd worn for days, were almost mesmerizing in their slow, steady movement. Wisps of dark hair, escaping messily from her chignon, trailed across her shoulders. Her breaths came deep, uneven, with a telltale heave and sniffle.

Despite his determination to be quiet and unnoticed, she turned to wring out her rag in the basin at her feet and caught a glimpse of him awake. In a blink or two, she'd composed her expression and met his gaze more fully for a moment. "Good afternoon."

"After—" He cleared his throat and tried again. "Afternoon."

"Do you need to get up?"

She started out of her chair, but he shook his head. "No. A drink would be appreciated, however."

He worked his way to sitting up while she fetched the cup, her skirt swirling with her. He accepted it with thanks, to which she responded with that sober nod. She watched him while he drank. "I expect you'll be needing something to eat soon."

"Soon," he murmured. For some reason, he was loath to get up the rest of the way.

Possibly because he didn't want to repeat the earlier debacle of nearly falling on his face in front of her. And the throbbing ache of his left arm warned that such a thing might be all too likely.

Another nod, then she seated herself again at the other man's bedside.

"All of us are prisoners of the recent battle?" Josh asked. In the meantime, it could not hurt to make inquiry on the full extent of his situation.

"Yes."

"And—two died already."

A slight hesitation, then, "Yes." The flatness of her voice recalled once again to his memory the feeling, by contrast, of her imploring whisper during his own fever.

"I'm surprised there aren't more of us here."

She glanced at him, her expression unreadable. "All our neighbors are conscripted into caring for the wounded, I'm told. Most have many more, true." She paused. "I'm not sure why we only have a handful, if things are as bad as described."

"And we are not all from the same regiment." None of the other men looked familiar, but one couldn't be sure in a situation such as this.

She shook her head. "This one's from. . .something Wisconsin. The other two are from Michigan and Indiana." She slanted him a glance. "Before you ask, no, I do not know why you were brought here. I've asked myself the same question often enough." Her hand went to the basin again to wring out the rag. "My cousin with the Army of Tennessee brought you."

He mulled this over for a moment.

Another glance. "Don't they send most of the prisoners to—Virginia, is it? Even the wounded ones?"

He combed his fingers through his hair, then his beard. "Yes. Libby Prison in Richmond. At least the officers go there. Enlisted I believe to Belle Isle. I can't imagine that they ran out of room on the trains north, but—"

She gave a soft snort. "Maybe they did. I had the feeling they half expected y'all to die anyway."

He watched the way her hand moved with gentle tenderness over the rugged features of the man across from him, despite the acerbic tone of her voice.

"Your cousin brought us," he mused aloud. "And where do your sympathies lie, Miss MacFarlane?"

The chill sweeping through the room was a palpable thing, like frost racing across a windowpane. Her eyes glinted as she looked at him, gaze holding longer this time. "With my country, Mister Wheeler. And kindly do not forget it."

He blew out a breath. "I will take care not to." He hesitated. "But it was a fair question."

"I suppose it is, at that," she answered crisply.

Dropping the rag into her basin, she swooped it off the floor and swept from the room, grand as any queen.

Well, that was a rousing success.

# CHAPTER 11

Blasted Yankee. That one would be better without a tongue. She was sorry now that she'd wished him awake. The nerve of him, to immediately pry at her loyalty to the Confederacy.

She came to a halt outside the bedroom door, halfway between the kitchen and sitting room. A wave of weariness swept over her. For a moment all she wished was to climb the stairs and collapse on the bed, sleep for hours. Maybe days.

Mr. Jackson and Mr. Shaw appeared to be asleep. Pa was nowhere in sight. Heart dropping, she set the basin down on her worktable and went to peek inside his bedroom.

And—he was there. On his side, back to her, but she could see the rise and fall of his breathing.

She let out her own breath in a rush. Thank the good Lord above. She didn't think her heart could take any more today.

After tossing the used water from her basin out the back door, she fetched the pail and went to the well for fresh. It would be time to think about starting supper again, here soon. She set her empty bucket on the stone wall encircling the well and sighed. With Pa sleeping off a spell and Clem out running the hills—could she even count on them for helping? She should get bandages changed before feeding everyone.

Another sigh, and she reached for the crank on the windlass that would lower the bucket they kept tied there to bring up water. She was just bringing it up again, full, when a call, barely audible over the creak of the windlass, drew her attention.

An officer in gray was just dismounting in the barnyard. What was Travis doing here, alone? He tethered the horse to a hitching post and sauntered over.

"How are you faring, Pearl?"

She drew herself up. A social call? After all this time? "Has Portius not reported back to you?"

He pulled off his hat and raked a hand through sandy-brown hair. "Yes, but I wanted to speak with you for myself." The pale blue eyes searched hers. "I'm sorry for simply leaving these men with you as I did. I—some weren't likely to survive, and I thought of you—it gave me a reason for coming and looking in on you."

She pressed her lips tightly together for a minute. "Why would you bother?"

His gaze faltered, and he only shook his head, turning the hat around and around in his hands.

"Pa's had another spell," she said. "I found him wandering on the other side of the ridge this morning, when I needed to be doing the laundry. Clem's—out wandering. Likely hunting, true, but I wonder for what. We've a few chickens left, but our horses and cows were taken weeks ago. I've another man in there who might not survive the night, and no one here able-bodied enough to help bury him. Another who's decided that the kindness I dared show one dying man is owed him in another manner entirely. How do you suppose I'm faring, Travis?"

Her cousin's shoulders squared. "I like this no better than you, but others have it much worse. Every one of the neighbors has their share of wounded—or will. Shoot, at the Clarks' there wasn't a bit of floor space either in the house or barn, and tents were being set up in the yard."

"Clarks have more hands to help, as well." Able-bodied women, at least.

"True, but—" He dragged a hand through his hair. "I'm trying to make this as easy as I can on you, but I'm afraid I'll have to bring you more at some point. Would it help if I sent Portius back?"

She sighed. No use arguing with him if orders came from elsewhere—even she knew that. "It might." She shot him her own speculating look.

"Is he one of yours? I don't recall any Negroes with his particular talents belonging to your family. Besides, I thought everyone's slaves would have run off by now to join the Federals."

His gaze flashed at her nettling. "He isn't a slave. And you know as well as I do that the Proclamation only takes effect where the Federals occupy."

She favored him with a stare.

"Look, I know our family and yours quarreled aplenty over that, in recent years. You and Uncle George have been all high-and-mighty because you managed to farm this place without using owned labor. Others weren't so fortunate. But"—he softened again, inexplicably—"I found Portius up around Nashville. He's a freedman, but some Yankee boys gave him a hard time. I saved his life. Guess he still feels beholden, though I told him he needn't."

Pearl searched her cousin's face. "All right, then," she said finally.

He gave a single, hard nod. "I also want to speak with the men who are left, if they're able."

"Three are." She glanced down at the bucket, then at the bandages still drying on the line. "If you can stick around awhile, stay for supper, I'd appreciate the help."

"I can do that," he said and offered a smile.

She knew the lure of a meal would be too much for him to resist. But she'd take the extra hands right now, no matter whose they were.

Josh listened to the approach of the rider, and the rise and fall of the unfamiliar voice alongside Miss MacFarlane's. His attentiveness and patience were rewarded with the booted footfalls crossing the house until the gray-coated man stood in the doorway. Three yellow chevrons marked his sleeves—a cavalry sergeant, then. Light brown hair and beard framed an angular face, young but weary—and wary—with pale eyes that looked barely a shade more blue than his dusty coat.

He glanced at the unconscious man in the other bed, then as Josh struggled to sit up, crossed the floor in one step. "Here, let me help."

Josh did not protest. Gritting his teeth against the sharpened ache in his wounded arm, he caught his breath for a moment then asked, "Who do I have the pleasure of greeting today?"

The corner of the man's mouth lifted in a way that reminded him much of Miss MacFarlane as he turned the chair around and seated himself. "I am Sergeant Travis Bledsoe, of the Fifth Tennessee Cavalry, Army of Tennessee. Partly responsible for your presence here."

Josh dipped his chin in the approximation of a nod. The rank was as he'd guessed. "Sergeant Joshua Wheeler of the First Ohio Infantry. And how do you know Miss MacFarlane?"

A definite smile this time, however tight. "She is my cousin, so any concern I have for her is warranted."

Josh tried to force a pleasant expression to his own face, though something in the man's tone set his teeth on edge. "Fair enough, I suppose. So—why are we here and not, say, elsewhere?"

Bledsoe regarded him sidelong for a moment. "Full of questions, aren't you? Do you *want* to be sent to Belle Isle?"

"Not particularly."

"Well then. I've no objection to your remaining here as long as you give my cousin and her family no trouble."

Josh did not waver. "I've no wish to give her trouble."

"Good. We understand each other, then."

He put out a hand then stopped. "At least one of the others might not."

Bledsoe hesitated at that. "Pearl already warned me," he admitted, then sat back. "Might I get you anything while she's busy cooking supper?"

"I could use help to the privy. My coat's hanging right there."

Bledsoe assisted with both, first with the coat and then with walking him outside. Once Josh was done with the privy, he stopped before crossing the yard again. "I also would beg news of the Army of the Cumberland, if you please."

A long, assessing look was Bledsoe's only response at first. Finally he said, "For the most part, they've holed up in Chattanooga. The action is, of course, being hailed as a great victory for the Confederacy." Bledsoe's smile was brief and sharp. "Any more than that I can't tell you. Word is, however, that Lincoln is none too happy with Rosecrans."

Josh snorted. "Old Rosey. We like him well enough, but—"

Bledsoe leaned toward him a little. "But?"

He shook his head. "I can say no more."

"Can, or should?"

Josh gave a rueful laugh and let Bledsoe escort him back to bed.

Pity the man wore gray and not blue. He'd a feeling they'd have been friends. Of course, there was his unaccountable tension where Miss Mac-Farlane was concerned...

And just what was behind that? Crossing the sitting room, Josh eyed her as she bustled about the kitchen, hesitating only slightly to watch his progress.

Travis saw Mr. Wheeler back to the bedroom, then reemerged a minute or two later to approach the two men bedded down in the sitting room. Quiet conversation ensued, which Pearl wished she could overhear, but— she likely didn't need to.

These men were her concern as well, an inner voice argued.

And the less she knew about them, the less likely she was to find her sympathies improperly engaged, she told the voice firmly. They should get as well as they could, as quickly as they could, and continue on to wherever the Confederate army sent its prisoners.

Especially the one with the rudest manners. Just the look in his eyes chilled her.

In the middle of supper preparations, Clem returned and presented her with a pair of squirrels, already skinned and dressed. His shirt hung half-untucked and grimy, and he sported a fresh tear across the knee of his trousers. His feet, predictably, were bare and covered in dust.

Pearl set one fist on her hip and regarded him sternly. "All these hours gone, and you only have two squirrels to show for it?"

He had the good grace to look chastened. "I went over east, Pearl. No game on the ridge to speak of. You know this."

She huffed. "Take those and wash them."

"I did."

To his credit, she saw now that his hands and forearms were indeed clean. Taking the scrawny carcasses from him, she carried them to the worktable and made quick work of cutting them in pieces. "I could have used your help today, with Portius gone and all."

"Sorry," he muttered.

She shot him a glance. "Pa wandered all the way up over the ridge. I liked to have a heart attack myself before finding him."

Clem's eyes went wide.

"And then one of our blasted bluebellies thought he'd get himself to the outhouse and back, alone, and fell."

Her brother snorted at that. "So let 'im lay."

She lowered her voice. "I very well couldn't do that, and you know it. Yankee or not."

"Why not?"

This time she favored him with a stare. "You know why. Isn't right. Regardless of what they do." When his eyes flashed defiance at her, she pressed harder. "No matter what, Harry Clement MacFarlane. You're God's child. You answer to Him. Do unto others as you'd *have* them do unto you, not as they've *done*."

His mouth thinned and nostrils flared. "You haven't seen what they've done."

"I've seen enough," she hissed. "I went over the hill to Lydia's. It was—it was unspeakable, yes. But that doesn't make us animals. We can choose to do better. And right now, doing better means taking care of them what might hate us, just for the soil on which we were born."

He stared back at her, scowling, then turned on his heel and stalked away.

"Go wash up!" she called after him.

He barely gave her a wave as he left the house.

"Fine, be that way," she muttered, and went to toss the bits of meat in the already-boiling pot of beans. A poor enough meal it would be, but hungry men might not notice the difference.

Travis came back in from tending his horse, carrying an armload of bandages. "What did you do to Clem?"

"Told him the truth."

Travis dumped the bandages on the table and pulled one out of the heap. "About?"

"Why we don't just let these men die."

He stopped, his face softening. "And that, Pearl MacFarlane, is why I love you."

Her heartbeat chugged to a halt. "Don't—you—be speaking to me about love."

The bandage fell from his fingers, and he stepped toward her. "I do, you know."

She put up a hand to fend him off—as if it would—and backed away. He blew out a breath and held his ground, watching her as her heart began to pound again.

"Still, Pearl? After all this time?"

"It's been *two years*." Although it could have been twenty, and it wouldn't have made a difference.

"And I was a fool for allowing it to slip by without writing."

"I—you—"

A crash from one of the side rooms brought them both around. Pearl was past Travis in a moment. A glance inside her former bedroom revealed nothing out of the ordinary there, so she dashed on to Pa's room, and there she found him sprawled on the floor.

"Pa! What—"

He groped toward her. "Pearl?"

Travis was there beside her, and together they raised him—but with difficulty—and seated him at the edge of the bed.

"Pearl—" Pa's hand came up to cup her cheek, shaking. "Pearl."

It seemed to be all he could say, and she couldn't seem to get a single sensible word out, either.

# CHAPTER 12

Josh lay, wide awake, wishing he were asleep. First the quiet but heated discussion between Miss MacFarlane and her brother, then between her cousin and herself, only to be followed by the muted desperation in the bedchamber next door. Was the woman's father ailing as well? What had her cousin been thinking, adding to her burden?

He was more determined than ever to recover his strength as quickly as he could and not be any more trouble than necessary.

He listened while they got the older man back to his bed and tucked in. Their footsteps brought them back to his room. He shut his eyes, pretending to be asleep, as they went about the work of tending the man in the other bed.

"That's a nasty set of wounds," Bledsoe said, examining the man, who was still unconscious. "I'm surprised they let him keep the leg."

"I thought so, as well," Miss MacFarlane said. "I've no wish for him to lose it, but—I've less wish for him to die. From my conversation with him, he seems a good man."

Silence, then, "What, from you, Pearl?"

She hissed at her cousin. "Pa keeps reminding me they are men, as any others. Sons, brothers, fathers." She hesitated. "Mister Thorsson told me he has a sweetheart waiting for him at home."

"And you claim not to be sentimental," her cousin chided her.

"I never claimed any such thing."

He chuckled, but it seemed without humor. "Only where I'm concerned."

Silence again. Josh peeked and saw them wrapping the other soldier's leg in fresh bandages.

"Pearl—"

"Not here," she snapped.

Josh gritted his teeth and wished he could shake Bledsoe by his scruff.

He expected them to leave the room right away, but she turned to him and said, "Are you awake, Mister Wheeler? I'd like to change your dressing as well."

Josh drew a deep breath and feigned being freshly wakened, which wasn't difficult, considering the state of affairs. Opening his eyes to Miss MacFarlane's cool gaze, he couldn't tell if she was convinced by his act or not.

He swung his legs over the side of the bed and sat up with increased dexterity, finishing the maneuver before either she or Bledsoe could assist, and was gratified at the surprise in both their faces. Setting his jaw a second time, he proffered the wounded arm for their examination.

Miss MacFarlane unwrapped the limb with amazing gentleness—and proficiency. How many times had she cause to do this the past several days?

And then—there it was. His arm, or what was left of it. Horribly raw and bloated and disfigured, and—aching. That awful, bone-deep ache, like he could almost feel the saw again.

Miss MacFarlane peered into his face. "Do you feel faint? You could lie down if you'd rather, and not—not look at it."

He sucked in a ragged breath. "I'll sit." And watch as well, but he'd not say that.

If she, a girl untrained—to the best of his knowledge—could bear tending it, he could bear being upright and aware of it all.

Not once did she flinch or shrink from the awfulness of it. Josh found himself watching the flicker of expressions across her face, waiting for disgust or even pity, but it never came. Her brows knit for a moment in what looked like concern, and the softly curving lips parted in apparent concentration before small, white teeth caught her bottom lip. The green eyes, sparkling in the room's dusk, met his for a heartbeat or two, and then her lashes dipped as a flush spread lightly across her cheeks.

For an instant, he nearly forgot the task she'd set herself to.

Pearl could not decide whether it was the presence of Travis, leaning in from one side to look at Mr. Wheeler's wound, or the intensity of the Yankee himself as she tended the arm, that drew the blush to her cheeks.

One thing was certain, those dark eyes riveted to hers—unfair how a man's lashes could be so long—nearly drove all thought of her task from her mind. Her fingers fumbled while applying the goldenseal powder, and with a wince, Mr. Wheeler's gaze dropped. Her face burned all the more, but she reached for the fresh length of cloth that Travis held out, and began the process of binding the wound again.

The damage had been done, however, and her thoughts remained not a little muddled.

And what on earth just happened between them?

She finished as quickly as she could, checked on supper, then had Travis help her with the other two men before they looked in on Pa once more. Sleeping, still. She caught her breath in a moment of thankfulness.

How was she to manage with him recovering from a bad spell yet again? And if he were to fall out of bed a second time?

Travis helped her lay supper on the table and carry bowls to the two men in the sitting room, now able to feed themselves but not to leave their beds. He helped Mr. Wheeler to the table and called Clem in. A curious tension wound around the four of them as they surrounded the table.

Clem thumped down into a chair, and Pearl could feel the eyes of both Travis, still standing and waiting for her to be seated, and Mr. Wheeler, already sitting, as she pulled out her chair and arranged her skirts. Quiet settled around them for a moment, and Travis offered the blessing. At his *amen*, Pearl looked up enough to make sure the three men were eating or preparing to before taking up her own spoon.

She tasted the stew cautiously. Not bad, for bean and squirrel. Travis ate without comment, Clem spooned his with a sullen air, and Mr.

Wheeler tucked himself around his bowl as before but ate more slowly this time, shooting occasional glances at the others.

"What news of the army, Travis?" Clem said.

Her cousin shot him a frown. "I can't talk about it here, Clem. You should know that."

Clem muttered something in return, bending his head over his bowl so that the dripping ends of his hair nearly touched the food.

The meal dragged on in silence. Clem and Travis went back for a second bowl, with Travis refilling Mr. Wheeler's, but at last Travis pushed back his chair. "I must be getting back. Pearl, a word with you, if you don't mind?"

She followed him out into the dusk to the hitching post, where he set to the task of bridling his mount. Away over the ridge to the west, clouds gathered, with the occasional flash of lightning and rumble of thunder. "Rain, finally. It's been so dry."

Travis buckled the bridle under the horse's jaw but made no move to untie the animal. After a moment, he swung toward her. "Pearl. Now that we're alone, hear me out, please."

Tightness gripped her throat. *No. . .oh Lord, please, no. . .*

She gave him a single, tiny nod.

His pale eyes shone in the twilight. "You know how I feel. How I've always felt. And even though you may not share the sentiment now—"

"Ever, Travis," she choked.

"You may not share it now, but—you need someone, Pearl. Uncle George is failing. Your brothers are gone, and Clem, I see he's itching for some action as well." Travis eased toward her a half step. "Let me be that one, Pearl. Marry me. Right now while the army is here at Chattanooga."

Her heart drummed with painful beats. The inside of her mouth had gone suddenly parched.

"Please, Pearl."

"I—I can't, Travis." Her head had begun to shake, just a little, then more emphatically. "I—you know I love you, we grew up together, and I know you as well as one of my brothers, but—I can't."

He stared at her for a long time then tucked his chin, one boot toe scuffing the earth. "You don't have to answer right away. Just—please think on it." To her silence, he added softly, "Promise me you'll consider it."

A huff escaped her. "I—will at least do that much. But I can't promise a yes."

In fact, she was more than certain her reply would always be a no. Not least of all because she didn't know if she could bear being hitched to a man who thought nothing of owning other human beings. No matter what Portius's loyalty bespoke of him.

But Travis looked so mournful that it nearly drew tears from her—again, after everything else this day. She swallowed hard. "I'm so sorry. I wish it could be a yes."

He glanced down again. "It could be a yes. But—I can't make you say it."

With that, he tugged the horse's lead rope loose, tossed the reins in place, and mounted.

"Travis."

He pulled the horse around to face her.

"Be well." There was suddenly nothing else she could say.

A hard nod as he heeled the horse about. "I'll send Portius back." And then he was gone, galloping down the road.

She stood, still choking back the tears. A rumble of thunder shook the ground, the storm closer now. *"I will lift up mine eyes unto the hills, from whence cometh my help."* How many times had she watched the clouds rolling in over the ridge, but each time the storm would pass.

This time, she wasn't so sure.

Finished with his second bowl, Josh was in no hurry to move, and the gangly MacFarlane boy seemed to be lingering as well. When his sister stepped inside at last, followed by the crackle of lightning, he turned to look at her. "What did Travis want?" the boy asked.

"Never you mind," she said, but with less heat than Josh suspected the words deserved. She glided up to the table and regarded her half-eaten bowl of stew with distraction.

"Do you want the rest of that?" Clem asked.

"No." She slid the bowl toward him and drifted toward the kitchen.

Even then, she simply stood there, one hand on her hip, the other rubbing her forehead.

What the blazes had that Rebel said to discomfit her so?

Carefully, so as not to jostle anything and humiliate himself again, Josh scooted his chair back and rose, then carried his bowl and spoon to the kitchen. Miss MacFarlane angled him a watery, abashed glance. "I could help with the washing," he said.

"You'll do no such thing," she snapped, then sighed. "Today, at least."

He offered a half smile then made his way back to his room.

The Norwegian tossed and moaned a little in his sleep. Josh lingered for a moment, but it didn't appear that there was much he could do.

Besides pray.

Did he even know how to do that anymore?

He had a feeling he best learn, if not.

By the time Pearl finished with washing up, making sure Pa hadn't fallen out of bed again, and meeting any reasonable requests from the two men in the sitting room, full dark had fallen, and the house shook from the lightning, thunder, and lashing of the rain. Clem had helped, reluctantly, then disappeared to the barn despite the storm. Oh, how she wished she could simply go fall into her own bed.

But—Mr. Thorsson.

Who was likely to die anyway, and—suddenly she could face none of it.

She scurried up the stairs and did exactly as she'd been longing to do, fairly diving into the coverlet and pulling the corner up over her head. As the rain beat on the roof, she let her own downpour come.

The look on Travis's face when she'd refused him. His insistence that he simply wanted what was best for her. How could she deny that she was in desperate straits here, or would be soon?

But to marry Travis. . .no. That was not a solution her heart could accept. At least—not yet. Could she ever? Was it fair to him to take her, the troublesome young girl cousin, who would likely always be a troublesome wife? And she, who once upon a time had let Travis kiss her but just thought the entire production strange. . .

*You know I love him, Lord, but—as a brother. Not like that.*

Yet she couldn't seem to stop the tears from flowing.

*Oh, gracious Lord.*

Finally, as the rain began to ease, so did her weeping.

# CHAPTER 13

Sometime later, she awoke with a start.

Had there been a sound? She was so used to awakening this way of late, it was beginning to feel normal. Regardless, there was a niggling urgency she could not rid herself of, so with a sigh, she rose, straightened her clothing, and trudged downstairs.

Pa still slept. So soundly, she wondered whether it a natural sleep, but a moaning and muttering from her bedroom drew her on. Predictably, it was Mr. Thorsson. She dutifully fetched her basin and cloth, made sure she had a cup and spoon for fresh water, and settled herself at his bedside.

She'd barely begun the task of bathing Mr. Thorsson's face and neck when Mr. Wheeler spoke behind her. "He's been like that for the past hour or two."

The pitch of his voice, low and quiet, minded her of the thunder, distant now, and not unpleasant to the ear. She glanced back and found him watching her.

"I'm hoping this helps him. It did seem to soothe you."

Mr. Thorsson had already quieted a little but still muttered incoherently. She wrung out the rag and started in again. "Come on now," she murmured. "You need to fight this too. You've so much to live for, back home."

Feeling abashed for the tender words, she cast another glance over her shoulder. Those dark eyes, surrounded by long lashes and scattering of freckles visible even in the candlelight, were still fastened on her, and she tucked her chin to hide whatever blush he might be able to see. Why she found herself responding so was a mystery.

"What about yourself," she went on. "Who did you leave behind?"

Her cheeks fairly burned now, but the darkness of night lent an illusion of intimacy. His slow intake of breath and noisy exhale told her the question was no easier for him to receive than for her to give.

"Oh, my ma and pa. An older sister and her brood. Two brothers and their families." He was quiet a moment. "One of those hasn't been heard from since Gettysburg."

Her hands slowed. The too-familiar ache rose in her chest. Of course the Federals would have suffered losses as well.

But again, they were the ones who had invaded the Confederacy.

"Why," she muttered. "Why do you feel it necessary to bring this fight to us?"

Another long exhale. "Why do you feel it necessary to hold on to Secession?"

She bent, forehead almost to the Norwegian man's shoulder. "Questions for which there are no good answers," she said at last, then straightened. "I am sorry for your loss. Three of my own brothers have died in three different battles."

"I'm most regretful of your loss as well," he said, his voice very low and rich with feeling.

As if he meant it.

She fetched a cup of water and went through the process of spooning it into Mr. Thorsson's mouth. After the first taste, he gulped it greedily.

Well, that was a good sign.

"Did you force-feed me water, as well?" Mr. Wheeler asked.

"Yes," she answered, not turning.

Another silence, then, "Why not simply let us die?"

The proper answer was on the tip of her tongue, but she found herself murmuring, "I considered it."

Now why had she said that, and to him of all folk?

To her surprise, he chuckled—then after a moment, broke into a genuine, if weak, laugh. "You, Miss MacFarlane, possess a singular honesty."

A rueful smile tugged at her mouth.

"Which battles, then, were the ones where your brothers fell?"

"Fishing Creek, Shiloh, and—the one just past."

His silence stretched on until she couldn't resist glancing at him.

"Let me guess, you were at all of them."

Those dark eyes had gone hooded. "Fishing Creek, no. But Shiloh—yes."

She sighed and turned in her chair to face him more fully, clutching the rag in her hands. She was so weary, she couldn't even find it in herself to be angry. Even the grief was but a hollowed shell, at the moment, despite how the all-too-familiar ache sharpened.

"I wish I could adequately convey how very sorry I am," he murmured. The quiet hung between them for another minute or so, and then he said, "What were their names?"

She cleared her throat. "Jefferson and Jeremiah were twins. Mama lost three before those two finally came along, strong enough to survive infancy. Then there was Gideon. Jeremiah, he left a wife and children—" She swallowed. Lydia deserved the title, even if the law had not recognized her brother's commitment to her as legitimate. "Jefferson and Gideon were too wild to settle, though."

"And your younger brother is called Clem?"

"Clement. Actually Harry Clement, but he insists on Clem."

A muted sparkle returned to Mr. Wheeler's eyes. "Truly a name to live up to."

Mr. Thorsson seemed to be sleeping soundly now, so Pearl set the rag back in the basin and made herself more comfortable. "It was a family name, on the MacFarlane side. Pa was never very clear on how." She smiled again, a little. "Word has it that my great-grandparents were Loyalists in the War for Independence, but rather than leaving with the British, they up and moved to north Georgia. So no relation to the McFarlands, for whom the gap over yonder is named."

Mr. Wheeler smiled in response. "My pa's family were from Virginia and were patriots."

"Of course," she said, and he grinned.

"Then my pa moved to southern Ohio, by way of the river, after the Shawnee cleared out."

"My mama's family was from Kentucky, by way of the Cumberland Gap. But we have family all across Tennessee and Kentucky and as far west as Independence, Missouri."

Mr. Wheeler's eyes crinkled. "Just think, if you'd grown up in Kentucky, you'd be a Yankee now."

Pearl snorted, and to his laughter she said, "Oh, there are good Confederates up that way as well."

"I do know that," he said, growing thoughtful. "We even have a few Confederate sympathizers up our way. We call them Copperheads."

"But you aren't one of them."

His gaze flickered to hers and held. Still thoughtful. Not condemning. Simply—assessing.

"Why—"

A thump and hoarse cry came from the other room—through the wall, from Pa's room.

"Oh no." She scrambled out of her chair, snatching up the candle.

Sure enough, Pa had fallen again and lay plaintively calling for help.

*Not again, not again, not again* beat the tattoo of her heart as she knelt beside him. "Are you hurt anywhere, Pa?"

"Pearl, I need to go to town."

Distress lashed at her. "It's the middle of the night. You should be sleeping."

"No, must—get to town. Willy Jones has promised me a good price on the fall colt."

"No, Pa. He—" She flailed for a reply. "He bought the colt last week. You're just dreaming, is all."

Pa's rheumy eyes fastened on hers, his mouth slack behind his gray beard. "Are you sure? I know it was today."

"No, Pa," she said more softly.

Mr. Wheeler was suddenly beside her. "How can I help?" he murmured.

She glanced at him. One strong arm was surely better than none, in this case—but had he energy enough to do this, after the day he'd had? "We should get him back in bed, but—this is the second time today he's fallen."

"Why don't we put his pallet on the floor?"

"I'll not sleep on the floor," Pa said indignantly.

Pearl sighed. His cross moods came seldom, but when they did, he could be a sore trial to everyone around him. "Pa, you need—I need—you to not fall out of bed. You've fallen twice now."

"Rubbish," he snapped.

Pearl sighed and sat back, scrubbing a hand across her face.

Mr. Wheeler edged forward. "Sir, if you would allow us to assist you back into your bed, I'd be honored to sit and visit with you."

He slid a glance toward Pearl, and she gave him a tiny nod in return.

"Oh, I suppose that would suit well enough," Pa grumbled. "I am tired of this hard floor, after all."

Between the two of them—Mr. Wheeler hooked his uninjured arm beneath Pa's on one side, and Pearl did the same on the other—they managed to lift Pa and get him situated again. But when they went to assist him in lying down, he planted his feet and announced, "I'm not sleepy."

Mr. Wheeler chuckled, surprising Pearl yet again. "Well then, we'll just sit and chat, sir." He reached for the straight-backed chair in the corner and pulled it closer, then waved Pearl away.

"Are you certain?" she said, and he flashed her a grin.

"Who did you say you were, again?" Pa asked, frowning hard at the younger man.

Mr. Wheeler settled himself, as calm and dignified as if he were properly dressed and not, as Pearl realized with a jolt, clad only in slightly threadbare wool trousers that had once been light blue. "I'm Joshua Wheeler, sir, from Ohio. Pleased to make your acquaintance."

Pearl held her breath. Would Pa even remember that they were at war?

"George MacFarlane. And likewise." With equal dignity, Pa put out his hand, and Mr. Wheeler shook it without hesitation. "Ohio, eh? I've been there a time or two. Beautiful country. What brings you to these parts?"

She darted a glance at Mr. Wheeler. A calm, friendly smile still played about his bearded mouth. "Ah—government business."

"Aha." Pa's face twisted in distaste. "Well, how long are you planning to stay?"

"Don't rightly know."

Pearl glanced about and seized a knitted throw lying across the end of Pa's bed then handed it off to Mr. Wheeler. With a grave nod, he pulled it around his shoulders. "Truly. I do not mind," he murmured to her. "Go get some sleep, or whatever else you need to do. I'll call if we need anything."

It was just. . .too strange, this Yankee soldier sitting there, conversing with Pa as if they were neighbors newly met. Yet she couldn't deny her relief at the sudden, unexpected reprieve.

This was not a duty he'd been expecting—sitting the night watch with an infirm but feisty old Confederate. One who, by all appearances, did not seem mindful at the moment of the fight between blue and gray, but only sought to sort out which way was up in his world, and which down.

And the man's daughter, so obviously wearied by all that was laid at her feet, Josh could not find it in his heart to leave her to it.

"Have you seen my sons?"

Josh's attention snapped back to Mr. MacFarlane.

"They've gone away, you understand. I'm not sure where, but I'm confident they'll be home soon."

Josh shifted, folding his arms against his middle, ignoring the ache.

"That's good to hear," he said finally.

*God, could this be any more difficult?*

Why yes. . .yes, it could. This man could be recognizing that Josh was on the side of war that had guaranteed his sons would most definitely not be coming home soon—or at all.

"Of course, with that trouble Mister Lincoln has stirred up, it's hard telling what might happen next."

Well, that would qualify as more difficult as well. "How so?"

Mr. MacFarlane's bristly eyebrows knitted. "What rock have you been living under, boy?"

Josh couldn't stop his grin. "That trouble means different things for different folk. I'd simply like to hear your opinion on it, sir."

The older man hmphed but sat back. "Well. Understand that, yes, we believe slavery is a dreadful institution. The South originally voted against it—did you know that?"

"I did not, sir." And in truth, this point of argument was fresh to Josh's ears.

"I am not surprised. They aren't fond of admitting it, in the North. It was New England ship captains and the like, however, who saw that importing slaves was big business. And then with time they learned that the northern climates are not well suited to the practice of slavery. But the Constitution itself remained silent on the issue, as the framers intended to let the states choose how to handle the issue."

Josh thought he could recall shreds of debate around various hearths and tables, where the names of Hamilton and Jefferson were invoked in the question of whether Union meant the states banded together under one central government, or whether the States were considered sovereign unto themselves, and the concept of *government* meant equality and cooperation between them.

The difference between Republic and Democracy, as they were originally conceived. It had all seemed to be but the talk of old men around a fire or a pint, once upon a time.

MacFarlane shifted on the edge of the bed, bracing himself with both hands upon his cane. "Even Lincoln said that slavery wasn't his concern. Not that I think leaving the Union was necessarily the right thing either." He shook his head. "So much trouble. Not like the old days when we fought the British and everything was cut-and-dried."

That Josh could agree wholeheartedly with. Recalling all he'd grown up hearing about the old wars was certainly more comfortable territory than political debate. "Both my daddy and granddaddy did their part. Revolution and War of 1812."

MacFarlane nodded emphatically. "Mine as well. Nothing like that kind of heroism, today. They had none of this nonsense about North and South, blue and gray." A smile flickered across his face then faded. "And here we are. How has it come to this? All men are created equal. Even the Founding Fathers knew it. Yet we are stuck in this awful dilemma. Threatened by the tyranny of a government trying to tell the people what's best for them, all over again, without proper representation."

Josh sucked on his teeth for a moment. "I admit, I had not thought of it from that perspective, sir. Thank you."

MacFarlane nodded as if he had done Josh a grand favor. "If a man cannot stay true to his country even if he disagrees with some things that country does, what sort of man does that make him?"

That statement could apply both ways, but Josh held his tongue.

The older man yawned suddenly. "I do believe I might sleep, after all."

He stretched himself out on the bed before Josh could offer to help. His breathing shortly settled into snores.

Josh sat for a few minutes, reflecting on the last hour or two. These people were not what he'd thought them to be—what he'd always been led to believe they were. True, their situation was humble enough, but— he glanced around the room—the house and its furnishings were well made, if sparse. This man, for all his infirmity and confusion, bore a quiet dignity that reminded Josh of his own family. And the man's daughter— there was a puzzle, for sure, one that Josh wished to examine more closely.

Secessionists they might be, but they were good people.

What was he, a soldier of the Union, supposed to do with that?

Arms still folded around his body, he curled his hands into fists—or more properly, his remaining hand into a fist, as a flare of pain in his left arm reminded him of what his service to the Union had cost so far because of these Rebels. Hot nausea flooded his body, and sucking a breath through his teeth, he curled even further in on himself.

It was easier, when other folk were awake and visiting with him, to ignore the hurt. The loss. How he'd have to write home and break it to his family that he'd lost a hand and would no longer be whole. At least he didn't have a sweetheart to similarly inform and doubtless disappoint with the news.

But what was he, a man with a maimed limb, to do with a sudden fascination for the young woman tasked with caring for him? No woman could possibly feel anything but revulsion at the thought of him touching her, much less one who had seen him—and the amputation wound—at its worst.

# CHAPTER 14

Pearl woke to quiet. For a long moment, she simply lay still and listened, straining for any sound. The breath in her lungs froze with the sudden thought that everyone else in the house had gone—or worse—expired.

Or could it be that they'd all simply, yes, fallen asleep at the same time?

Drifting through the floorboards came the sound of humming, rich and low. Her heartbeat stuttered and breathing started again. Portius had returned.

She rose, straightened her clothing and hair—at some point she should do washing for herself, and bathe, and wash her hair—and hurried downstairs. It was barely daylight.

Portius stood at the stove, tending a pot of something cooking, but he turned with a smile. "Morning, Miss Pearl."

She summoned her most welcoming smile. "Morning. It's good to see you, if you don't mind my saying so."

He chuckled softly, and tapping the wooden spoon on the side of the pot, he set it aside. "I don't. It's a whole sight more quiet here than in camp, I assure you."

A half laugh bubbled out of her at that. "I imagine so."

As difficult as things had been here, it was probably the truth.

"And what news of the camp this morning?" she asked, more softly.

Portius's smile faded somewhat. "Well, now. Confederates hold Missionary Ridge and Lookout Mountain. The Federals are all locked up tight in Chattanooga. The Confederates did take out a big Federal supply train up on Walden Ridge." He flashed her a look. "Nice if they could have brought us some of it, but no, I hear tell they burned it."

"A pity," she murmured. Such waste made no sense to her, but then, so little of war did.

"Mister Travis insisted I bring you a few things, however." His gaze was more pointed this time.

"Good of him. And thank you, Portius."

"Of course, Miss Pearl."

She went then to check on Pa. The sitting room was still mostly dark, and a stirring told her the men sleeping there were awake, or would be soon.

Outside Pa's window, dawn colored the horizon and lent enough light for her to see that he still lay snugly in his bed—and a second form adorned the floor. It was Mr. Wheeler, wrapped in the throw she'd offered him the evening before.

That Yankee had spent the entire night there?

"What in the world happened here?" Portius asked, suddenly behind her. "He get tired of his own bed?"

Pearl's breath caught. "You startled me."

He chuckled. "My apologies."

"No, but—Pa had a bad spell yesterday. Wandered outside, all the way up and over the ridge, alone. Then he fell out of bed twice. Mister Wheeler helped me get him back up the second time."

"The second time."

Her cheeks warmed at the memory. "Travis was here, the first time."

"Aha." The Negro held his breath a moment. "He does seem mighty concerned for you."

*Well he might be.* She gritted back the words and forced her voice to mildness. "Good of him. I appreciate his sending you back to us." Suddenly remembering Mr. Thorsson, she slid past Portius and sped to her bedroom.

Would this never end, the frantic checking to see if men still breathed or no?

To her astonishment, he not only still breathed but—opened his eyes as she stumbled to a halt in the doorway.

*Oh—thank the good Lord above!*

The day's demands caught her up then and carried her along, from tending a still-weak Mr. Thorsson to feeding everyone breakfast. Portius had brought supplies, and Pearl did not even care from where. Portius and Clem helped Pa to the table, with Mr. Wheeler following, while Mr. Shaw and Mr. Jackson stayed in their beds. Pa seemed more clear minded this morning. Mr. Wheeler met her eyes and nodded but otherwise seemed subdued.

Perhaps it was only the night spent on the hard floor, although she knew a soldier's life was hardly one of ease, and surely he was well used to sleeping wherever he could find a stretch.

She was looking in on Mr. Thorsson one more time when Mr. Wheeler entered. Still holding himself in that slightly hunched position, Pa's throw wrapped about him, he shuffled up to the bed and regarded the Norwegian gravely.

"He awoke enough to drink and eat a little," Pearl said.

"Glad to hear it."

She looked more closely at him. Hair rumpled, dark shadows beneath darker eyes, mouth tight. "Are you in pain?"

His gaze snapped to her with a suddenness that almost make her flinch. "Sometimes," he said, at last.

She chewed her lip, trying not to look away. Last night, conversation had seemed so easy, so comfortable. But in the light of day—

Clearing her throat, she swung toward the wall where his coat and the Norwegian's hung on her dress hooks, and their boots and bundles of belongings lay tucked against the wall. "I promised to help you find a shirt."

"I don't recall a promise being part of that conversation," he said, an odd catch in his voice.

"Wasn't it?" Her own voice felt strangely tight, and her cheeks were burning so intensely she dared not face him. But when she crouched and put her hand on his knapsack, to riffle further felt wrong. Gulping a breath, she turned back and presented it to him.

With another searching look she could not interpret, he sat on the edge of the bed and let the wrap fall from his shoulders before reaching for the bag. She stood carefully back, giving him at least the illusion of privacy as he balanced the thing across his knees and fumbled inside.

"I—I should also ask, now that you're up and feeling somewhat better, would you care for a bath? I could have Portius or Clem bring in the tub and haul the water."

His gaze came up again, betraying surprise.

"You'd have to keep the hurt arm out of the water, of course—"

"That would be most kind of you, Miss MacFarlane."

Pearl winced a little. "It's. . .simple hospitality, bluebelly."

A grin stole across his face, for a moment banishing the weariness, then he pulled his expression to sobriety again. "And most appreciated, secesh."

She felt an eyebrow going up. "Secesh?"

The grin reappeared, abashed. An actual sparkle lit the brown eyes. And somehow the jibe, usually aimed at folks' choice to support Secession, seemed like mere teasing from him.

"Well, if we're reduced to insulting each other, you might as well call me Pearl."

To her amazement, color crept across his face as well. "I'm not sure I can do that, Miss MacFarlane."

Well then.

A little more riffling, and he drew out a much crumpled roll of what she was sure had once been crisp, white cotton. A flick of his wrist, and he shook it out. It was, indeed, a shirt.

"There you are. I could—I could also wash that for you, and your trousers. Or anything else you'd want," she stammered.

Just what ailed her this morning?

The color in his cheeks deepened, but he bobbed a nod. "Very much appreciated, Miss MacFarlane."

What ailed both of them, more like. "Pearl," she blurted.

He blinked. "Then you can call me Josh."

Something squirmed in her middle under the warm brown of his gaze. "That I'll have to think about," she snapped with mock severity and, with a little smile, swept from the room.

A chuckle followed her.

Out in the kitchen, she could hardly breathe. Mr. Wheeler's initial response was probably the truest. She was becoming far too familiar with someone she should keep firmly in mind was a Yankee and by all accounts still very much the enemy.

Josh closed a fist around the shirt. How could he have ever thought her plain? Her face was so full of life and feeling. The way the morning light caught her eyes, green and sparkling—

And he'd no business thinking any of this. Doubtless as soon as he was recovered enough, Bledsoe would have him on a train north to Richmond, despite what he'd said yesterday. And even if not—he was half a man now. Useless to a girl as capable as Pearl MacFarlane.

*Pearl.* Why the devil had she done that, asked him to use her given name, as if they were on their way to being the best of friends, instead of mere acquaintances across this gulf that necessity had made of what had once been one nation?

Or worse, enemies on either side of a war that should have been over with long since. He was so weary of it all. Strange how principle and resolution to a cause faded in the face of the day-to-day struggle—he'd seen that already while on the march, in camp, on the field after battle. They talked so often of glory in death—was there truly any glory in what he'd witnessed?

And for himself—would it not have been better to die outright than become a useless casualty of a battle that by all appearances did nothing for the Union but impoverish it?

With a deep breath, he forced himself to stir. Set aside the shirt and peer inside the knapsack. It wasn't his bag, but he wasn't going to tell Miss MacFarlane that. He'd seen before that when the wounded were collected off the field, it was impossible to make sure each man's own belongings went with him, so oftentimes the abandoned blanket bundles and knapsacks were also collected and dispersed to whoever needed them. This one held not only the customary tin eating utensils, sewing kit, and hardtack crumbs, but a bundle of letters.

He drew those out. What he could make out of the name was unfamiliar. A return address read Wisconsin. Shaking his head, he slid the string over one corner of the bundle and thumbed through the envelopes, scanning return addresses. All Wisconsin, and Minnesota.

He looked across at the other man. Mr.—Thorsson? Is that what Miss MacFarlane had said? The letters looked to be to someone else—something Halvorson, if he was making the name out correctly. Not the man in the bed across from him, but perhaps someone he knew.

Josh secured the string again and slid the bundle back into the knapsack. Those perhaps could be returned to their rightful owner, eventually, but the shirt could not be helped. He needed to be decently dressed, to preserve his dignity—and that of Miss MacFarlane—if nothing else.

# CHAPTER 15

Pearl left the drawing of baths to Portius and Clem and set herself to preparing laundry. She'd a smaller tub for soaking the soiled clothing, and the familiarity of the task soothed her mind and helped her not dwell on the details of what she was doing or for whom.

Also it allowed her to be outdoors. And though the day was still overcast and a little windy, she was able to tuck her washtub in behind the house to shield from the worst of it. From here, she could look up and still see the hillside rising beyond the fields, where late fall wildflowers nodded in the breeze while reddening maples and sourwoods waved from the slope. Graceful chestnuts would be ready to drop their nuts soon and, if Pearl was quick enough, would add a welcome change to their provender.

Portius had gathered up all the men's clothing, bundled the men themselves in blankets, and handed everything off to Pearl to wash. Clem had helped, though grumbling about his lack of freedom for the day. After letting the garments soak awhile in warmish water—what could be spared from bath preparations—she poured in a bucket of cold and started scrubbing.

She never knew such a tedious task could be so satisfying. After drawing water for rinsing, she wrung out each garment then hung them on the line. The wind would thankfully dry them quickly.

Afterward, she went to the barn and, taking a lantern, descended to their hidden cellar to take inventory of what they had left by way of foodstuffs. In past years, she and Mama had labored the entire summer and fall to pickle and preserve and dry all they could, from beets and carrots and turnips to peaches and apples and berries. But because of the army's predations on their garden, she'd put up only a fraction of what they'd always had before.

A bin of apples she'd managed to pick before others did and squirrel away. Another of sweet potatoes, rapidly dwindling. Half-a-dozen jars of blackberry preserves that she stubbornly refused to break into. She might be able to scrabble a few carrots, onions, and sweet potatoes from the earth, if the foragers had missed any.

She turned a slow circle in the middle of the floor, lantern lifted. "Lord, I don't know what You've got in mind here, but. . .please do something with this situation."

After picking a half-dozen apples from the bin and tucking them in her apron, she left the cellar and headed back to the house.

Three figures sat on the porch. Pearl recognized Pa right away, dressed and hair combed and looking neater than he had for many a week. He looked to be feeling better, sitting upright in his chair with both hands gripping the handle of his cane before him. He was at the moment engaged in conversation with the two men beside him but saw her coming and smiled. "Ah, there you are, Daughter! Do you see, our guests from the North are greatly improved. Is this not a wonder?"

She couldn't help a laugh. Guests from the North? And speaking of those—the man nearest to Pa, also chuckling and shaking his head, had the vivid auburn hair and beard of Mr. Wheeler, but also so neatly combed she'd not have recognized him.

Her feet dragged to a halt, heart thudding in her chest before settling back to a more manageable beat. Mercy, but—all cleaned up, blue coat draped about his shoulders over a clean shirt and an obviously borrowed pair of trousers—he was fine to look at.

The laughter faded from his expression, and he rose slowly from his chair to greet her. "Miss MacFarlane," he said with a nod. "We wondered where you'd gotten off to."

She forced a smile—likewise forced her feet to move forward, and for her gaze to register the third man. Fair hair also combed, blue eyes regarding her with humor and warmth, though his face was yet a bit pale.

"Oh! Mister Thorsson. I am much relieved to see you up and about."

She suppressed a wince at the pitch of her own voice. Was the sudden squeak of nerves obvious to anyone but herself?

He gave her a boyish grin and bob of the head. "Tank you. I am still not feeling all myself, but God is full of grace, is He not?"

"Indeed He is." Another shaky, broken laugh as she made herself meet Mr. Wheeler's deep brown gaze once more. A hesitant smile curved his mouth.

Oh Lord, why? Why did he have to be so very handsome—and why was she reacting this way to a bluebelly?

"It's good to see you looking better as well, Mister Wheeler," she managed, at last.

His smile deepened, so warm it was like a breath of summer over her. He bowed a little. "Thank you, Miss MacFarlane, for your hospitality."

The ridiculousness of their playacting wrung another chuckle from her. "Of course. Now, if y'all will excuse me, I have work in the kitchen."

She moved toward the steps, but Mr. Wheeler preempted her. "Ah, I am bid tell you to use the back door. Our good Portius has the sitting room curtained off so everyone can be scrubbed down, but the kitchen is safe for you to enter."

The sparkle in those brown eyes would not be refused, but somehow she tore herself away. "Thank you."

She fairly fled to the other side of the house, to the back door, where Clem and Portius were just emerging with yet another tub of filthy bath water. "Just one more," Portius huffed.

"Thank you for taking on this task," she said, as the two men lugged the tub into the yard and tipped it out.

"They needed it."

Even Clem nodded his agreement to the older man's statement. "Full o' lice, they are. Every one of 'em."

"Clem!"

"It's true, Miss Pearl." Portius set down his edge of the tub and wiped his brow. "The men themselves own up to it. Just part of camp life. Our own gray troops suffer the same."

Pearl was seized by the sudden urge to scrub at her scalp. Just barely did she keep both hands knotted in her apron, where the apples were bundled. "Well then," she said.

He grinned, white teeth shining against his dark skin. "You have some good lye soap, Miss Pearl. I've no doubt it'll help."

She lingered, doubtful, but he made a shooing motion. "Get yourself inside. Or wherever you need to be. We got this."

"What about the bedding?"

"Tomorrow is good enough, if it ain't raining."

Gritting her teeth, she stepped inside the kitchen. *Lice.* She should have guessed. Should have observed it herself.

It was not such a terrible thing, she reprimanded herself. They'd contended with such, before, when she and Clem were very young. And it wasn't like the men could help it, being all crammed together in camp.

But—she thought of sitting there, so close to Mr. Wheeler's bed-side—and that of Mr. Thorsson—and how she'd tended both of them—

Well. Nothing to be done about it now, except what they already were.

She lifted her apron and carefully spilled the apples onto the table. Found a bowl and knife, set to work cutting and paring them. She'd little flour, so no pie, but perhaps a cobbler or crisp. Yes, a crisp would be just the thing, with cornmeal.

*"If thine enemy hunger. . ."*

It was, as she'd told Mr. Wheeler, just simple hospitality.

She'd do the same for anyone.

Josh reckoned it had been, oh, possibly before he'd enlisted since the last time he'd had a real bath inside a house. He'd nearly forgotten what a difference it made to be completely clean, with fresh clothing. Even if it wasn't his own. . .

He thought back on the long months on campaign. Sleeping on the ground, marching through muck and dust, over rocks and through creeks and rivers. Sometimes not even a fire on cold nights. Subsisting on coffee and hardtack.

The terrible march south to Chattanooga, across the rugged,

unforgiving terrain of middle Tennessee. An even more terrible pair of days and nights spent in the agony of waiting for battle interspersed with the terrors of battle itself, until that minié ball shattered his wrist bones and took his hand. The agony of being moved to a hospital and then here.

And now. . . He leaned his chair back enough to rest his head on the outside wall of the house. Mr. MacFarlane had gone inside after Portius and Clem came for Mr. Thorsson, but Josh had asked to stay outside awhile. Though cool and breezy, it felt too good to be outdoors.

And clean. And halfway well groomed.

That startled expression on Miss MacFarlane's face when she'd caught sight of him. . . He knew the look well enough from years of trying to charm this girl or that back home. This one, however, was doing her best not to be charmed, he was sure.

And he'd be doing his best not to charm, except—she was just so charming herself. He was coming to look forward to every instance of speaking with her, just to hear whatever surprising thing she'd say or do next. Even when caught off guard, or maybe especially then—like the burst of laughter from her pa's comment, completely transforming her for a moment and lighting up those green eyes, which then caught his and widened.

The knowledge of what that response meant lit through his blood like, well, a stolen shot of his father's best whiskey, and left him twice as addled.

Even the memory of it was heady. He drew a deep breath, seeking to steady his thoughts and his heartbeat, and the aroma of apples set him nearly to salivating.

Was she—baking in there? An apple pie, maybe? And where on earth had she found apples, at this time and place, where an army occupied and had for a while?

He sat up, just a little too quickly, and was rewarded with a stabbing ache in his left arm that left him gasping.

And like a bucket of cold water over his head, the sure knowledge of his position—and that he had absolutely no grounds for pursuing such frivolous thoughts—doused any fire that might be lingering in his veins. It left him shivering.

# CHAPTER 16

Pearl worked steadily the rest of the afternoon, finishing the apple crisp and setting dinner to cooking on the stove in between trips outside to check the dryness of the laundry hanging on the line and peer at the thickening clouds. She'd likely not get the bedding laundered tomorrow after all.

She pulled the shirts off the line and brought those inside. The men could wear damp trousers if necessary, but this at least would be a start. Portius and Clem had gotten everyone washed up and the tub back outside and tipped upside down against the back of the house, but they left the blanket between the kitchen and rest of the house hanging to preserve Pearl's sensibilities. She smiled thinly. Others had it worse, Travis had said. She should be thankful that Portius was here and mindful of sparing her such things.

And she was thankful. If Travis's prediction that he'd be bringing her more wounded was any indication, such delicacy might yet meet a sudden death.

*Lord God, thank You for helping me thus far. Please. . .please keep giving me strength in this. I don't know how we're to continue on. . .but if others do have it worse, and very much so, then help them and give them strength as well.*

Late that afternoon, as the first drops of another squall spattered her, she pulled the last of the laundry off the line and hauled it inside, then handed everything off to Portius and Clem for the men to sort. Portius was just taking down the dividing curtain, and she'd decided supper was as ready as she could make it, when a commotion came at the door, and someone called out that they had company.

She turned, half expecting Travis, but it was a shorter man, slightly stout in a knee-length fawn coat and black hat, which he removed to expose a greatly balding head of still-black hair. "Ah, Reverend Mason!" Pa exclaimed, from his chair. "Come in, and welcome!"

Pearl gritted her teeth and put on a smile. Reverend Mason's gaze swept the room, widening as he almost visibly counted the number of men there, and doubtless made note of the color of their clothing. "Well. I had heard you have guests, but this. . ."

He crossed the room to stand near Pa. "I am making rounds today to inform everyone that we'll not be having services on the morrow because the church has been taken for hospital purposes."

"Well that is very much too bad," Pa said. "But understandable."

Reverend Mason looked about as if he doubted that. Mr. Shaw and Mr. Jackson were just being reinstalled in their beds, while Mr. Thorsson sat on one of the kitchen chairs, Mr. Wheeler standing nearby, both steadfastly giving their attention to the pastor.

"Will you stay to supper?" Pa asked.

Even from across the room, Pearl could see the conflict in the preacher's face. The willingness to be fed must have won out, however, because at last he nodded, forcing pleasantness into his expression. "I would be glad to stay."

Pearl laid an extra place at the table, and after the two men across the sitting room had been served bowls of corn bread and beans, the rest of them assembled for supper. She did her best to ignore the somber handsomeness of Mr. Wheeler as he stood beside his chair, waiting ostensibly for her—or Pa—to be settled, and though his gaze flicked toward her once, he likewise did not acknowledge her.

Whether that was a relief or a disappointment, she could not say.

They sat, among introductions that Pa insisted on. Reverend Mason peered into his bowl with a frown, and Pearl squashed any feeling she might have at his response to such a humble meal. This was what they had to offer, and if he found himself offended by it, well then perhaps he shouldn't have accepted the invitation to stay.

She likewise squashed the successive wave of guilt that came for having such thoughts about a man of the cloth.

Reverend Mason was not too proud to bolt down half of his bowl before pausing long enough to pat his lips with his handkerchief and take a breath. "Such a fine victory we have won this week, George, would you not say?"

Complete stillness fell over the house. Did the man have no regard for half those present being already wounded and at the mercy of the Confederacy, that he felt the need to insult them further?

Pa favored him with a look of shock. "Have we, then?"

Pearl choked down the bubble of laughter that rose in her chest unbidden and bent over her bowl.

"Why yes." A frown flickered across Reverend Mason's face, and his gaze skimmed around the table. Though Mr. Thorsson's expression remained mild, Pearl took unaccountable satisfaction in the way Mr. Wheeler turned that calm, intent gaze of his on the preacher and that the older man glanced away, clearing his throat. "Well. Perhaps best to not speak of such things in polite company."

"Hm, yes, thank you," Pa said gravely. Pearl bit her lips together, not daring to look up. "We have missed hearing your messages these past weeks, Reverend Mason. What was the text of your sermon Sunday?"

The preacher hemmed and hawed for a moment. Pearl stole a glance and found him looking imploringly at her. She shook her head slightly. "It was on 1 Corinthians 13, of course," he said. "You were there, after all."

Pa huffed. "I have no memory of that."

"Well, 1 Corinthians 13 it was, on the subject of charity." Another cautious look around the table, this time more lingering. "How nothing we can accomplish for our Lord is of worth if—if we do not show charity to our fellow man."

Reverend Mason had the good grace to flush after those words.

Pearl tried her hardest to look prim and ladylike. "We are certainly doing our best to fulfill that command, here. 'If thine enemy hunger, feed him; if he thirst, give him drink.'"

" 'For in so doing thou shalt heap coals of fire on his head,' "

Pa finished, with a note of triumph.

Though his head was likewise now ducked to hide it, Pearl spied Mr. Wheeler's telltale smile over across the table. In the next instant, he flashed her the barest wink.

It was very nearly her undoing.

Reverend Mason looked thoroughly abashed, but did not refuse a helping of the apple crisp when she offered it once everyone had their fill of the beans and corn bread. He tasted it and made no comment—indeed, looked surprised at its flavor. "I am sorry we have no cream to pour over it," she said. "The cow was taken some time back, but I'd saved back some of the summer's honey."

"It's quite toothsome," he admitted.

She smiled thinly. And there, in the edge of her vision, was—confound him, anyway—Mr. Wheeler nodding emphatically as he shoveled in another bite.

And suddenly her smile was not so thin after all. But Reverend Mason didn't have to know the true reason why.

He ate quickly and made his excuses. Pearl offered to see him out. A shepherd should know the true state of his flock, after all, and Pearl would not speak of Pa's spells in front of Pa himself.

She walked with Reverend Mason to where his mount, a rather worn-looking bay horse, was tethered beside the barn. "I wonder that you dared leave him unattended," she said. "Neither army would care that they'd be taking an animal from a man of God."

He did not answer but fixed her with a look of deepest alarm and concern. "You are in a precarious position here, no mistake."

"I am perfectly aware of that fact, sir."

That mollified him a bit. "Has your father had another spell, then?"

She let out her breath in a rush. "Yes. It was—so frightening, Reverend. I was busy doing laundry, and he slipped out and climbed all the way over the ridge."

Proper shock registered on the pastor's face at last. "It's a miracle you found him."

"That was my thought. And he's—not been himself since. He refers to our unfortunate houseguests as if they were honored guests indeed, and—"

"And you merely wish to keep the peace." Reverend Mason reached out to seize her hand and patted it. "You are a good Southern girl, Pearl MacFarlane. Pray do not let yourself be swayed by anything they might say. You know our cause is a righteous one."

How to answer that? Eyes stinging, she swallowed and stammered, "I—I will trust God to lead me as He wills. And to give me the strength to serve as He requires."

Reverend Mason gave her hand a last squeeze then took up his horse's reins. "And I will pray for you and your father."

"Thank you, Reverend."

She suppressed the urge to scrub her palm on her skirts in his presence and contented herself instead with clenching her hands in her skirts as he rode away.

It wasn't that she doubted his sincerity. It certainly wasn't that she doubted the good Lord either. Why, then, did his words unsettle her so?

Near dawn, Josh dozed fitfully and woke by turns. The house was blessedly quiet. The burning ache in his arm had faded to a dull throb, though he guessed he must have smacked it against the wall sometime in the night...again. The bandages at the end of the stump were oozing a bright red, visible even in the gloom.

Another day in which he had to wake, rise eventually, and face this.

He blew out a breath and blinked. The soughing of Mr. Thorsson's breathing was ordinarily deep and even enough to soothe him back to sleep, but his thoughts were noisy this morning. Just as the house would be in less than an hour.

The minister's visit the night before was upsetting, to say the least. The way the man had thought to gloat over them, and in their very presence—Josh had met better treatment while actually being taken prisoner. Even the men he'd fought against weren't without simple compassion for his wounded state.

But the way Mr. MacFarlane had turned it right back on the good reverend—completely inadvertently—and the almost palpable amusement flowing from his daughter, across the table. . . Josh was sure they'd both nearly disgraced themselves in the moment.

He grinned, despite himself. It was disrespect to a man of God, perhaps, but did the preacher's own words not convict him?

The words were convicting enough to Josh, especially here in the dusk before dawn.

He wrenched his thoughts away and turned instead to how he might gain word of the armies' movements—how things fared with his regiment and Old Rosey's plans so far. He knew enough of the way things went that if the two armies didn't reengage sometime soon, there might be talk of parole, or prisoner exchange—or if time allowed, he'd just be sent to Richmond.

The prospect of the former held less appeal than it might have a day or two ago.

How on earth did that happen?

Not his concern, he told himself firmly, the fate of one Confederate family. And his place was with the army—and country—he'd sworn to uphold and fight for.

The creak of footsteps across the floorboards above his bed announced that Miss MacFarlane was awake and up.

He sighed. Nothing for it but to manfully face the day.

He'd faced battle, after all. This should be easy.

# CHAPTER 17

The first order of Pearl's day, of course, was breakfast. From the provisions Portius had brought, she was happy to have salt pork to fry alongside the morning's corn mush. It wasn't what she wished she had to offer, but it was something. Although Travis better be supplying her with more if he expected her to house more wounded.

*Others have it much worse.* She was tired of thinking about it.

Outside, a steady rain fell. No laundry would be done today, unless she could set up her washtub in the kitchen and hang things to dry upstairs. Yes, that would work, at least for her own clothing. Blankets might be another thing entirely. She'd had Clem take them outside after the men had all dressed again yesterday and give them a good beating on the line, even as the first rain shower started. Even so, several were past needing attention.

Clem was actually up, bringing in an armful of split wood for the stove. Portius was helping Pa to his chair in the sitting room, and Mr. Wheeler was over assisting Mr. Jackson and Mr. Shaw to an upright position in their beds.

She nodded to herself and commenced to dishing the food.

After breakfast, she set Clem to bringing in buckets of water to heat on the stove and started in on the task of washing the blankets. It took all morning, since she could only do one or two at a time, but Portius built a fire in the hearth to keep the men warm while their wraps were taken away. The satisfaction of seeing the dirt and filth float away in the soapy water carried her through the nagging ache creeping across her shoulders and the pain of her increasingly chapped hands.

At one point, she heard the stove door being opened just behind her, and thinking it Clem, she turned to snap something at him. The words died on her tongue. Mr. Wheeler knelt there, door opened, reaching for a stick of wood from the box beside the stove. The reflection of the fire inside the stove cast a ruddy glow across his face and lit his hair and beard to a vivid hue. Teeth bared in a grimace, he moved slowly and deliberately but with an admirable air of capability, keeping the elbow of his wounded arm anchored firmly against his upraised knee while he poked the stick about and finally settled it into the fire.

She should not stare. It was unspeakably rude.

As he swung the door shut and turned the handle to latch it, she finally tore her gaze away and returned to scrubbing. He rose, but hesitated, so she chanced another glance upward. "Thank you."

A quick nod and he moved away.

"Wait."

Another hesitation, as she rocked back on her heels and rose. Wiping her hands on her apron, she nodded toward the dark stain at the end of his bandage. "You've not been resting enough?"

He tucked the limb against his belly. "Thumped it on the wall last night in my sleep, is all."

She gave him a hard look. "You've quite a way to full recovery, yet. Don't feel like you have to be busy every minute."

The look was suddenly returned with equal weight.

"You still need to rest," she added, stubbornly.

"I will," he said and, turning, walked away.

She huffed and went back to the washing.

Josh watched her, scrubbing blanket after blanket, tirelessly. Sending Clem out into the rain for more water as needed, her back going ramrod straight during the times her brother dared give her guff about doing so, then sending him to the fire to warm up and dry off when he'd return from the errand.

And each blanket, after she'd wrung it out—a task he didn't dare offer to help with yet, with only one good hand—she carried upstairs.

Was there room enough to lay them all out, up there?

Once she was done with those, she carried her small washtub up the stairs, while heating yet one more pot of water on the stove, then followed with the hot water and a bucket of cold. The door shut behind her, and that was all he saw of her for a while.

Doing her own laundry now, or. . . ?

*Not his concern.* Though before he could stop it, he had the image of that wayward dark hair all tumbling loose down her back. . .

The rumble of a wagon in the yard, the sound carrying even over the rain, drew everyone's attention. Josh peered out a window. Bledsoe, if he didn't miss his guess, with another load of wounded prisoners. At least they'd covered the wagon this time.

Portius, already standing at the door, turned and made a long, slow perusal of the room, then gave a nod to no one in particular and headed out. Bledsoe and the driver were getting down.

Though still barefoot, Josh went out to stand on the porch. Out in the rain, Portius conferred with Bledsoe then glanced back. "Three this time, more to come. Let's put these in the house, and we'll begin preparing the barn for more."

Speaking of the barn. . . Clem emerged, looking none too happy at that news.

Josh did what he could to assist preparing the two empty beds, which they hadn't gotten around to taking down yet. "We'll put the third on the floor for now," Portius said, as he and Bledsoe carried one man in on a stretcher.

They all looked up in surprise when Miss MacFarlane came pattering down the stairs, dressed in fresh clothing and—yes, dark hair down, but her fingers flew, binding the mass in a sober braid.

Josh caught a glimpse of bare feet peeking out beneath the skirt of blue calico, despite the obvious addition of a stiffened petticoat or modest set of hoops.

She hadn't time to say a word before Bledsoe said, "I told you I'd need to bring more."

Her mouth hardened, but she remained silent, producing a ribbon from somewhere and tying off the end of the braid. From the corner of his eye, Josh saw Bledsoe watching her as intently as—well, as Josh himself was.

He couldn't blame the man—the blue of her dress brought a fetching flush to her cheeks and heightened the green sparkle of her eyes. Her trim waist just begged for a man's arm around it. But that niggling desire to box Bledsoe's ears crept under his skin again.

"What in the world did you do to these poor souls?" she said at last. "They look absolutely wretched."

"These men have lain on the field all week," Bledsoe said. "We've worked as quickly as we could, and still it hasn't been enough."

Her face paled, and cold settled deep in Josh's own gut.

That could have been him.

*Thank You, merciful God.*

Miss MacFarlane whisked off to make her own preparations. Josh did what he could to assist getting the three additions settled, and once that was done, Bledsoe beckoned him out onto the porch and to the far corner. "You're recovering remarkably well."

Josh didn't know whether or not to admit how weary he truly felt.

Bledsoe sucked his cheek for a moment. "We're making some prisoner exchanges for wounded, if you still need time in hospital. Recovery for losing a limb is about two months, as I recall. Or I could leave you here, on parole."

He should rightfully prefer an exchange, return to his regiment. How were his companions there faring? His mind skipped over the faces he often saw around the campfires—Ross, Thacker, Ainsley—good men who'd saved his neck more than once.

Had any of them fallen?

"What are the terms of parole?" he found himself asking.

The pale eyes flickered. "One, you'd not be allowed back north of Tennessee."

"And just how far back has the Army of the Cumberland fallen?"

Another long moment of consideration. "At the moment, they're holed up in Chattanooga."

Josh thought fast. Old Rosey's entire goal was to take and hold that town. But the Rebs would surely strike, and soon, and drive the Federals farther north. He might not have another opportunity to be exchanged back into his own lines.

Another opportunity to fight again, despite the loss of a hand. Others had been known to continue under such circumstances.

He shifted his weight from one foot to another. "I'd like to stay here for now. Assist the MacFarlanes in any way I can."

Bledsoe's eyes narrowed. "And why would you feel the need to do that?"

He scrambled for an excuse. "There's an obvious shortage of able-bodied men here. Miss MacFarlane can't do it all alone, not with her pa failing."

"You're mighty concerned for her."

"And you are not?"

Bledsoe's mouth curved, a thin but cool smile. "Since I've asked *Miss MacFarlane* to consider becoming my wife, I think I've more right to concern than you."

So that was it. His thoughts flashed back to Miss MacFarlane's complete discomposure after reentering the house two days ago. The verbal sparring between the two that Josh couldn't help but overhear.

Could it be that she wasn't altogether welcoming of such a proposal?

"I should think that *consider* is the operative word here. If she chooses not to—"

Bledsoe spat an oath. "She's best served by accepting it, and she knows it."

Josh held the other man's gaze, his resolve to stay hardening.

By all that was holy, he'd not flit off and leave Miss MacFarlane to her cousin's determination. Not without knowing where she stood.

"I'll keep that in mind," he said, slowly. "In the meantime, I can be of help. You are—busy elsewhere much of the time, unless I miss my guess. I can help her nurse the other sick, and stay out of her way.

Perhaps even keep an eye out and send you word if need be."

Bledsoe gave a reluctant nod, some of the tightness leaving his face. "I would—be most appreciative of that."

Josh was going to regret this, he just knew.

# CHAPTER 18

Travis did indeed bring more. Wagon after wagon, until not just the house was filled but the barn too, both the main floor and the hayloft. The only space reserved for Pearl was her attic bedroom, stolen from Clem.

After a couple of days' relief from the terrible resentment, she found herself indignant all over again that it was when she'd dared take an hour to wash up herself, and put on her best dress complete with corded petticoat and a nice collar, while her other clothing dried, that Travis came. And these poor wretches were indeed covered with all manner of battlefield filth. The house stank, and no amount of vinegar or lye soap or lavender simmered on the stove, so carefully hoarded until now, completely alleviated it.

Nothing for it but to braid back her still-wet hair, discard her petticoat, tie her least-soiled apron over the dress, and plunge into the work.

Pa thankfully sat still, near the hearth, occasionally making conversation with those around him, while she and Portius and Clem—and Mr. Wheeler too, though she watched him carefully for signs of weariness—bustled about, offering water, washing wounds, and rebandaging where necessary, laying aside soiled garments for borrowed blankets only slightly less so.

Travis did also bring provisions. Yankee supplies left behind after the battle, he said.

Pa recovered enough to hold the Bible on his lap and read, this time from Psalms. Pearl wondered whether it was simply that the volume of scripture most naturally fell open in the middle, to this book of prayer, or if there were other reasons.

"'This is my infirmity: but I will remember the years of the right hand of the most High.'"

Dusk came early, as the rain continued. Portius lit a lamp and set it near Pa so he could keep reading, and Pearl did not argue the use of precious kerosene. It was a comfort for all of them to hear it.

Supper was finished at last, and a modicum of settlement accomplished with all their charges. Pearl couldn't bring herself to count yet. The sounds of whimpering and moaning echoed through the house, and she knew the barn was the same. Portius and Clem retired there, promising to tend that portion of their guests so Pearl would have no need to cross the yard in the rainy dark. By unspoken agreement, Mr. Wheeler lingered to help Pearl make sure everyone was made reasonably comfortable, and even shepherded Pa to bed once night had fully fallen.

Pearl could not help but be grateful.

At last the house was moderately quiet, and when at last Mr. Wheeler turned for his own bed, Pearl made him sit at the kitchen table so she could tend his bandage. She felt his eyes upon her while she gathered lamp and washbasin. From the pocket of her dress she pulled a jar of ointment—Mama's recipe, like other things hoarded until now—and a length of clean cloth she'd saved back during the day's ministrations.

"I thought we'd used everything up," he murmured.

She angled him a tight smile.

"Not giving me special treatment, are you?"

Confound the blasted Yankee. She bit back the grin tugging at her mouth. "No. I simply refuse to let you lapse back into infection after expending so much effort upon you already."

"Good. Because I'd hate to have to explain that to your fiancé."

Heart, breath, and motion stopped.

Mr. Wheeler's eyes were like deep wells, all expectation and question.

Of course. *Travis.*

"He is not my fiancé," she snapped, barely above a whisper.

"He seems to think himself so."

She struggled to pull air into her lungs. "He—I—" She huffed. "He is my cousin."

Mr. Wheeler sat, completely undeterred. "Cousins marry sometimes." A half shrug. "I've one who my mama has pestered me to consider sparking."

Her head wagged. "Travis isn't like that. Not to me. He's. . .more like a brother." Another breath, this one deep and clean. "Despite what he thinks. Or might have told you."

She forced herself back into motion, reaching toward his wounded arm. Mr. Wheeler extended the limb, rolling his blouse sleeve up above the elbow and then bracing it on the tabletop.

"What *did* he tell you?" Her fingers struggled to free the tied ends of the bandage.

"That he'd asked you to consider becoming his wife," Mr. Wheeler murmured. "I thought it telling that he didn't simply say *asked* you to be his wife."

Heat swept her body. Suddenly the Yankee was just too close, but she had to finish this task. The stubborn knot came free at last.

"Are you considering it?" he pressed.

The limb half-unwrapped, she stopped again. Met his too-knowing gaze. Half-a-dozen pert replies came to mind, but finally she settled for a simple, "No."

The bandage unwound easily to the very end, where the bleeding had seeped through and dried. With cupped hand, she scooped water onto the spot, as Portius had taught her, and worked it loose.

"Why, do you think I should?" What was it about this man that made her own tongue so loose?

"I know neither of you well enough to be able to make that recommendation," he said, all mildness, and the end of the bandage lifted free at last.

He turned the limb this way and that, examining it along with her. The wound itself appeared less raw and angry, despite the bleeding from earlier, and what was left of the forearm, less swollen. Deep bruising still marred the flesh to the elbow and a little above, but the color bespoke healing.

Without thinking, she laid the backs of her fingers against his forearm, to feel for fever there, a telltale sign of infection. He flinched.

"Does that hurt?"

The dark eyes were wide, startled, this time. "No." He cleared his throat, and she took her hand away.

"Hm, it's a wonder if not. Your arm's a little warm, I'm guessing because you've been up and about so much today." Feeling foolish, she touched his forehead this time, brushing aside his hair to do so. "No fever overall, though. That's good."

She'd swear she was the one with a fever.

He made no comment as she went briskly back to work, dipping out ointment with her littlest finger and gently applying it to the amputation wound, then rewrapping it with the clean bandage. After, he rolled the sleeve back down and tucked in the end. "Thank you," he said at last.

"Of course." She still couldn't meet his gaze. "You should get to bed now."

He made no move to get up, and finally she did look directly at him. The lamplight drew fire from his hair and beard but underscored the shadows beneath his eyes. "I could take the first turn sitting up," he said.

She should refuse. . . She should. Insist on him retiring for the night, that she would wake him when she could no longer stay awake. But the thought of how grueling the next several days were likely to be. . .

Her breath escaped her in a rush. "Very well. But please wake me if need be."

His expression warmed in what was very nearly a smile.

She woke sometime in the night and came down to find him seated in Pa's chair, asleep, head propped against the wall, arms folded, and legs outstretched. A few of the men stirred, and one groaned. She picked her way across the floor to that one, offered water, and on the way back to fetch a cup and pitcher, nudged Mr. Wheeler awake.

He shambled off to bed, leaving her to make the rounds, checking on their various charges.

For some reason, it all seemed far less terrifying this time. Perhaps because she knew she had help, if she needed it. Or because of those few men who seemed to be thriving after just a few days under her care, despite the two who had died.

Dawn came, and still it rained. She and Portius had discussed how best to feed everyone, and they'd agreed that Pearl would start a pot of gruel or soup and keep something simmering at all times. She'd just started in on the first batch of the day, and Portius had come in to help take men to the necessary and such, when children's voices and that of a woman could be heard from outside.

Portius opened the door, and in came Lydia and her two children. With a cry, Pearl ran to embrace her as Clem lugged in a pair of bundles and carried them toward the stairs. "I heard you needed help," Lydia said. "So I came. I hope you don't mind."

"Oh—no, of course not!" Pearl's mind was already sorting details as she crossed back to the kitchen. The morning's gruel would scorch if not stirred constantly. "You can all sleep in the attic with me."

Lydia nodded, hanging her damp shawl and bonnet on pegs by the door, then shepherding the children through the room toward the kitchen. Her lips pressed firm as she glanced around.

"There are more in the barn," Pearl said with a rueful laugh, then caught the other woman's gaze as she approached. "I wouldn't have asked you to come," she said, softly.

Lydia's warm golden gaze was steady. "You know I would have. And did."

"How did you know?"

Lydia nodded toward Portius. "He came yesterday and told me you had need of more hands. Figured it was better than sitting at home by ourselves." She angled her head toward the very full sitting room. "We missed being pressed into service, apparently because, well, either the house is too hidden or Travis didn't know I was there."

"You are always welcome, regardless," Pearl breathed.

A real smile this time. "I know."

Pearl hugged her again. "I. . .am sorry this has been so difficult for you."

Lydia clung to her. "Your brother ain't coming back, Pearl. I know this."

"Doesn't mean we don't grieve," she choked. But there was no time for lingering over tears.

The rain continued for days. Josh was glad to have plenty of work to keep himself busy, but with everyone mostly stuck indoors, each day felt interminable. And he lost count of how many times he'd go to do a task, reaching with both hands, only to remember that he only had. . .one.

And the weariness never quite went away. But still he pushed himself, inspired by the quiet, uncomplaining faithfulness of Miss MacFarlane. Her companion was likewise industrious, managing both the two children and assisting Miss MacFarlane in caring for the wounded. Josh could not figure whether Lydia was a friend or if the two were somehow related—and George MacFarlane did not seem the type to have taken advantage of a slave woman, although such things were common enough.

Two men died by the end of the first day. Another the second day. Three the third. Josh could see the toll it took in Miss MacFarlane's face—Lydia's as well—but the young woman visibly pulled herself together and kept working. Kept ministering to those who needed even the most menial tasks done for them.

Josh talked with all of them, gathered names and regiments and assorted injuries. None were from his own regiment, but there was another man from Ohio, just a couple of counties over from Josh's family; one from Michigan; a handful from Kentucky; and the rest from Illinois and Indiana.

The range of injuries staggered him. One poor soul had half his jaw blown off, it seemed, which required someone to hold the side of his face closed while he chewed, oh so carefully, and swallowed. Likewise when he drank water. The blue eyes peering out of the mangled, bruised, powder-burned face were barely human, but the man clung to life and looked upon Josh with desperate, shamed gratitude for his assistance, since he also had sustained a shoulder injury which prevented him from performing this service for himself.

All of them shared bits and pieces of what they'd seen in the battle. All were hungry for news of Federal lines, but Portius would only say that Rosecrans remained holed up in Chattanooga, until the day Clem came running in while Josh was helping in the barn with the news that Federal reinforcements had arrived in Chattanooga. Portius asked whether the Confederate lines were on the move, and when Clem replied that he didn't think so, the Negro retorted that it didn't matter, then, and returned to work.

Clem heaved a sigh. Josh gathered cups and dishes to return to the house for washing, doing his best to appear as if he was minding his own business but watching the tall boy. After a moment, Clem lifted his head and caught Josh's eye, looking for all the world as if he wanted to say more. Josh beckoned him near.

"You've no more word than that, regarding reinforcements?" he asked softly.

"Nah. I've asked around—I have. General Bragg is just sitting there, waiting for something to happen, and Longstreet ain't happy because provisions are short." He hesitated. "I think Travis practically stole what he brought us."

It was likely not far from the truth.

"Newspapers, what I can get of 'em, are saying we've won a great victory. That we put the Federals on the run. 'Scuse me, of course, for saying so—I know they's your side—"

Josh gave a dismissive wave.

"They've been working on getting the rail line from Catoosa Springs and Chattanooga Station rebuilt, but that's been slow, especially with the rain."

He nodded at the boy as if that was information he knew already. Of course, it stood to reason that the Rebs would rebuild what the Federals had torn down, so it came as no surprise.

Clem tipped his head, shaggy dark hair falling over one eye. They were more blue than his sister's, Josh noticed. "What regiment were you in, again?"

"The First Ohio." Josh had been in an all-fired hurry to rush out and enlist the moment the war broke out, despite both Mama and Pa advising him to wait and see how things went. He'd likewise rushed into each engagement his regiment took part in. Never hesitating. Never looking back.

And then there was Snodgrass Hill....

The boy still looked at him curiously. "What weapon did you carry?"

He couldn't resist the smile this time and let himself relax into a more comfortable stance, shifting to set his good shoulder against the barn wall. "A Henry repeater, but of course I lost it. Had the chance to handle a Sharps carbine a time or two, though, and liked it."

Clem's eyes rounded. Obviously the renown of both the expensive lever-action repeating rifle—he'd spent all his savings on that one—and the new breechloader used by the cavalry, though merely a single-shot firearm, was already widespread.

The boy cut his gaze to the side, glancing around as if just now realizing that he was treating Josh in a most un-prisoner-like manner. Then he twitched his head to the side. "Come with me. I've something to show you."

He led Josh around the edge of the barn's main floor, into a side room holding an ancient set of harness and a cart with a broken wheel, standing up against one wall. He hefted the cart aside to reveal a ladder built into the wall, then peered inquiringly at Josh. "Can you climb that, do you think? I've done it one-handed, carrying things."

Josh smiled grimly at the challenge—and the boy's calm acceptance of his new limitation. "I'll do my best."

Clem scampered up first, lifting a panel in the ceiling above and setting it aside, then wriggling through the opening. Josh followed after, slowly but with determination, and to his own faint surprise and intense satisfaction, he made it. He emerged into a dusty but surprisingly well-lit attic room. Outside the unshuttered window, rain pattered and ran from the barn eaves.

It was the floor that drew his attention, though. Josh pulled himself the rest of the way through and tried not to let his jaw sag.

The boy had an entire arsenal up here. Muskets and rifles lay beside revolvers and assorted piles of round shot and minié balls. A half-dozen sabers and combat swords rounded out the collection.

Josh let out a low whistle. "So that's where you'd run off to, half worrying your sister to death."

Clem's expression was half chagrin, half pride. "I been scoutin' the battlefields, yes. Ain't no one else using these now."

"I see that." And he'd made no distinction between gray and blue, by the looks of it. "Are you planning on holding off the entire Union army, then?"

The boy's face crinkled in a laugh that minded Josh so suddenly of Pearl that a pang resounded through his chest, like the concussion from a cannon.

*Miss MacFarlane.* Not Pearl.

As he'd already reminded himself dozens of times that week.

"Might at that." He sobered then angled another glance at Josh. "So which of these looks like what you carried?"

"Well, let's see." Yes, there was a Sharps, over there in the far corner. He picked his way across the floor and lifted it. Careful to point the barrel toward the outside wall and away from Clem, he braced it between his elbow and side and checked to make sure it was unloaded. Then he hefted it again, looking it over more carefully. Nicks and cuts here and there, but to all appearances still in good working order.

"She's a beauty," Clem murmured, leaning close.

For an instant, Josh had an image of Pearl, eyes sparkling, mouth tipped in laughter, face framed by loose strands of hair. But of course the boy meant the carbine. "Yes. . .yes, she is."

"So what kind of load does she take?" Clem turned to glance across the floor.

"Well, let's see."

And with that, they spent a companionable half hour or so talking over Clem's finds, and what went where, until a call from somewhere made them both aware of where they were and how much time they'd spent. Clem glanced up, face pale. "I'll go down first. Can you make it alone?"

"I should," he said. The entire escapade made him think of happier times with his own brothers.

They exchanged a grin, and Clem disappeared down the ladder.

# CHAPTER 19

September had long since whiled away into October. Pearl settled into a routine of cooking, washing, tending wounds, and, with Portius and Lydia assisting, overseeing the general well-being of their house- and barn-fulls of guests, as Pa still was wont to call them.

Pa himself was little better, but he was at least no worse. The constant activity about the house apparently thoroughly engaged his attention, because there had been no repeat of the day Pearl had found him out wandering over the ridge. And for that at least, she was most grateful.

The longing to do the same, however, tugged at her, almost unceasingly. That same constant activity—when she finally allowed herself to stop and count, she found there were thirteen men populating their downstairs, not including Pa, and easily twice that in the barn—caring for those men, keeping them fed, their wounds washed and dressed, only half attempting to keeping them clean, comforting the suffering and even the dying where needed, was nigh on overwhelming. Jem and Sally, Lydia's two little ones, were both a counterpoint for the gravity of the situation, and wearing on her nerves and Lydia's by turns. Pa did enjoy their presence, which was also something. Sally spent as much time in his lap as with her mama.

More than two weeks of rain left it nearly impossible to do proper washing or provide the men with baths. Firewood they at least had in abundance, with Portius and Clem working together to bring some in. Few of their charges were recovered enough to help with any great regularity, but Mr. Wheeler remained determined to be of as much use as possible. More than once Pearl looked up from cooking or other tasks in the kitchen to see him standing out by the woodpile, chopping or splitting. The first time she'd seen him struggling to swing the ax, one-armed, her heart had nearly stopped. Surely he'd cause himself the loss of a foot as well as the hand, doing that.

But somehow he hadn't. He did, after a few attempts, toss the ax aside and switch to a hatchet instead, with which he made surprisingly quick work of the job. Pearl found herself shaking her head at the spectacle.

And now—on a morning where the rain had miraculously stopped, though the clouds still hung heavy and low, obscuring the ridge beyond the house—instead of working, she stood at the window, transfixed by his intensity and determination. And not a little admiring of his growing dexterity with just that hatchet.

"You spend an awful lot of time watching him," came Lydia's murmur at her shoulder.

Pearl slapped a hand over her heart, her pulse and breath both chugging. "Gracious, woman. Shouldn't you be cooking?"

Lydia's full lips tweaked in a smile, golden eyes gleaming, and she pursed her lips and leaned toward the window as well. At least half a minute went by. "Can't say as I blame you much, though."

That drew another gasp from Pearl's throat. "Lydia!"

"Well? You gonna try to deny that he's easy on the eyes?"

"Lydia."

The other woman chuckled then whisked herself back to the stove. "Too bad he's a Yankee."

Pearl bit her lip.

Too bad indeed.

He laid aside the hatchet and collected half an armload of pieces. Pearl shook her head as he stacked them—incredibly—on what remained of his left arm. She hadn't noticed him doing so before, but—

He rose and headed for the house. Startled to realization, Pearl yanked herself from the window and scurried across the kitchen. It was high time she found some other occupation.

The back door opened, and he walked in. "Why, thank you, Mister

Wheeler!" Lydia sang out, her voice thick with amusement.

"You're most welcome, Miz Lydia," he responded with an edge of puzzlement and released his load into the box by the stove.

Pearl could not help but glance over her shoulder and found herself meeting his eyes as he brushed off his shirt. After an awkward little dip of her head and the barest smile, she turned back toward the sitting room, gritted her teeth, and tried to place her attention anywhere other than on the man behind her.

The sitting room currently was about half-empty from its usual state of late. Some of the men occupied the front porch, Pa was holding court around the hearth, and only the worst wounded still lay in the beds over against the opposite wall. Of these, one very young man who they all simply called Johnny was her main concern these last days, and he shifted with a particular restless movement she was coming to know all too well.

*Oh Lord. . .*

It was beginning to feel as though her prayers were just pebbles tossed into the river, sinking below the surface and lost to the tumbling of the current.

She went to the man's bedside and laid a hand across his forehead. He'd been feverish for many a day, and she knew the cause. He'd a leg wound very like Mr. Thorsson's—which had improved greatly and appeared to be healing well, although she still watched it with great concern—but Johnny had lain, as Travis told them, on the battlefield for days untended.

*If only someone had gotten to it sooner. . .*

Portius looked at the wound often, his expression graver every time. Pearl used some of the rapidly dwindling goldenseal, and though it seemed to help at first, the worst of the damage had been done, and this time, the soldier seemed to be fighting a losing battle.

The man opened his eyes. Something in his face, whether the eyes or how impossibly young he appeared, tugged at her heart.

As it did nearly every time she helped tend him, directly.

He smiled drowsily, and this time her heart just broke. "Might I get you anything, Johnny?" she whispered.

He shook his head, then, "A drink would be most welcome, miss."

"Of course. I'd be glad to get that for you."

She turned, ready to spring into motion, but Mr. Wheeler was already halfway across the room with a cup.

He handed it to her, and she helped Johnny sit up and drink. After, he sank back with another smile. A sigh, then he met her gaze again. "I'm not long for this world, am I?"

Pearl's breath seized. "I—don't know rightly, sir. I'm not God, to tell a man his time."

The smile widened to a grin. "Well. I think it must be mine, and very soon. I'm not afraid, mind you. The river I cross might be dark, but I know I'm going to a happier place." He hesitated. "I do wish, though, that I could somehow let my mother know."

Pearl swallowed and finally was able to say, "I could help you write a letter, if you like."

The young man's eyes brightened. "I would be most appreciative, Miss MacFarlane."

Choking back the tears, she fetched her lap desk, made sure she had ink and paper, then seated herself at his bedside.

Josh tended the fire, then grabbed a broom and attempted to sweep the sitting room—anything to keep himself busy, when all he wished was to simply watch Miss MacFarlane at work.

He knew he was behaving like a hopeless sot. But her simple act of compassion—lingering over a dying man, performing the service of writing a letter to the man's family—mesmerized as fancy dress or hair could not.

No wonder Bledsoe was so smitten with her.

He'd nearly mastered using the broom, at least. About halfway across the floor, he glanced up and found Miz Lydia regarding him with a wry smile as she stirred the stew on the stove. With a slow shake of her dark head, she turned back to the pot.

Was that because of his clumsy insistence at sweeping, or something else entirely?

Miss MacFarlane finished up the letter, blotted and folded it, and patiently had Johnny dictate the address. Then, after tucking the packet into her lap desk, she set it aside. "Might I get you anything else?"

Johnny sank back with a satisfied sigh. "Not presently. Thank you."

From the corner of his eye, Josh saw her nod—just a little too tightly—and heard her murmur, "Please do excuse me, then," in a voice that pitched a little too high.

Snatching her woolen shawl from the peg by the door, with one hand clutching her skirt, she fairly fled the house.

He angled toward the window to watch, but instead of the barn or even privy, she headed for the open field leading toward the hillside, running.

Where the devil was she going?

And should he follow, just to make sure she came to no harm?

He'd barely time to think the thought before one of the men loitering outside by the barn pushed himself upright and wandered in the same direction. His companions jostled each other and laughed.

He didn't think. He simply went. Thankfully, he already wore his boots, having gone out to chop wood and whatnot.

The wind held an edge, but he hardly felt it. Someone greeted him as he crossed the porch, but he threw them a wave and kept going.

*God. . .oh God. . .keep her safe.*

She'd already disappeared into the cover of the timbered hillside, with that no-account still following.

Josh broke into a run, though his arm ached with the exertion and his body felt oddly off balance. He was a fast runner—or had been, because apparently losing a hand made him clumsy, but he drove himself harder up the slope.

# CHAPTER 20

Pearl simply could not bear it a moment longer. The closeness of the house, indeed, the despondency which hung about the entire farm these last few weeks—Lydia was there and could surely spare her a half hour.

She had a vague idea of running to Mama's grave—which now shared the family plot with an assortment of Yankees—but once her feet were on the hillside, she decided against it and kept running until she'd gained the timber. And even then, she climbed steadily, over rocks and around boulders, through the brush, until she'd nearly gained the top of the ridge and lack of breath forced her to stop.

So—much—hurt. So much sorrow. Too much death, and blood, and—where would it end?

She collapsed against a boulder, half gasping, half sobbing. *Lord, where are You in all this? Are You even here? Have You forgotten us? My eye wastes away with grief, my years with sighing...*

A snapping of twigs brought her upright, and she whirled to find a shabbily dressed man approaching—one of their wounded Yankees from the barn, although she couldn't be completely sure in the moment. An all-too-intent gleam shone in his eyes. "Hullo there, missy. It's lonely out here. Care for some company?"

A ragged gasp rattled from her throat. "I—no. I prefer to be alone, sir. Pray return to the house."

His smile grew more oily. "Ah, but your talent for comfort is renowned. I thought I might get me a taste of it meself, iffen ya don't mind."

Anger fired through her veins, hot and desperate. "I do mind, very much." She scrambled away, sliding along the boulder, the burning in her side forgotten as she poised to dive away and take flight once more.

And then—a roar came from behind the man, and he jerked around to look just as a second man plowed into him. The impact sent them both tumbling, until they slammed against another rocky outcropping. Pearl caught a glimpse of fire-red auburn hair.

*Mr. Wheeler?*

Indeed, though she hardly recognized him in his fury, it was he, rearing back now to slam his fist into the jaw of her would-be assailant, then rising to haul him to his feet. "Get—get out of here, right now," he snarled. "And don't let me catch you within thirty feet of Miss MacFarlane without Portius or myself present." He shook the man so hard even Pearl heard his teeth rattling. "Do—you—hear—me?"

With a single, hasty nod and the barest glance toward Pearl, the soldier stumbled away, limping and clutching his shoulder.

Mr. Wheeler watched him go before swinging toward Pearl, eyes dark as night, face flushed, teeth bared. The ferocity faded only a little as his gaze swept her. "Are you unhurt?"

Hands across her mouth, she nodded, unable to move, unable to speak. Trembling seized her.

As her knees buckled, he was suddenly there, at her side, catching her before she too tumbled. And all she could do in the moment was let herself fall against him, cheek pressed to his chest, hands reflexively clutching his shoulders.

"All's well now," came the soothing rumble of his voice, under her ear. "He won't touch you, I promise."

A whimper tore from her throat. His arms tightened around her, and as the weeping took over, she sank into him.

How could his embrace be so unexpectedly comforting? But it was— and he seemed not to mind that she was blubbering all over the front of his blouse, or that she was clinging to him as if her life depended upon it. His warm strength not only held her up but also soaked through her like the heat of the fire in the hearth at home, or her best quilt wrapping her about. Even as the sobs lessened, he held on to her, and she found herself content to be held.

More than content, actually. It eased a hurt she didn't even know she had until this moment.

She became aware of him rocking her slightly, of his bearded cheek pressed to the top of her head. He shifted, and as his lips brushed her forehead, a shiver coursed through her, this time for a very different reason.

With a long, unsteady breath, she straightened. Those deep brown eyes stared into hers, fiery hair wild about his face. His arms fell away, and the chill rushed back in.

"Thank you," she whispered.

His mouth compressed, and he nodded. "I saw him take off after you—"

Fresh tears poured down her cheeks. His hand came up to brush them away then lingered on her cheek. Pearl found herself swaying toward him again, but—surely that was mere weakness from the fright she'd just had.

Of course she'd find his embrace comforting. It had been so long since she'd felt such from Pa or any of her brothers—

No, Mr. Wheeler was somehow not like her brothers at all.

His thumb traced the corner of her mouth. Her breath caught. And before she could react, he was the one leaning in, oh so gently pressing his lips to hers, shifting, caressing, his fingers cupping her jaw and sliding into her hair.

For a long moment—or was it an hour?—she was floating.

It was also most decidedly not like being kissed by Travis, either.

Holding her was one thing, kissing another entirely. He shouldn't let himself do this.

Wind moaning in the trees above them, and a riot of warning bells clamoring in his head, Josh couldn't bring himself to let go, quite yet.

And she didn't seem to want him to let go.

He pulled away only enough to set his lips against her cheekbone, then simply breathed her in, sweet and soft, smelling faintly of lavender and beeswax. "Pearl," he sighed.

Her sigh answered his, and she settled a little deeper into his arms.

Why did it feel as if she belonged there?

"I didn't mean to cause any trouble," she murmured. "I just wanted half an hour alone."

He could well understand that, with the noisy press her home had become. Life in the army afforded very little quiet—or privacy either, for that matter. "Are you sure you're unhurt?"

She nodded against his shoulder then drew away. Her eyes were wide, a dark green sea, shining like stars. Her cheeks flushed pink.

Oh, but she was lovely. He nearly dived back for another kiss.

"Mister Wheeler—"

"Josh. Please. Surely we are not so formal with each other still."

She went completely crimson at that, and consternation filled her gaze. "Surely we must be."

Must they, truly? Josh's mind stuttered over the possibilities. Couldn't he, a Federal soldier, and she, a Rebel girl, be more than enemies across a line? Didn't these last few minutes prove that?

Tightening her shawl about her shoulders, she edged away. "I—I thank you again for assisting me. Now I must get back."

"Pearl—"

But she was gone, skipping across the hillside as if he were the villain and not the one he'd just chased off.

Pearl slipped inside the back door, avoiding the crowd on the front porch, but feeling the sharpness of Lydia's gaze as she took off her shawl and hung it beside the door. She refused to meet the other woman's eyes, lingering to smooth her apron and tuck the wayward strands of her hair back in place. Not that such things would matter, but it gave her an extra minute to collect herself.

Lydia sidled up to her. Of course. "Is everything all right?" At her tight nod, Lydia pressed, "I saw Mister Wheeler skedaddle after you—"

"I'm perfectly well, Lydia. Thank you." Sorry for her sharpness, she faced Lydia and met the golden eyes full of concern. "Is supper ready?"

Lydia's mouth compressed for a moment. "Not yet."

Pearl glanced past her. Nothing had changed about the scene inside the house. How could that be? Everything in her world had shifted in the past half hour.

Through the window on the other side of the room, she caught a glimpse of a figure in simple blouse and trousers, with vivid hair and beard, crossing the yard toward the barn.

Her heart faltered. *Josh.* Oh, how she'd wanted to answer him in kind. But she dared not.

"Did he hurt you?" Lydia demanded, under her breath.

She shook her head. "Not him." *Never him.* "But. . .someone else nearly did. Mister Wheeler. . .stopped him."

Lydia's mouth dropped open. Pearl smiled a little. No small feat, that—Lydia was rarely so impressed.

She sighed. Lydia would also be undeterred. Especially since she'd spilled that much.

"I. . .went up on the ridge. I just needed to pray, compose my thoughts. And one of those ruffians out in the barn saw me and followed. Thought I owed him more than simple food and shelter." She raised a brow, and Lydia's expression hardened in understanding. "And then—Mister Wheeler was there. Dusted him off and sent him back down, tail between his legs."

Lydia's brow also popped, her mouth quirking. "Good for him."

"But then. . .of course he lingered to make sure I was not hurt." Her eyes snapped shut. The memory of the rough tenderness in his voice nearly undid her even now. "And of course in my female weakness I cried, and then. . .well. . .he thought to comfort me—"

Lydia seized her elbows. "Tell me already, woman."

A sound bubbled from her chest, half a giggle, half a sob. "He ended up kissing me."

The breath escaping Lydia was pure bliss. Even Pearl could hear it. "And then what?"

"What do you mean? That was all. I had to come back to the house. What else could there be?"

Lydia just looked at her.

Pearl rubbed a hand across her face. Why, oh why, had she given in and told Lydia anything? "He's a Yankee, Lydia. That's the plain truth. And we"—her next breath hurt—"we are in the middle of a terrible war. There can be no good end to this."

"Oh Pearl."

Lydia's arms came around her, and then Pearl found herself weeping on the other woman's shoulder, as well.

It was easier, here, to compose herself, because Lydia had to dash to the stove and stir the stew before it scorched, while Pearl wiped her face with her apron, but the woman was back at her side in double time. She set her hands on Pearl's shoulders and leaned close once more. "You listen to me." Thankfully, the men's chatter from the sitting room covered their conversation. "When your brother first told me he loved me, you know well how scared I was to believe him, much less act on it. How impossible it seemed that he and I could have a life together. And though now, yes, I've lost him, it was worth the risk. I have Jem and Sally. I have—you."

The tears threatened again.

"Has it been an easy road? Not at all. I am still learning to trust our God in all of it. But He has never let us suffer want, though times have been lean enough."

Pearl had no response. She was the one scrambling day to day to find enough to feed their motley group of houseguests. Watching Pa fail, week by week. Still mourning Mama's death, and the loss of her older brothers. Granted, one of those brothers had become Lydia's entire life—but hadn't the woman grown up suffering hardship, being born Negro as she was? Easy enough for her to speak of faith, in this moment.

Or was it? Pearl searched the beautiful face of her sister-friend, hardly seeing the difference in their skin and features. *Some things more important than color,*" Portius had said. And if they truly believed, as the Declaration of Independence had said and scripture itself attested, that all men were created equal—

That did not change the fact that bluebellies were the invaders. That it was wrong to force political policy on people who had not consented to it. Slavery was a horror, for sure, but to simply sever ties to a practice without giving all involved time enough to find a solution, to adapt to the changes—

The front door opened, and Josh stepped inside. His gaze met Pearl's from across the room. He hesitated then shut the door behind himself.

She glanced away, but the damage was done. Her arguments had already collapsed in ruins.

# CHAPTER 21

After everyone in the house had been served, Josh carried the pot of stew to the barn. His arm ached more than usual from the climb up the hill and back, not to mention sending that poor excuse for a Kentucky soldier running, but he could still heft the pot. And he would not show weakness in front of Pearl, who opened the door and accompanied him, but still refused to meet his eyes—just as she had all throughout supper.

They started across the yard together. "Pearl—"

"Nothing is changed between us," she snapped, very quietly.

He huffed. "It is, and you know it."

Not a line of her stance altered as she marched across the yard before him.

Stubborn, beautiful woman. Hearts such as this one were the reason the Union had found it so difficult to prevail over the Confederacy, he was sure.

He wouldn't tell Pearl he'd gone straight to Portius and reported how that reprobate had threatened her. How Portius made no hesitation but turned to Clem and directed him to run to take a message to Bledsoe, and be "most particular" about mentioning that the trouble involved Clem's sister.

Nor would he mention the long, speculating look Portius gave Josh after delivering the order. "It goes without saying that if you likewise give Miss Pearl trouble, I'll gladly pass that word on to Mister Travis as well," the black man had said.

"I understand perfectly," Josh answered, and he did—both the sentiment and Portius's willingness to carry out such a thing.

Head tucked, Pearl opened the barn door and stood back while Josh entered. How hard was it for her to enter, knowing her would-be assailant was within? Yet she did not shrink from the duty.

A cheer rose at their appearance, and the clattering of tin cups and plates—a usual occurrence with men who were in high enough spirits to appreciate being fed. It was handy that most if not all the men here had their own dishes for receiving their portions, and while they were collected after a meal and washed at once, they were always returned shortly after.

Another bit of organization by the sterling Miss Pearl MacFarlane that Josh could not help admiring.

She moved about the men now, one by one taking a cup or plate and filling it from the pot as Josh held it, or holding it for him if he'd set the pot down and was handling the ladle. About halfway around the room they stopped before the Kentucky man who had accosted her earlier. The only sign Pearl gave of discomfiture was the slight tremor of her hand as she filled the man's cup. Josh fixed the worthless fellow with a steady glare, and he kept his own head properly bowed while Pearl dished his supper.

They moved on to the next man, where Josh noted a little more belligerence toward himself and open ogling toward Pearl. Josh had to chew back a snarl. This one certainly bore a closer watch. Hungry men, and for more than mere food, and a comely woman trying to show simple kindness were not a good match under any circumstances.

As Josh and Pearl moved on to the next in line, the man met Josh's stare with one of his own, but Josh refused to break eye contact until the other did.

At last supper was finished, dishes washed, wounds tended, and everyone fed, bedded down, or otherwise settled in for a quiet evening. Pearl sat near a candle, bent over a piece of mending, and Josh perched on the hearth as the other men took turns telling stories of where they'd come from and things they'd seen. It was at the behest of Johnny, who'd grown markedly weaker, and his breathing more labored.

Would he even survive the night?

Still the young man commented when he could, and prompted the others with questions. Josh felt oddly reluctant to chime in, and over on the other side of the room, Pearl gave all her attention to the mending.

Her indifference cut far more deeply than he expected, after that moment up on the hillside, when she'd simply fallen into his arms and he'd forgotten his wound, forgotten even why he was there, except to ensure she was kept safe from harm. And of course, after their kiss—especially after that, brief as it was, but oh, so sweet.

Could things be different between them if they were not surrounded by an entire room of people, and the two of them could speak only with each other? If he had the leisure to court her properly?

If indeed they didn't have the whole Union and Confederacy between them?

He tipped his head back against the stone surrounding the fireplace. Lord willing, if he continued recovering and wasn't shunted off to Richmond and prison, he'd be returning to duty and then—no telling where he'd be sent next, or what would befall him there. He'd nothing to offer Pearl under the best of circumstances.

Likely Pearl's perspective on it was the wisest view after all, that what had happened changed nothing of their relation to each other.

Between the shadow over his thoughts, the warmth of the hearthstones at his back, and the rise and fall of the other men's voices, his attention drifted, and the world around him shifted and blurred until dreams took its place. A warm summer day, and his mother's voice urging him to go get his chores done, but all he wished to do was linger and—

He woke abruptly to someone tapping his foot. Looked up, bleary eyed, to Lydia standing over him. The room was quiet except for the hiss of coals in the fire beside him, and nearly dark.

"You should get to bed," she said, an odd smile twisting her mouth and a gleam in her eye.

"Of course," he mumbled and climbed to his feet.

Once there, it was sweet relief to stretch out. His last waking thought was of mighty trees on a steep hillside, swaying with the rushing wind, and the soft surrender of a Rebel girl in his embrace.

He should hold on to that memory, because it could never happen again.

Pearl lay staring into the dark, exhausted, but somehow unable to quiet her thoughts and fall asleep.

"If you sigh one more time," Lydia said from her pallet on the floor, "I'm a gonna come up there and slap you."

"I'll slap you right back," Pearl murmured. "And then your babies will wake up because you be caterwauling."

A chuckle answered her, and the rustle of bedding as Lydia turned over, then Lydia sighed as well. "Travis ain't gonna like this."

Pearl sniffed. "What he likes doesn't matter."

"You think not? Your man's a Yankee prisoner. Don't think Travis won't see that he's sent up to Virginia, in a moment."

Pearl's heartbeat stuttered. "He isn't—my man."

"Shoo, girl. I see how he looks at you. Especially—this evening."

"It—" She swallowed hard, then forced the words out. "It doesn't matter."

"You still gonna camp on that?" More rustling, then Lydia was there beside her, nudging her. "Move on over."

Pearl turned on her side, making room on the narrow bed for the other woman, as they often did. Lydia settled, back to back. The warmth was comforting—not in the same way as Josh's embrace, but comforting nevertheless.

Utter nonsense that being in that man's arms suddenly became the standard she measured by.

"There you go again," Lydia groused.

"My apologies," Pearl mumbled. Her eyelids stung.

"So. What are you gonna do when Travis pushes you for an answer?"

"Tell him no. What else can I do?"

"Mm-mm. It's hard, for sure."

Silence hung between them. Pearl whispered, "I—just—can't—marry him."

"And you shouldn't marry a man you don't love. No matter how hard things be here."

Because regardless of what she felt about what had happened up there on the ridge, she absolutely knew now that she couldn't bear giving herself to someone whose kiss did not make her feel what she'd felt standing on that cold, windswept hillside.

"Women marry for convenience or necessity all the time," she said.

Lydia snorted. "You'd do whatever you needed, if you were convinced it was the right thing. But Travis? No, girl." She hesitated. "Especially not with the likes of Mister Wheeler bein' a possibility."

Pearl yawned. "It's too early to know if he's a possibility or not. And I'm fairly certain he is not. But regardless—" A second yawn nearly cracked her jaw. "I'm sleepy now, thank you."

"That's convenient," Lydia snipped.

With a chuckle, Pearl shut her eyes and burrowed a little deeper into her covers.

Her last waking thought was of strong, warm arms around her, rocking gently as the wind rushed overhead. If only she could be held like that for always.

Josh woke to rain pattering outside the window. Again.

He rose, dressed, and headed out to the privy. Lydia was up and at work in the kitchen, both her children seated at the table with half a gnawed-on apple each, but Pearl was nowhere in sight. About half the other men were awake and stirring as well.

In short, an ordinary morning as these last couple of weeks had gone. Lord willing it would stay that way.

The rain was a mere drizzle at the moment, but he was glad for the extra layer of his coat so early. At the front steps he stopped, glancing around. Still no Pearl—not at the well nor anywhere else. He frowned. Was she in the barn? Maybe he'd best go check on her. It didn't set well with him for her to be wandering alone after the events of yesterday.

He'd finished his business and was coming out when something hit the door of the outhouse, slamming into him and knocking him backward. He threw himself against the inside, but then it flew open too abruptly and rough hands hauled him outside and upright. "Become a secesh lover, have you?" came a low growl.

Josh fought with all his might, and at finding himself suddenly free, he scrambled away so he was no longer surrounded. Three men faced him—the Kentucky scoundrel and his two cronies, also from yesterday.

Such a surprise, that.

Josh stayed in a half crouch, backing up as they edged toward him. "It's a yellow-bellied thing to force your attentions on a woman," he snarled.

"And she needs a one-armed soldier to guard her?" the Kentucky man sneered.

"This one-armed soldier whipped your tail and sent you back."

"Yeah, well, won't happen today. And then we'll be happy to show *Miss Pearl* what she be missing in the way of manhood." He and his companions snickered.

Josh unclenched his teeth and struggled to keep his vision clear through a haze of red. "Have some respect for a woman who's fed you and tended your wounds, when she could just leave you to die."

Another ugly laugh. "She ain't nothin' but a darky-lovin' Rebel chit. Although I wouldn't have figured on putting those two in the same breath."

Blast it, there were three of them, and Josh could only sidestep and angle away so long. He glanced around for something, anything, to use as a weapon, but Pearl kept her yard just too tidy.

Wait—there, a stick, left by one of Lydia's little ones. He dived, seized it, came up swinging just as the three closed in on him. He landed a good three or four blows before it was wrested from him and their fury descended.

# CHAPTER 22

In the root cellar, Pearl heard the commotion but dimly, and was already on her way, apron full of sweet potatoes, when Clem appeared at the top of the steps. "Come—right now! Fight outside!"

She dumped the sweet potatoes and dashed up the steps. Clem thrust a revolver into her hands. He held another and had a third tucked into his waistband. "Here. It's Josh. Three of the others have jumped him."

A crowd of men blocked the door, commenting and cheering, but Clem led in shoving their way through. They parted readily enough when they saw that she and Clem were armed.

They burst out into the yard, and Pearl wasted no time in leveling her gun on the knot of men. "Stop! Right now, or get yourselves shot!"

They minded her of a pack of dogs, savaging. *Dear God, please let me not hit Josh!*

"I said, *stop!*" She punctuated her scream with a pull of the trigger.

One of the three attackers reeled away, howling. The other two scattered back as well, but more slowly, glancing between her and the huddled form on the ground.

*Oh Josh. . .*

"Farther back," she ordered, motioning with the revolver barrel. "Get clear away from him, right this minute. That's it. Now what were y'all thinking, here?"

The man who'd threatened her the day before offered what he doubtless thought a conciliatory smile. It came across as a leer. "Don't be hasty now, miss. Just put that thing down, or someone might get hurt."

"Someone already has," she gritted out. Aside, to Clem, "Where's Portius?"

"Not here," he hissed. "I think he went to fetch Travis. I couldn't find him last night."

Travis...or Portius? Either way, clearly this task fell to her and Clem.

The two men still standing took a couple of steps forward. "Do you truly want to die, here?" Pearl demanded. Their companion huddled nearby, clutching his side, whimpering. "Or maybe you'd prefer waiting until my cousin hauls you off for a long train ride ending in prison."

He laughed, but with a nervous note this time. "Like I said—"

"Do not move another step," Pearl said. "Or I will shoot you."

"You'll hang if you do," he snapped, suddenly grim.

"I've a dozen men at my back to bear witness to the fact that the three of you attacked an unarmed man, and one of your own, to boot. And then you've threatened me."

His hands lifted, fingers splayed, and his eyes widened with mock innocence. "I've done nothing of the kind."

"I heard you," Clem growled beside her, in a voice she was sure he'd never used before. "And I ain't the only one."

Pearl saw the change when it came, the resolve hardening in the man's face. And when he launched toward her, she had no choice but to fire again.

Two cracks sounded, nearly simultaneous, then a third. Incredibly the man's feet carried him forward until he fell, facedown, so close she had to jump back to avoid him. In the breath of silence that followed, she caught Clem's face beside her, completely white. Josh's third attacker threw his hands up and sat down, where he was. And then a babble of voices rushed over her from all sides.

Shoving the revolver in her skirt pocket, she ran to Josh's side, dropping to her knees on the muddy ground and murmuring his name.

He breathed, at least, but she hardly knew where to touch him. After a moment's hesitation, she laid a hand on his shoulder, and he rolled to his back, moaning.

She brushed his hair aside. His face was a mess of cuts and bruising, his clothing completely soiled. The front of his blouse gaped open, torn, revealing more bruising. "Josh—can you hear me?"

He rolled his head to the side, and his eyelids fluttered open. His hand flailed out and seized hers. "Pearl?"

"I'm here, Josh." She was suddenly weeping. "How—how bad is it?"

"I'll—live."

"You'd better," she sobbed.

He offered a weak smile, heartbreaking against the blood and dirt, and closed his eyes.

She looked around, wildly. Someone was helping Clem tie up the third attacker, and her brother glanced up. "What do we do with the other one who's shot?"

Heat fired through her veins. "Tie him up as well. We'll tend him—eventually." She bent over Josh again but found herself at a loss, beyond holding his hand. Could she even properly assess his injuries without Portius here to help?

As if in response to her thoughts, hoofbeats thudded beneath the sound of the other commotion. "What's going on here?" came the strident voice of Travis.

His gaze swept the scene and landed on Pearl. Squashing whatever chagrin she might feel at being caught at Josh's side, she laid his arm carefully across his chest before clambering to her feet. "Three of the other men attacked this one, presumably because he had acted in my defense."

Travis dismounted from his horse, and Portius from another, behind him, and strode across to her, eyes wide and mouth tight. "What do you mean, in your defense?"

"Yesterday, that one"—she stabbed a finger at the man lying face-down—"came seeking a little more hospitality than I am prepared to give. Josh—Mister Wheeler—intervened."

Travis noted the slip and its correction—couldn't help noting it, she was sure. The flicker in his expression found an answering pang in her breast. She truly did not mean to wound him.

"Well. I'm glad for his intervention." He glanced around again, saw

Clem still holding the brace of revolvers. "Did you shoot?"

Clem nodded toward Pearl. "That was mostly her. I just helped."

They'd fired two shots apiece, Pearl remembered—but who was counting?

Travis swung back to her, approval and consternation at war in his features. "And I ask again, what happened?"

She huffed. "They—apparently they jumped Mister Wheeler." A glance at Clem to confirm, and he nodded. "Clem came and got me, and we—put an end to it."

"You certainly did," he murmured.

Portius rose from the side of the one who lay unmoving. "He's dead, Mister Travis."

Under his breath, Travis swore bitterly. "Confound it all, Pearl, you can't just go shooting the men who are here to receive medical care—"

"Is a woman not allowed to defend her own honor, then?"

"Of course, just—"

"Just what? Should I have let them kill Mister Wheeler, then submitted quietly to my own violation? Would that have seen the situation justified? You left me to care for wounded enemy soldiers, Travis. I had no other recourse. Nor time to think of any."

Her cousin stood, body stiff, face scarlet, doubtless from such a public tongue-lashing. Suddenly weary, Pearl swiped a hand over her eyes and released a hard breath. "Could I please obtain your assistance in moving Mister Wheeler inside?"

Travis went to one side, Portius to the other, and after a false start or two, they lifted Josh between them. Pearl trailed after, but once they'd laid him on the bed, Portius shooed her back out into the sitting room and shut the door. She hovered a moment, limbs trembling, but Lydia ushered her to the kitchen and made her sit, then pressed a cup of something warm into her hands. "Drink this," she whispered.

Hands shaking, Pearl could hardly lift the cup. She tasted mint and—was that whiskey? She shot Lydia a glance, but the other woman only put a finger to her lips.

Travis came out of the bedroom and squatted next to her. Pearl refused to meet his searching gaze. "Why such distress over a Yankee soldier?" he murmured, at last.

She could feel her cheeks heating and tried to hide it behind another sip of Lydia's concoction. "He defended me. Does that not deserve gratitude?"

His lips thinned. "This is more than gratitude, Pearl. I've never seen you so upset—not over a stranger."

"I just shot a man," she snapped. "Two, actually."

And Josh was not a stranger, not anymore.

"You were holding his hand, Pearl."

She set the tea on the table with a solid thump then deliberately met his gaze. "I am not your wife, Travis. I'm not even your fiancée. Not yet, and likely not ever. But even if I were—you asked me to nurse these men. And he appears to be gravely wounded. Again. Forgive my distress in the moment, wherein I only sought to ascertain the extent of his injuries."

He watched her for another moment, then sighed, gave a quick nod, and rose. "I'll see what I can do about moving the men who are able to travel."

He angled toward her bedroom, and with a quick knock, he disappeared inside.

"Well." Lydia spoke from the stove.

Pearl glanced over, found her staring into the pot, brow raised. Eyes burning, she didn't even have the strength to ask Lydia's thoughts. After a gulp of her tea, she folded an arm on the tabletop, lay her head upon it, and let the tears come.

Every breath hurt. Even the agony of amputation seemed a dim memory by comparison.

Portius was gentle enough while removing Josh's clothing and assessing his injuries, but it was still no picnic to be examined and tended as if he were fresh off the battlefield. And in truth, Josh felt like his body had taken the brunt of an exploding shell this time, and not simply a minié ball to the wrist.

"At least two broken ribs. Your limbs seem to be. . .fine."

Josh knew the hesitation in the man's deep voice could bode nothing good. Especially when Portius lingered overlong when examining the amputation wound.

Josh thought he remembered at least one of those ruffians stomping that limb.

"As far as everything else," Portius went on, "only time will tell."

"Is Pearl—safe?" It hurt to speak, and his head throbbed with the effort, but he had to know.

"Miss Pearl is very much safe." Portius's voice was edged with amusement this time. "She and Clem made pretty quick work of those scoundrels, in fact."

Memory drifted back of her voice, ringing out above the haze of the attack, just before the first shot. . .then sudden quiet, and her voice again, taking charge of the situation. He breathed out a long sigh. *Thank You, Lord, for that much at least.*

A rustle came from the other side of the room, and Travis Bledsoe loomed into view. His pale eyes were like ice.

"I told you I'd look out for her," Josh rasped, before the man could say a word.

"So you did," Bledsoe admitted. "Might you explain to me what happened?"

Josh closed his eyes against the searing ache in his brain then refocused on the man. "Those three who jumped me this morning were all standing out by the barn yesterday, and when Miss MacFarlane walked past, the one followed her, thinking to start trouble."

Bledsoe's face remained hard, whether because of Josh's dissembling over his familiarity with using Pearl's given name or the gravity of the situation itself, Josh wasn't sure. "The others weren't around to come to her aid? Or they left it to you?"

Josh thought about how to reply. "She headed up the hill, into the timber, alone. And no one else noticed him following her."

Bledsoe chewed his cheek for a long moment. "So you sent him packing?"

"I did." Never mind that Josh had caught the ruffian off guard, or he might not have had such advantage. "And apparently he didn't take so kindly to it."

Bledsoe snorted. "So it would seem." His eyes flicked over Josh's body. "I'm a little surprised you're still awake and conversing with us."

"No more surprised than I," Josh said.

Grudging respect glinted in the other man's eyes. "You still refuse exchange?"

Breath in, then out. "I do."

Bledsoe shook his head, slowly at first, then with more vigor. "I do not understand you." His gaze flicked toward the door, then back. "Would that you were a Confederate."

"Or that you were a Federal," Josh said.

A thin-lipped smile was Bledsoe's only reply. He shifted. "Clem tells me he went to fetch Pearl when he saw the three lurking about while you were in the privy. Where, though, did he find arms?"

"Field salvage," Josh said, with a little smile of his own. Would Bledsoe see fit to confiscate those, if he knew?

But Bledsoe only grunted. "If anyone asks," he said, finally, "the man died of his wounds. Nothing more."

"The yard was full of men watching what happened," Portius said.

"You'll not speak of it," came Bledsoe's sharp reply. "I won't expose Pearl to possible recrimination, if I can help it."

Josh peered at the two of them, locked in a silent battle of wills with their gazes. Finally the Negro broke and swung away. "Very well, sir."

Judging by the mocking edge to his voice, nothing had been ceded at all, there.

Travis returned later that day and, as he promised, collected all the men Portius deemed ready to travel—including, to her surprise, Mr. Shaw, who was suddenly much more respectful and had apparently improved enough to be moved. Or perhaps Travis and Portius decided not to risk his causing trouble again, later. Pearl was not a little relieved to see that the effort reduced the number of men they tended by at least half, although several of their neighbors still hosted many more.

After he'd gotten the men loaded in the hospital wagon, Travis approached Pearl, his face grave and thoughtful. "I may not be able to return in the next few days, but I'll do what I can to send more provisions."

She nodded. His words were a mere formality, she knew—not that she wasn't grateful for anything he could send, given the circumstance.

"And—if questioned about what took place today, admit nothing."

She made her gaze more searching this time, but he stood turning his hat round and round in his hands for a long moment, refusing to meet her eyes.

"You know I'd never do anything to deliberately endanger you, don't you?" he said at last.

A corner of her heart softened. "I do know that."

"And—I'm thankful you weren't hurt, either today or yesterday." His voice thickened. "Very thankful that Wheeler was there to intervene."

She bobbed a nod. "As am I."

He cleared his throat. His hands stilled, holding the hat. "Please. . . please promise me you'll not go running off alone, again."

That wasn't something she felt she could promise, but—"I'll try."

His gaze was earnest this time. "Please, Pearl. I couldn't bear if you came to harm."

More of her heart melted. "I promise I won't deliberately endanger myself, if I can help it."

As if he realized that was the best she could do, he nodded, then jammed his hat back on his head. "Be well, Pearl," he murmured, and before she could stop him, he leaned in to brush a kiss on her forehead.

Her breath caught, and heat washed through her. All it did was remind her of that windy hillside, and Josh.

# CHAPTER 23

The rain returned with a vengeance the next several days. Josh slept, and woke, and slept again to the sound of it running steadily off the eaves outside his window.

During that time, Clem was as likely to look in on him, and sometimes linger to talk, as Portius or Pearl or Lydia. In fact, Pearl was there less often than she was wont, or at least not when he was awake enough to know it, and—he missed her.

He shouldn't miss her. He'd no business doing so.

Breathe in, breathe out. After three days, it hurt only slightly less. Why he hadn't accepted Bledsoe's offer to send him back, he wasn't sure, except that he didn't think he could face jostling in a wagon even a few miles. It was bad enough to have the two men lift and carry him inside the house.

Clem had no more news of either army, except for reports of dissent within the ranks of the Confederate forces over General Bragg's decisions—or lack thereof. The Federals were still holed up in Chattanooga. Josh thought about that—how Rosecrans's goal had been to take the town. Did he consider himself the victor after everything, in the battle just a few weeks past? And if Bragg considered that the Confederacy were at a point of strength, why hadn't they moved more decisively, since?

None of these were his to have an opinion on, of course. He was not one of those in authority. Technically he knew nothing of battle strategy and had never been to West Point or studied law, as many officers had.

Yet the situation niggled at him.

And how—how best to protect Pearl in all this, and her family? Because once the Federal army found its footing and moved—and surely they would, because President Lincoln would not stand by and leave them undefended, not with reinforcements already arriving—and word got back about her having shot down a Union soldier, even if it was in her own defense, she'd be hauled before a court-martial at least. Other women had in similar cases.

His chest ached. Or was that simply his cracked and bruised rib cage?

A sound came from the other side of the room, in the dark. Likely Thorsson, stirring in his sleep. He'd improved so greatly, Josh was surprised Bledsoe hadn't taken him with the others.

Then there was a creak, and the door swung open, and a bit of candle-light filtered in. A female figure hovered in the doorway, leaning in, then away, swaying with obvious startlement. "Oh! I didn't mean to awaken you," she whispered.

For a moment, he forgot all the aches. "I was already awake."

She hesitated then glided inside.

"What time is it?" he asked. "I seem to have lost all sense of day and night, again."

"I'm not sure. After midnight, likely." The light from her candle made her eyes shine like stars.

"Is it your turn to sit up, then?"

Another hesitation. "No. I simply couldn't sleep." She slipped inside the rest of the way, leaving the door ajar, and set the candlestick on the wash-stand before reaching for the chair, which still stood between the beds. She tugged it closer to his side before settling herself there.

For a long moment she only gazed back at him. It wasn't that he hadn't seen her at all these past few days, during the usual tasks of tending his wounds, both new and old, or of seeing him fed and watered. But there had been none of this, the lingering, as if they could truly just enjoy each other's company with no thought of North and South and the war between them.

"Are you feeling any better?" she asked, finally.

"A bit."

"You look—" She leaned forward, examining his face. Her hand lifted and twitched as if she wanted to brush his hair back, and a part of him craved that touch, though he tamped the feeling down. But then she drew back. "The bruising might be fading already. It looked a little better when I saw it this afternoon, in daylight."

So she did come to look in on him more often than he knew.

"Your arm, though, is worrisome—" She winced, and then her eyes, wide and earnest, fastened on his again. "I am so sorry you've had to endure this," she murmured, "simply for coming to my defense."

He started to reach for her hand then pulled his back as well. "I would gladly do so again." At the shake of her head, he did reach out, letting his fingertips brush her forearm. "In fact, it might just have been the most useful thing I've done since joining the army two years ago."

She looked startled but didn't pull away from his touch. "How can you say that? I am. . .I'm not even on the Union side. I expect, in fact, that we represent everything you enlisted to fight against."

"Not. . .everything. There's much, truth be told, that you represent about what we all feel we're fighting for."

She caught her breath, lips parting, eyes wide. "But we are—Secessionists."

"There is that." He shifted so his hand covered hers. "But you're brave. Hardworking. Strong in both mind and faith. And whatever the Confederacy stands for in regards to slavery. . ." He peered at her. "Just how is it, anyway, that one who so obviously believes in the dignity of the human soul can support a government which approves of keeping a whole people in bondage?"

Her mouth compressed, trembling. Her gaze filled but held his. "I will tell you something, Joshua Wheeler. My own brother loved a woman he was not allowed to marry, simply because of the color of her skin. My pa has been slow to accept my brother's choices, mostly because he knows how cruel a polite society can be about things they do not approve of, but also because it's hard to see the fault in a way of thinking that one has been brought up in." She stopped to catch her breath. "But those children sleeping in the attic above us are his grandchildren, whatever our society says, and they give him joy. Have we not all wished for a better world, one in which my brother would be free to call Lydia his wife without recrimination or shame? Of course we have. But we do not believe Lincoln has done one thing to make such a world. His grand Proclamation earlier this year did very little to undo slavery, and even less to help those who it claims to free. Many of us feel it just a ploy to add men to the Federal army."

Josh closed his eyes. He'd heard such before. There was no answer to it—Pearl herself had said so when last they'd tried to discuss it—at least none that any would listen to in these times.

The worst thing about it, however, was the way the question rattled inside him, stirred up a fluttering panic that all the expense of enlisting, of going to war and clamoring to fight had truly been for naught. It was the question that haunted him in the dark of night, when the ache in his arm was the worst, when pain seemed to come from the hand he'd lost, itself, when in reality that hand was no longer even there to suffer pain. He'd never feared dying. What if now he'd just become a useless sacrifice in a war that would accomplish nothing?

Especially after a loss like this last one. Especially with the awfulness of battle, all by itself.

Pearl's hand started to slide out from beneath his, but he gripped it a little tighter. "Please. Do not leave, just yet."

"Why?" she breathed.

"Because. . .I can't face the dark alone. Not tonight."

Her chin tucked, and her expression was lost to shadow. Slowly, she turned her hand over until she could clasp his in return. "You still haven't explained why coming to my rescue was so much more worthwhile."

"Accosting women is a blight on any army, regardless of politics." He thought about how much more to say. "But on either side, war is terrible," he admitted at last. "Before any of us had seen battle, we couldn't wait to get a taste of the fight, show those Rebs what we were made of—but then we all found it a horror. You don't know—I could never explain—men and horses and mules torn to pieces. The whine and scream of bullet and shell. Men crying, no, sobbing for their mothers." He hesitated. "I might have done that myself a time or two."

She tipped her head, a tiny, sympathetic smile on her lips.

"And then to have battles like the one weeks ago—or Shiloh, or Gettysburg—where it's day after day of run to the front, and fight, and fall back, then get up and fight again. Where you see your best companions lifeless on the field—" He swallowed. It was too much, but he couldn't seem to stop the flow of words. "You wonder if you'll ever see those you love again, this side of heaven. Or if you'll ever have the chance at a wife and family of your own, of a plain, ordinary life."

Head tucked again, Pearl's chest rose and fell sharply. Her hand clutched his. "It is a valid enough thing to wonder at."

"And it seems madness that the scrap we had a few days ago should be so frowned upon. Or that you, as Bledsoe is rightly concerned, should be indicted for taking up arms to defend yourself or your own." And brilliantly so, although he'd not say it in this moment. "But in battle, they lead us out to the field, line us up, and tell us to have at it. Not that I disagree with the reasons why, but—" He huffed. "And here you and I sit, so. . . companionable."

She sighed, leaning forward, cradling his hand now in both of hers. "And it cannot last."

"Exactly."

Or—could it?

"Would you—wish it to last?" he whispered.

A squeak escaped her—or was that a sob? "Do not ask me such a thing. Do *not*."

"Why not?"

Her head snapped up, her eyes wet. "You know why, as well as I do. And we are only enamored of the sentiment here because—because it's so very impossible that we can do anything about it."

His turn to let out a long breath. Oh. . .if he could only pull her into his arms again, as he had the other day—but it was neither fitting, nor convenient, not with his added injuries or—

He should really send her away, but he couldn't bring himself to do so. "How is your pa faring?"

"He—I don't know. There are moments he's better. He sits with the Bible in his lap but doesn't read. He has enough memorized to quote this or that and does regularly." Pearl sniffled. "I know he is at peace with his Creator. If. . .if the worst were to happen. . ." She cleared her throat. "Speaking of. . .the young man with the gangrenous leg—Johnny—expired about sunset that next day. You were—asleep."

Josh shut his eyes. "He too at least was at peace with God. So many are not."

"And what of yourself?"

"I suppose I am."

"You suppose?"

"Very well, so I am. Washed in the blood of the Lamb and all that." He hoped his smile wouldn't make her think he was being irreverent.

But she only looked at him gravely. "How is it that a man who believes so strongly in protecting others can be just fine with tromping all over people's land and freedoms?"

It took him several moments to grasp her meaning. "It's the Union that is worth fighting for," he answered finally. "When our nation was founded, we were the United States of America. The concepts our Founding Fathers fought for, then wrote into the Constitution—it depends upon all the states staying together. Not half of them gallivanting off just because they can't agree that slavery must come to an end."

"Not all of us disagree with that," she said. "In fact you and I talked about this once before."

He sighed. "I do realize that."

"And such conversations are why there could be no lasting friendship between us."

But she still did not release his hand.

If he could only change her stubborn mind about this. There yet remained, however, the problem of him not being whole.

And she deserved nothing if not a whole man, who could hold both her hands with his, as he longed to do.

Which left him nothing but the longing, when all was said and done.

Impossible it might be, but Pearl woke, hours later as the sky was lightening, from her seat on the floor beside Josh's bed, where she'd moved during the course of their conversation. She sat propped against the frame, her arm outstretched, still holding Josh's hand as it lay now across his chest.

With a little start, she disentangled herself and rose. Her arm was still quite asleep, and she rubbed it to bring the feeling back.

Josh slumbered on, those long lashes fanned out over cheeks that, yes, were not quite as bruised as before. His mouth was parted slightly, lips looking so soft that she felt the urge to bend and kiss them—just once, very lightly.

No one would ever know.

But by the same token, she wanted Josh to know. To be assured that she did not hate him for being born a Northerner. And to have something to remember her by when Fate took him far away, because—that was bound to happen, sooner rather than later.

It was a wretched idea, all around.

Pearl caught her breath and held it, blinking against the sting in her eyelids, and walked resolutely out of the room.

# CHAPTER 24

*October 24*

The rain went on unrelentingly for what felt like days, until it seemed a living, breathing thing that sucked all the color and joy out of life. As if that were not already the case, in the wake of battle and loss.

It was all Pearl could do to drag herself through a day. At least this time Lydia was there to help cook, and tend wounds. And with the numbers of wounded being reduced, Portius and Clem were able to bring in those from the barn, at least for meals and gathering around the hearth at night.

At first there were songs and stories, a nearly endless litany of the latter, where names and places and regiments all blurred into one, but even that faded after a few days, and the men were increasingly short with each other. A fistfight nearly broke out over a louse race—which was itself such a horror to Pearl that she could scarce believe the men engaged in such for entertainment, picking the vermin from their own bodies and setting them on a plate or other flat surface to see whose was fastest.

But with the rain and all else happening, there was also no time, or space, for proper washing. She'd done bedding once, after the most recent death, but that was all.

And she thought she might go mad if she had to hear one more Yankee camp song.

There were rare moments of peace, such as when Pa, sitting perennially with the Bible open on his lap, handed the volume of scripture over to Josh, seated in a chair beside him, and ordered him to read. And read

Josh did, with a fine cadence and volume that made everyone quiet down and pay attention.

And then, even a few discussions about scripture and other things spiritual broke out. In spite of her determination not to notice what he said, Pearl could not help but be impressed at the depth of Josh's faith and understanding of scripture.

After a few days, the rain slackened to a drizzle. While the men were having a quiet moment with Josh reading and discussing the Bible text with Pa, and Pearl was contemplating the work of hauling in water and subjecting the men to a round of baths, Clem burst inside, panting. He glanced about then made his way around the edge of the room to Pearl, where he leaned in and whispered, "Just heard word—Rosecrans has been removed from being in charge of the Federals, and Grant is now in his place."

This was news she could not ignore, though she'd been trying in that area as well. "So that means—"

"The Federals will likely be on the move again soon." Clem's gaze darted about the room. "I don't want to noise it about, but—Josh made me promise to share anything I heard."

"*Josh* made you promise. . ."

Clem's eyes were wide and earnest. "He's not a bad man, Pearl. Not like—those others. I—trust him."

Pearl was inclined to trust him as well, which was terrifying all by itself. But she wouldn't admit that to Clem.

"And can you blame him?" He scrubbed his fingertips through his shaggy hair. "For wanting to know?"

"As long as it's that, and not that he's using us to spy for the Federals."

Clem's gaze dropped, and his cheek flushed. "I don't think it's that, Pearl. I really don't."

"I hope not," she muttered.

"Besides. Travis and Portius hardly tell me anything, where all that's concerned. I overhear them talking a bit, but it's nothing useful."

She nodded reluctantly. "Well then. Tell Josh if you must, but don't you dare let it slip to the others. We'd have a riot, for sure."

Clem whisked away again, and Pearl took the moment to slip out the back door, despite the pattering rain, and just breathe in the cold, fresh air.

As bad as things had been, they were about to get worse.

Much worse.

Josh digested the news with mingled excitement and anxiety. First on his mind, though it should have taken second to reconnecting with his regiment, was how to protect Pearl and her family. Obviously, there was little he could do at the moment besides keep his head down and pray Bledsoe didn't decide to pack him off to Richmond.

Of course, they could always attempt escape. Any sane man would do that rather than wait around here, especially since they weren't really guarded. Or he could request official parole, but Bledsoe had been scarce of late.

Anything would be better than lying here awake in the darkness, aching fiercely where a hand should be but was not, and wishing for the company of a young woman whom he missed but should not.

His thoughts strayed back to the scripture reading Mr. MacFarlane had prevailed upon him to perform. The man had an uncanny knack for choosing passages that not only brought holy conviction but comfort as well.

*"My soul shall be satisfied as with marrow and fatness; and my mouth shall praise thee with joyful lips: when I remember thee upon my bed, and meditate on thee in the night watches."*

Apparently the psalmist suffered from the same problem Josh did.

He needed a strategy. Word would reach the other men, and not all of them could be counted upon to protect the MacFarlanes. And Josh couldn't protect Pearl on his own.

There was only one other he trusted to have her best interests at heart. Portius.

The next day being unusually warm for so late in fall, Josh found the black man out very early, chopping wood. Taking up the hatchet that had served him well enough before, Josh joined him. Portius leveled him a searching look. "Can you handle that yet?"

"We'll see."

Setting up a chunk to split, Josh gave it a swing. Ribs squalled in protest. He set the hatchet down, breathing hard and trying not to cry.

Portius chuckled, long and low. "Ten days ain't long enough for cracked ribs to knit properly. But I give you credit for trying."

"Thank you. I think." Josh eased himself to sit on another chunk of log. "I actually came out here to discuss something of importance with you."

Portius eyed him again, took up the ax, and gave it a swing. His piece split with the single blow.

"I'm concerned for the MacFarlanes if the Union breaks through the siege."

Portius stopped, slowly let the ax sink to the earth, and leaned on the handle. His gaze went severe. "Just how much do you know?"

Josh held his gaze. "Only what Clem has told me."

"You have the boy sneakin' around for you?"

"No. Most emphatically no." Josh relented a little. "Although the thought had crossed my mind, I'll admit."

"Good." He hefted the ax again. " 'Cause I've had a dozen others thinkin' they could do so, or turn me to spyin' for them."

"That thought crossed my mind as well," Josh deadpanned.

Portius peered at him, and then he shook his head with a laugh and set up another piece to split. "If your ribs were in better shape"—he huffed, then swung the ax—"I'd have you help me saw that log in pieces."

"What, Clem isn't strapping enough for that?"

Portius just grinned.

He worked a bit longer then stopped and considered Josh again. "Listen up. If you truly want to help the MacFarlanes—"

"I do," Josh said, quietly but vehemently into the Negro's hesitation.

The dark eyes regarded him in silence for yet another handful of moments.

It was hard enough in such circumstances for any of them to trust each other when it came to mere life and breath. Harder still when it was the lives of others, or when oaths of loyalty snarled all else.

"My life is completely in your hands," Josh said. "Has been for weeks. I simply want this family's care of us to not go unrewarded, by either side."

"All righty then," Portius rumbled. "Here's what we need from you."

A little later, Josh found himself being buttonholed by Pearl. Almost without preamble, she pinned him with a mere look. "I need to know, Joshua Wheeler, are you a spy?"

He fought the urge to groan. "I just had this conversation with Portius." But her steady gaze compelled as no words could. Leaning back against the wall, he folded his arms. "I am not. At least, not yet."

Her cheeks flushed, lips parting and eyes sparking wide. It was rather all he could do not to drag her into his arms and—

A now-familiar ache in one of those arms reminded him of why he must not give in to that impulse.

*Lord, You made her as fair as the day is long. It's a sore trial to be confined here with her and only be able to look.*

But mere looks it must be.

"Have you become a Confederate sympathizer, Mister Wheeler?"

Where one particular Confederate was concerned? Absolutely.

He held her gaze, not replying, and at last she flushed scarlet and tucked her head. "Please. If you have any regard for us at all, I ask that you at least not help deliver us into the hands of the Federal army."

"That is precisely what I seek to avoid, Pearl," he said, very low. "And you know I have only the highest regard for you. Or your family."

Did he imagine it, or did she sway toward him the tiniest bit?

"I know Clem has been bringing you news," she whispered.

"He has," Josh agreed. "But I would not betray you. In fact"—he leaned closer—"Portius has asked me to begin advising all of you in a somewhat official capacity, as he and Clem gather intelligence. Only as pertains to your family's defense, of course." He smiled a little. "I'd not relish being hung or shot by my own government as a spy. But neither will I stand by and leave you without protection, if I can help it."

Her eyes widened. After the longest moment, she nodded, turned on her heel, and strode away. There was no other word for the pace she set, regardless of how short the space she crossed or the skirts she wore.

And so began the quiet meetings, after all had gone to bed, or early in the mornings, between them—Portius, Clem, Pearl, Josh, and Lydia— discussing whatever news anyone could glean each day. They did their best to be discreet, and Josh felt conflicted at best, keeping such things from his fellow soldiers.

But he'd meant every word of his vow that he'd not leave the Mac-Farlanes without defense, whether that be forewarning of either Federal or Confederate troop movements or knowledge of how to use the small arsenal Clem had collected. And as October slid into November, the weather continuing rainy but turning colder, it became apparent that the Federals had grown more restless and Grant would not wait around as Old Rosey had.

# CHAPTER 25

*November 6*

The household was at last bedded down for the night, with Pa tucked in his own bed and nine Yankee convalescents scattered about the sitting room, the worst in beds and those nearer to getting well on the floor. All those remaining from Travis's cullings, with the exception of Josh, who was as usual up until the last moment helping Pearl and Lydia get everything settled before they'd all quietly and separately slip out—sometimes to the woodpile but more often to the barn, depending on how heavily the rain was falling.

On this particular night, Pearl went first, taking her gathering basket on the pretext—not entirely false—of fetching supplies for tomorrow's breakfast from the cellar. She wrapped not just her shawl about her against the deepening cold but also Pa's overcoat and hurried out into the downpour.

On a night such as this one, tempting it was to just linger on the porch, but they dared not gather where the others might overhear. As strenuously as Josh had assured her that he had only her family's welfare in mind, she was as determined not to jeopardize him with his fellow Federals.

A fool's sentiment, that, she was sure. Because she could no longer deny that he'd become tangled up among her other concerns.

*Gracious Lord, please. . .*

The prayer died on her lips as she gained the barn door, already ajar. Inside, a lamp revealed Portius and Clem seated, one on a short stool and the other on a half-broken packing box. Portius looked up as she entered and swung the door shut after herself. "I hate to break this piece of news to you," he said, "but the cellar is flooding."

She froze. "How badly?"

"An inch or two. Clem and I moved the barrels and crates up to the tack room. I think whatever's on the shelves will be safe enough for now, but we can look again in the morning."

One more thing to be concerned over. Pearl gritted her teeth then sighed. Nothing for it, this moment. "Wasn't much left in those barrels, anyway," she muttered, snagging another stool.

The door swung open behind her, and Josh slipped inside. Their gazes met, and he nodded without comment and moved past her. Their party would be complete once Lydia, their designated watch, arrived from tucking in Jem and Sally.

Which she did, in just a few minutes. It perhaps seemed longer because Josh dragged his own chosen seat a little closer to her than she found comfortable. Not that she wouldn't have remained acutely aware of him had he remained standing outside in the rain.

Or in the house.

"So," Clem began, once Lydia was stationed at a window, unshuttered in the dark for ease of listening outside, "what we heard about Wauhatchie is true. Yanks tried a pontoon bridge across the river on the morning of the twenty-seventh, and then on the night of the twenty-ninth, Yanks skirmished over on Lookout Creek with our boys. All night long. And ain't nobody happy about how it turned out. Bragg's gone and sent Longstreet up to Knoxville or some such. I heard it over at the railroad, as they're trying to move troops up that way. It was President Davis's own suggestion, so they say."

Quiet descended. Across from Pearl, Portius chewed the inside of his cheek, looking thoughtfully at Josh, who leaned toward Clem, his dark eyes intent as always. "So Confederates and Federals continue to grapple for control of the Tennessee River crossings."

Clem bobbed a nod. "Neighbors all agree that everyone feels stretched just 'bout beyond bearing, waiting to see what's gonna happen. Like before Chickamauga, but maybe worse."

"Bragg withdrew from Chattanooga at least ten days before Chicka-mauga," Josh mused.

Pearl knew better than to think the almost distracted quality of his voice meant he took no interest in what was happening. Her only worry was, what part would he choose to play in the events to come?

"How many does Longstreet have on the move?" Josh asked.

"Oh, 'bout fifteen to twenty thousand, depending upon who I talked to," Clem answered.

"So if the Federals break out of Chattanooga," Josh said, "or more like when the Federals break out, with Bragg shorting himself on troops—"

"You so sure about that?" Portius challenged softly.

Josh's gaze flashed toward him. "Grant isn't going to sit around long, I can about guarantee that. And my only concern here is not, as you and I have discussed before, my taking intelligence back to the Union lines, but simply making sure *y'all* are prepared once things change."

He said the word with a slight Northern edge that made Pearl want to giggle, despite the seriousness of the conversation. She fixed a stern frown on her face in an attempt to make sure such unseemly amusement did not escape.

"To that end," Josh went on, more quietly, "a Federal break in the siege should be treated as a probability and not merely a possibility."

Well, that was enough to strike the laughter from her heart.

They'd all seen for themselves the awful aftermath of battle. Heard the reports of homes burned southward into Georgia, beyond Rossville, and that was even with the Confederates pushing the Yankees back into Chattanooga. How much more terrible would it be were the Federals to break out and push the Confederate forces back?

Pearl resettled herself on the stool, rubbing the back of her neck against a growing headache. Did she not have enough to worry about day by day, with the usual washing and cooking and whatnot? She could just hear Pa's voice admonishing her, *"Pray without ceasing."* She was doing so—very nearly without ceasing, anyway—but the more she prayed, the less it felt that God was listening, much less answering.

Possibly a blasphemous thought, that, but—

"Miss Pearl? Have you anything to add?"

She startled and shook her head. She never had anything to add.

Clem and Portius rose, with Clem drifting over to say something to Josh about carbines and the proper caliber of ammunition. Pearl felt Josh's gaze upon her but turned away. She should go look at the contents of the cellar—or perhaps that could wait until tomorrow.

After setting aside her stool, she hied herself back to the house. As she hung up Pa's overcoat, one of the children was crying upstairs. A couple of the men lifted their heads. One, an artilleryman from Indiana named Tattersall, pushed up on an elbow as she passed. "There's an awful lot of you going out to the necessary at the same time, these last few days."

Pearl cast him but a glance and hurried up the steps.

That was all they needed—for the rest of the men to become suspicious.

The next morning, she found a moment to pull Portius off to the side and warn him that they needed to be more discreet about their meetings. "Perhaps leave me out of them, since I'm not contributing anything."

"It's important that you be there," Portius said soothingly.

"Well I wonder."

"Miss Pearl."

She set her jaw and did not reply but turned away, intending to go on to her next task.

"If you must know"—the Negro's deep, calm voice pulled her back— "it was Mister Wheeler who insisted you be included. Because, he said, he didn't want you to think we was doing anything nefarious behind your back."

She hazarded a glance toward him and found the dark eyes twinkling, a slight smile playing about his full mouth.

"Do you trust him?" she found herself asking.

He pulled in a deep breath. "I do. He's a Yankee, through and through, but—a good man, all things considered."

Why she found that comforting, she was not sure. The backs of her eyelids burned. "Thank you," she murmured at last.

"We just need to get up a little earlier, or something. Wait a little longer at night."

"Perhaps."

But as the days went on, it was increasingly difficult to find those moments when they weren't all being watched.

Everyone seemed possessed of an unstated dread. As Pearl's own desperation rose, Pa continued to fade and became more fractious. The wounded Yankees grew stronger each day and many of them more troublesome, especially Mr. Tattersall. She found it laughably easy to obey Travis's injunction that she go nowhere alone.

Even the mild Mr. Thorsson, left behind because of the lingering uncertainty of his leg wound, grew pensive and withdrawn, proving that the long weeks of waiting wore on even the most cheerful.

Portius organized the men into a motley workforce, setting several to such odd work as mending things around the house and barn, and the most able-bodied to digging in the mud of her garden for the last of the vegetables, thus sparing her that much.

On that particular morning, Clem dragged her out to the barn and into the tack room. Assorted firearms stood stacked against a wall, and bowls of bullets and musket balls, with a collection of powder horns and the revolvers she remembered using on Josh's attackers, lay on a makeshift table. Josh himself was seated on a stool, also leaning against a wall. "What is this?" she demanded.

Clem peered at her through his dangling forelock. "Josh wants to make sure we all know how to load the guns. Just in case."

While she stood staring at the array before her, Josh pushed stiffly upright, but with a little more ease than a week ago, and moved the stool to the other side of the table, indicating she should take it.

"I know how to load a gun," she protested, but sat down anyway, still dazzled. "Where in the world. . ."

Clem and Josh exchanged a look. "I found them," Clem said. "Here and there."

She gave him the benefit of a full glare. "Mm-hmm."

Josh snickered, but she ignored him.

Clem tried his best to be diffident. "What? It isn't like having the revolvers, at least, wasn't useful."

Pearl could only shake her head. She'd been beyond grateful for them, true. But to suddenly discover just how her brother had been occupying himself these past weeks. . .

For the next half hour, she let Josh instruct them on simply loading the revolvers and a pair of carbines, first with salvaged cartridges and then making their own loads. The latter she was only slightly less familiar with, since Pa and her brothers had made theirs as often as they'd purchased cartridges already prepared.

Mostly, however, she watched Josh converse and banter with Clem and noted the admiration that shone in her youngest brother's eyes.

She did not know how to feel about that. It had been entirely too long since Clem had the example and guidance of a strong older man. But to rail, even inwardly, at the ease at which Josh insinuated himself with her family's favor would be to indict herself.

He and Clem bent over one of the rifles, discussing some aspect of its works with an absorption she envied. It was tempting to simply rise and tiptoe out of the room and leave them to the task.

Josh's head came up at that moment, his gaze meeting hers. Neither moved for a moment.

"What was your occupation before the war?" she asked without thought.

He sat back, his hand braced on the tabletop. "Oh, a little of this, a little of that. My father started out years ago as a wagonmaster and wound up a merchant in Athens, Ohio. One of my brothers worked alongside him, while another took up gunsmithing." Josh's mouth twisted in a rueful smile, and he looked away. "I was more drawn to gunsmithing. But I suppose it would be best if I turned my attention to something else, given present circumstances."

He turned his hand over and tapped his knuckles on the table, among the firearms and accoutrements spread before them.

"I think," Pearl said slowly, "you could do most anything you set your mind to." She lifted her gaze to meet his once more. "Even given present circumstances."

His cheeks colored, but his eyes held hers. "Thank you," he said finally.

"So about this," Clem said, obviously impatient with the turn of conversation, and drawing Josh's attention once more.

Pearl took the opportunity to excuse herself and withdraw to where the air was markedly cooler and she could draw an easier breath.

How did she do that? Take all the color and life out of a room just by leaving it?

And to look at him like that, as if—as if losing a hand was merely a minor inconvenience and not something that had upended his entire world. *"I think you could do most anything you set your mind to."*

Except the one thing he possibly wanted most in the moment, which was to take a certain Rebel girl in his arms and kiss her until she swooned. Because that particular Rebel girl had made it oh so clear she would have no such thing.

But then, she slipped away and left him to continue prattling on to her younger brother about the falling-block action of a Sharps rifle, which he usually would find fascinating to study and explain, when all he wanted was to run after her.

Obviously his thoughts were already gone.

"Josh." Clem's sober voice and expression yanked him abruptly back. "How—how does a man know which side is the right one to be fighting on?"

He opened his mouth, shut it again. Thought back on the months—no, years—before the war, of the newspaper articles, the speeches, discussions among his family. *"A man has to do what he thinks is right,"* Pa had said in response to Josh's decision to run off and enlist the first chance he got. For the first time Josh wondered if that was a defense or a warning.

The boy's blue eyes remained on him, steadily.

"I suppose…we listen to all the reasons why, and we measure it against scripture, and—we pray, of course—"

Josh wanted badly to simply say, *I don't know.* It was as much a matter of where one grew up, except that he knew several of Copperhead bent who were as avid about their views as any who rose up to defend the Union, even going so far as to call for President Lincoln's death.

He blew out a hard breath. "There's no easy answer. I could explain all the reasons why I enlisted to fight for the Union. Why I still think it's the right thing. Some of it, yes, is what we grow up hearing from those whose opinions we respect and trust. Some of it boils down to what President Lincoln himself said, that a house divided against itself cannot stand."

Clem's face twisted. "Faugh. Lincoln."

Josh smiled a little. "And there you're just echoing what you've heard others say."

The boy couldn't argue that but looked none too happy about it.

"Ultimately we defend that which we love," Josh said, at last.

And was it that for himself?

# CHAPTER 26

*Sunday morning, November 22*

Ten blue-coated men, sitting as close to upright as possible around the sitting room. Pa, in his favorite chair, seated but restless. Clem beside him, in case he grew unsteady, but equally restless. Lydia, seated in the kitchen, hushing her two, with Portius nearby, carved from obsidian. The Negro reached over and swooped Jem onto his lap and whispered something that drew a smile from the small boy, but made him instantly settle.

Pearl sat on the other side of the table, hands folded, doing her best not to stare out the window while Reverend Mason stood near it, delivering a sermon, weaving a little to the cadence of his own voice. A steady rain fell outside.

Again. As usual.

She tried to pay proper attention to Reverend Mason, but her gnawing restlessness—and dread—kept tugging her attention to the window and the cold, gray mist beyond.

It was a fitting reflection of her heart, when she should be finding herself warmed by the fire on the hearth and Reverend Mason's discourse on scripture. Except that the smoothness of his recitation betrayed the likelihood that he'd given the same one all over the neighborhood, in similar gatherings. His visit did seem to give Pa a modicum of comfort and cheer, even if Pearl felt the minister's prayers and exhortations seemed stiff and as rehearsed as his sermon.

*Lord, what ails me? Besides the fact that it's been two long months since Travis first dragged wretched, wounded Yankees to my door and insisted we care for them.*

Her eyes drifted across the assembly. Most of the men were listening respectfully, or trying to, including Josh, across the room from her, sitting on the floor with his back against the wall. The neatness of his appearance, with hair and beard combed, and coat lying smoothly across his shoulders, still drew a flutter from her insides.

It was the only sign of life in days from her traitor heart.

She brought her wayward gaze back to Reverend Mason. The minister must have noticed her glance lingering overlong, because in the barest hesitation between words, he shot a glare at Josh, and an equally hard look at her.

Well, she could look forward to a separate sermon from him over that, she was sure.

Just one more thing to dread in an increasing array of late.

She glanced again over at Lydia and Portius. The clandestine meetings of their group of five were more difficult to arrange, but still they managed it. Things appeared increasingly grave for the Confederate side, and rumbles from over the ridge, across the mountains, grew more frequent.

Somehow Josh also managed to appear as concerned as the rest of them. And what could his true purpose possibly be in all of it? Were the Federals to break through, would they all perish in fire or be turned out destitute? Or would Josh truly try to protect them?

And could he even truly accomplish such a thing? Pearl couldn't imagine so.

Josh was troublesome in his own ways. He'd finally regained enough strength to be up and moderately helpful again, although he moved more stiffly than before, and the bruising and abrasions on his stump remained worrisome.

Conversations were more difficult as well. He seemed distracted and tense and even more focused than before on accomplishing as many tasks as he could, alone. When they did speak, it was mostly about domestic matters. . .or strange, searching questions.

When the sermon was finished and Reverend Mason had completed his prayers, Pearl and Lydia both rose to get dinner laid on the table. She could feel the minister's gaze on her periodically throughout the meal—or was that his unhappiness with the situation in general?

It was hard to say, given that she caught him casting dark looks at Lydia and Portius and the Yankees as much as herself.

Afterward, before she could even get her apron on for helping with washing up, Reverend Mason was tugging at her sleeve, quite literally. "A word with you, Miss MacFarlane."

"Of course," she murmured and followed him outside, wrapping herself in her shawl as she went.

"I am shocked, first of all, to find that your cousin hasn't removed the rest of these men. They appear to be hale and hearty enough for transfer or exchange."

She held herself still beneath his regard, though she wished fervently to fidget like one of the children. "Travis has been otherwise occupied," she said as mildly as she could. "And most of these men are still convalescing from serious wounds."

"One or two appear a little more solicitous than is proper," he said.

She lifted an eyebrow.

"Very well, one in particular, and I think you know which one I mean."

"He has been. . .very kind and helpful in regards to caring for the other prisoners," Pearl said. "Not to mention, he was wounded a second time some weeks ago, while engaged in my defense."

Reverend Mason's eyes fairly popped, and he lowered his gaze. "Too long the fair daughters of our Southland have suffered indignity at the hands of our invaders. Something should be done."

At that, she did shift from one foot to the other. "I believe our brave soldiers are doing as much as they can under the circumstances."

He regarded her quietly for a moment. "And to have colored folk sitting with you during Sunday worship and dinner—"

"You yourself said it was but prayer and scripture reading, not a formal service, when you came this morning. Surely I can extend the hospitality of such to those who have served me so faithfully these last weeks, as well as to the enemy whose presence we patiently suffer."

Reverend Mason's face washed pale. "Those Unionists have infected you."

Steel seemed to infuse her spine, and the words simply tumbled out. "It's nothing to do with Union or not. You know well that we didn't hold with owning folk long before this ridiculous war began."

She winced inwardly. The good reverend was bound to hear only insult in her speech, since he hadn't seen a thing wrong with owning a pair of house slaves, himself, before they'd run away six months ago. Surely enough, he drew a sharp breath, rearing back his head as if she'd struck him. "Well then. I should be taking my leave. Have a good day, Miss MacFarlane. Extend my regards to your father."

She sketched a curtsy and barely waited for him to leave the yard before turning back toward the door. But once she'd laid her hand on the latch, she suddenly could not face the press inside. She stepped past to the edge of the porch and stood peering up at the fog-shrouded slope of the ridge.

The door opened behind her. It should have been no surprise when it was Josh who slipped through and came to her side.

Pearl could hardly breathe. If nothing else, Reverend Mason's words brought home to her just how certain it was—and likely sooner rather than later—that their unintended guests would leave and take Josh with them.

"Pearl? Is all well?"

She could not reply. Could not even look at him other than to notice that he still wore his coat, a brighter blue than it had been when first he came, because of her ministrations. She'd managed to clean most if not all of the grime and blood, then trimmed and mended the shredded sleeve.

And he looked very well—quite well indeed—with the color providing a foil for the red of his hair and beard.

Why in the name of all that was holy did she have to keep noticing that?

He folded his arms across his chest and settled back against the porch rail. "I do not like that man," he murmured. "I realize it's disrespect of a man of the cloth, and that he's a staunch Confederate, so a certain amount of hostility is to be expected, but—there it is."

Her eyes burned, and she let out a broken laugh. "To be fair, Reverend Mason has done much good in our church body. I believe this recent unpleasantness has tried him beyond bearing, however."

Josh's chuckle warmed her through. " 'Recent unpleasantness'?"

A smile wrung her lips, despite the heaviness of her heart. "I must admit to some surprise at his lack of human feeling toward this situation."

"I'm sure his concern for you and your family outweigh any he might have for the rest of us."

Pearl peeked at him and saw him still smiling. "No doubt," she said. "But he has a way of expressing said concern which grates horribly."

"His intentions are doubtless pure."

"Oh, doubtless." She sighed. "He expressed surprise that you and the rest of our, ah, guests are still here."

Josh's smile faded. "Yes. That is. . .surprising, perhaps."

He looked as if he'd like to make further comment, but the door opened again and two of the other men, Tattersall and Johnson, emerged, each carrying a chair. They both bobbed a nod at Pearl. "Miss MacFarlane. I hope you don't mind if we sit outside and take the fresh air for a spell."

"Not at all. I should return to washing up." And with the barest glance toward Josh, she went back in.

Josh watched Pearl go and tried not to think about the hollowing of his middle in the wake of her words.

Or the extreme annoyance at being interrupted.

Tattersall set his chair down with a thump and dropped into it. "So," he said very quietly. "When are we going to try to get out of here?"

Evening fell at last, hastened by rain and mist, and with it the first hint of relief Pearl had felt all day. Pa went early to bed, while their convalescents gathered around the hearth for storytelling—Pa turned a blind eye to card games, but it was Sunday after all, and with Reverend Mason having been there earlier, everyone seemed to stay mindful of that. Lydia carried a crying Sally up the stairs while Pearl puttered around the kitchen, putting away a few things that remained from the supper dishes. It was with no small startlement that she looked up to find Clem at her elbow, reaching for a dish towel and a wet platter.

"And what is it you want?" she murmured with a half smile.

He shot a glance toward the sitting room. "Pearl. Is God really on our side?"

She fumbled the bowl in her hands and nearly dropped it. "What would make you ask such a thing?"

Clem wiped the platter with slow, careful strokes. "I—just want to know. Everyone says He is. Preacher always says so. But what if we lose the war? What then? Did the older boys die for nothing?"

"Oh Clem."

Pearl set the bowl on its shelf. What could she say, when he only echoed the unspoken questions of her heart?

"Pa and others talk about General Lee and Jackson and others, and how God must surely favor our cause because how could such fine Christian men choose the wrong side? But. . .Yankees believe too, at least some of 'em."

Pearl smiled a little, hot wetness blurring her eyes. "That they do. Some of them."

"So—who's got the right of it? And how do we know?"

"I—" She took a breath, set both hands on the table, and leaned on them. "I don't rightly know. Seems all we can do sometimes is just keep choosing whatever seems the right thing to do, right in front of us, and trust He'll bring good of it."

Where did all that come from? She sounded almost like Pa.

And did she truly believe it, herself?

Clem dried another dish, eyeing her, clearly unconvinced.

"Not sure I've anything better to give you," she said. "I wish I did. Other than—the South is our homeland, Clem. Our country. And we best stay true to her."

*November 23, 1863*

About midday, the sound of battle came again, in earnest.

They were cleaning up from lunch, and a game of chess was being organized in the sitting room, when someone lifted his head and hushed the others. "Is that thunder—or guns?"

A faint rumbling could be discerned from somewhere in the distance.

"It's guns," another replied, and they all scrambled outdoors to listen.

Pearl followed, dish towel still clutched in her hands, not bothering with her shawl despite the cold.

Sure enough, the grumbling that rolled from over the ridge, ebbing and flowing in a way that chilled Pearl to the bone, was too sustained to be mere thunder. She could only listen for a minute or two before heading back into the house.

*Lord. . .oh Lord. . .*

"What's going on, Pearl?" Pa asked plaintively, from his chair.

She did not know how to answer.

"Pearl?"

The words clogged her throat. "There is—"

"It's just artillery over across the mountains, sir," came Josh's voice, low and soothing. "Nothing to be alarmed by, here."

"Well." Pa scowled, clearing his throat. "They best not be spoiling my repose. Would you help me to bed, young man?"

Pearl could not even voice her gratitude at the moment as Josh slipped past her to assist Pa, as if it were his greatest honor to do so.

Lydia had already taken the children upstairs to nap, and one of them, likely Sally by the pitch of it, started to cry, followed by the sound of Lydia shushing her. Soft singing followed, and the crying subsided.

Pearl returned to the washtub and her task. Two months ago, they'd endured three days of this, the growl of battle from over the ridge—and then every day since had been filled with sorrow, hardship, and the nev-er-ending work of caring for their guests. Being raised on a farm, she was used to being busy from sunup to sundown, but this—

And was this time about to come to an end?

Josh emerged from Pa's room, but rather than return outside with the others, he crossed the house to Pearl.

"Thank you," she said. "As always."

He smiled a little, then considered the towel that Pearl held and the dishes still lying in the washtub. After a slight hesitation, he held out his good arm. "I'll wash if you'd be so kind as to roll up my sleeve."

"Of course." She set aside the towel and made quick work of unbuttoning his blouse cuff and folding it back. Her fingers itched to linger, to twine again with his strong, warm grip, as they had that night weeks ago, but she forced herself to finish and pull away. "There you are."

"Thank you." He plunged the hand into the dishwater, searching about until he came up with the washcloth, and set to washing as if he'd done it this way all his life.

Pearl had to likewise force herself to turn away and not stare. How did he make even such a mundane task seem so heroic?

Above them, Lydia's voice continued, soft but strong. Soothing even as it wrung an ache from her throat.

"What will you do if the Federals break the siege for good?" he asked suddenly. "And if the Union prevails overall?"

A chill gripped her. Had he overheard Clem's questions the evening before?

She forced herself to lift her gaze calmly to his. "What will *you* do if the Confederacy prevails and y'all aren't able to force us back into the Union?"

He laughed quietly, but there was little genuine humor in his face. One plate finished, he set it into the rinse water and started on another. "I do not know. Go west, perhaps."

She lifted the clean plate from the water and wiped it dry. When his face remained turned away, she gave his upper arm a playful backhanded tap. "You could be fitted with a hook, and go to sea. Take up piracy."

His dark eyes flashed to hers, and he gave in to a long laugh that shook his entire body. "You—are the most singular woman—" He swiped at his eyes with his wounded arm, and still chuckling, he peered at her.

She allowed herself a little smile in return.

"If the Confederacy wins," he said, still grinning, "what would you do? Come live a life of piracy on the open seas, as well?"

For a moment, she entertained the most vivid and nonsensical image of the two of them dressed like the illustrations in the Dumas novel over on her shelf, with high boots and ridiculously oversized and out-of-fashion coats, Josh with a cocked and plumed hat, and herself with a kerchief round her head and a patch over one eye—

"Or would you stay and marry your cousin?"

His tone was teasing, but it completely knocked the breath from her. She stood, gaping. "Why would you ask such a thing?"

Suddenly he did not look as though he were teasing at all. The intensity in his dark eyes continued to steal the air from the room.

Why did conversation with her always wind up going further than he expected or even planned?

And why on earth had he dared ask her about marrying Bledsoe? Especially after that fool comment about becoming a pirate?

Because the very next words that wanted to come out of his mouth were *While you're considering whether or not to be his wife, please consider becoming mine.*

Sweet Lord in heaven, have mercy. Had she not already proven she'd no interest in him that way? And he'd sure not ask a woman to marry him out of pity.

Especially not Pearl MacFarlane. She deserved so much better than that.

A shout came from outside, but neither of them moved.

"Pearl!" Clem came tumbling through the door. "Pa! Lydia! You will never believe—"

Pearl turned slowly, pulling in a deep breath. Mingled disappointment and relief rushed through Josh at yet another interruption.

But her brother stood there, gasping openmouthed, his face utterly white. Distress, or excitement? The figure of a man full grown filled the doorway behind him and entered, clothed in a grimy, tattered Rebel butternut uniform. His gaunt frame bore a startling resemblance in mannerism to Clem.

The man swept off a kepi-style hat, his hair and beard long and wild but damp from a recent washing or the rain.

"Pearl!" he uttered, then as his gaze suddenly fell on the colored woman standing on the stairs, he gave a strangled cry. "Lydia! Do you not know me?"

Both women pressed hands across their mouths, but Lydia was the first to recover. "Jeremiah? Is it really you?"

The two couldn't get to each other fast enough, falling into each other's arms in the middle of the room, crying and laughing. Pearl stood, trembling, bent, but still unable to take her gaze off the pair.

Could it be—this was one of her older brothers?

The man turned from embracing Lydia and went to gather up Pearl. "We thought you dead!" she said. "We were told you were dead!" Her tone was almost accusatory, even as she clutched at him and buried her face in his shoulder.

He laughed brokenly. "Nearly so. I was in Alton Prison, in Illinois."

"Prison!" She pulled back and stared at him, then promptly dissolved into tears again.

From the far bedroom, old Mr. MacFarlane emerged, leaning on his cane and shaking. "Gideon, is that you?"

Pearl's brother turned, the blue eyes full of tears. "No, Pa. I'm Jeremiah." He let go of Pearl only to embrace his father, glancing around the room. "But speaking of Gideon—"

Pearl had covered her face with her apron, but she pulled it away to murmur, "He. . .died at Chickamauga these few weeks past."

Her brother looked stricken. "Ah, no."

After a few hard breaths, she choked out, "As did Jeff at Fishing Creek, we were told." Silence for a few moments, as her brother slowly shook his head, then she added, "We thought all three of you gone. It's been near more than we could bear."

At this admission of weakness on Pearl's part, Josh snapped into motion. He dried his hand on the towel Pearl had dropped on the table, then quietly began gathering up those of his fellow Federals who had crowded back inside to see who the visitor was, herding them out the door and across to the barn.

Giving an overjoyed but still-grieving family a little privacy was the least they could do. Heaven knew it was something Josh would want were it him.

If, Lord willing, someday it was him returning home.

# CHAPTER 27

They clung to each other for so long, Jeremiah and Pa and Clem, then Lydia and herself again, weeping without shame, that Pearl lost all sense of time. She only knew that when she came to herself and looked around, the house was still completely devoid of their Yankee guests.

"So—you been quartering Yanks all this time?" Jeremiah said, taking in the beds along the wall and the myriad other signs of occupation around the house.

"Wounded prisoners," Pearl said. Jeremiah looked to have no comfort in that. "What is it?" she prompted him.

He only shook his head, frowning.

Pearl drank him in. "I still can't believe you're here. You're. . .so thin."

His blue eyes flicked toward her. "Prison ain't a picnic."

Her heart chilled. The men she'd helped care for. . .and the ones who were still here, avoiding that fate, just yet.

*Josh.*

She pushed that thought to the back of her mind. A new one took hold, laced with suspicion. "How did you manage to get out?"

Jeremiah stepped back, made a show of hanging his cap on a peg by the door while the rest of them looked at him. Stayed there for a moment, dragging his hand through his shaggy hair.

"Jeremiah." It was Lydia's smooth, firm voice which broke the silence.

He whirled back to face them. "I did something terrible. I. . .took an oath. The oath of allegiance. And just that easy, they wrote me a pass and sent me home."

To a chorus of cries and exclamations, one of them her own, she was sure, Pearl stumbled back into a chair. Jeremiah—her own brother, who had enlisted two years and more ago with all the fire of any son of the Confederacy—had sworn allegiance to the Union.

He was trembling, teeth gritted. "Turn me out if you will, but. . .I couldn't take it no more. The cold, the hunger, the sickness. The missing you, Lydia. And from what I seen getting home, it won't matter anyway, for long."

None of them could move, even now.

Jeremiah lifted reddened eyes, met each of their gazes in turn, then lastly looked at Lydia. "It seemed like. . .the best way. The only way to come back to you. And—if the Federals win, as it's looking like they will—maybe you and me, we'll have a chance to finally live as man and wife without hiding. For me to finally do right by you. Don't you want that, Lydia?"

With a sob, Lydia flew into his arms.

Pa cleared his throat, thumped his cane a couple of times on the floor. "My son has come back to me. It's enough for now."

Pearl could only sit weeping into her apron.

Though they'd just finished lunch, she was determined to celebrate the occasion with the best supper she and Lydia could pull together, which meant going to the barn to forage.

It also gave her just a few moments to think through everything with Jeremiah.

A cold fear lodged in the pit of her belly. He still had no good plan for explaining to Travis, who was bound to show up sooner or later, or to Portius either for that matter, how he managed to be released, besides that he was on convalescent leave. Travis might shoot him on sight for desertion or treason, or both, once he found out Jeremiah had taken the oath, and at odd moments Pearl was not entirely sure she would blame him.

But then with a little thrill, she'd recall that one of the brothers they'd thought dead was very much alive and home.

Crossing the yard, she looked up to see Josh leaning in the open doorway of the barn. An entirely different sort of thrill swept through her, but whether it was comprised of anticipation or guilt—or both—she could not say.

He pushed upright as she approached, his dark eyes intent.

"I need to gather things for supper," she murmured. "Will you. . . accompany me?"

It felt strange and overbold to ask him to do something she knew well that he'd do regardless of whether or not she asked, indeed would insist on even if she didn't. And with all the other men inside the barn looking on as she entered—

She hesitated for a moment, meeting their gazes.

"Is all well, Miss MacFarlane?" Mr. Thorsson asked, his blue gaze shadowed but as earnest as ever.

"It is, thank you." Finding her voice unsteady, she cleared her throat. "My brother, who had been reported killed after the action at Shiloh, has returned. Needless to say, we are beside ourselves with joy."

A murmur of surprise and agreement rippled through the group. They all could appreciate the sentiment, even if—as she did—they doubtless wondered how this would change their own situation here. Or what news Jeremiah brought with him.

She dipped a little curtsy. "You will excuse me while I find provender for supper."

By now they all knew, as well, that the entrance for their root cellar was located inside that storage room, and it was silly to pretend otherwise. They were all polite smiles and nods in the moment, however, and she ducked away and into that room.

Josh already had the floor cleared and the door open. Pearl gathered her skirts and descended the stairs, ignoring as she always did the dust, cobwebs, and increasingly musty odor from the recent rains. Her lantern illuminated the space before her, and as she approached the bottom of the stairs, Pearl could see that though the floor was darker than usual, there was no standing water.

That might change with the last few days' downpour, though.

She stopped in front of a shelf of blackberry jam but suddenly could not make herself focus on what was actually there.

"Is all truly well with your brother?" Josh asked softly.

Pearl started to answer yes and brush off his question as she habitually did the strange, prickling awareness his presence always stirred. Then she sighed, her head already wagging. "He took an oath of allegiance in order to be released from prison."

She could guess well enough what his response to that would be by his intake of breath, but he let it out again and only said, "That is a surprise."

"You've no idea. Or...perhaps you have." She angled him a glance. He stood near—too near for her comfort—watching her gravely. "But in his heart, he's already given up on the Confederacy. I...I can scarce believe it." She hesitated. "I suppose you will say I should do the same."

He was silent so long, she almost peeked at him again. "At one time," he said, his voice almost a caress, "I might have. But no longer."

She did turn toward him then, unable to mask her startlement.

"The depth of your conviction is a beautiful thing, Pearl MacFarlane. It's part of the strength which makes you the woman you are. And I'd—I'd not change that."

The warmth in his brown eyes was a tangible thing, wrapping her about, filling her as it were with the very sort of strength he talked about.

"But things are changing," she said. "We all know it. Jeremiah bears witness to it—he'll be telling us more at supper. And we cannot help any of it."

His gaze was unwavering. "If I could leave the Confederacy intact, somehow—change slavery, yes, but otherwise, for your sake—yes, I would."

Her jaw had fallen open and somehow she could not close it again. He smiled, and the heat of a midsummer day swept through her.

Mercy but he was handsome. Why did he have to be so handsome?

"See how much you've affected me, Pearl?"

"How much I—" She shut her mouth with a snap, her eyes burning anew. Did he not see what a simpleton she became, merely standing in his presence?

The corners of his eyes crinkled farther. "Now. What sort of goodies do you have here? Is that blackberry jam I see, honest and true?"

This woman was going to be the death of him. He couldn't seem to stay away from her—even as—yes, she'd said it—they could all feel the change in the air and knew nothing could stay the same. He could not hope to have anything lasting where she was concerned, but he could barely resist the growing impulse to pull her into his arms and kiss her insensible.

And he could, here in the cellar, away from prying eyes. Just a taste of those sweet lips, a moment of her lithe form in his embrace—

It would not be enough. It could never be enough. It could never even *be*. And so he forced a grin and prattled about blackberry jam. Instead let the thought of berries remind him of his own best boyhood summer memories, make his mouth water, and place far to the back of his mind that it was the tart sweetness of this Tennessee Rebel girl he wanted to be savoring.

He only wanted what he could not have, she'd maintained once.

No. It wasn't that at all.

Even here, by lantern light, as she also turned stiffly away to the jams and other canned goods, she was so comely, so brilliant that he could not look at her, yet could hardly tear his eyes away. She was the loveliest thing he'd ever seen, he was sure. And all he wanted was to linger here at her side for hours.

For the rest of his life, if he could finagle it.

*I cannot. It's impossible. She deserves—so much better. A whole man. Not one who sacrificed a hand to a cause she hates and fears.*

He would only ever represent loss and degradation to her, he knew. No matter how they chatted and smiled while gathering things for the joyful feast to come.

But the longing for things to be different had seized him by the throat and would not let go.

# CHAPTER 28

M uch later, they sat around the table, Jeremiah telling his story between shoveling in bites of supper. "So, I was shot at Shiloh, then captured and sent off to Alton." He cast nervous glances around the table, first at Portius, then Josh, then the sitting room full of convalescent Federals. "While there, we caught—oh, I don't know, there were several rounds of sickness. I most earnestly doubted my own survival more than once." He chewed, swallowed, looked down at his plate. "Many of my companions perished."

Lydia leaned close to his shoulder, pressing her cheek to his arm.

"In all," he continued, "the Yankees treated us most deplorably."

"And yet here you are," Portius said, his voice mild, but it made Pearl want to laugh, were she not all too aware of how carefully Jeremiah was trying to conceal his true reason for being there.

Jeremiah lifted his head and fixed Portius with a stare. "Pardon me," he said at last, "but who are you?"

"This is Portius," Pearl interposed. "Travis sent him to give us aid and watch over us. He's been invaluable."

As if realizing the contradiction inherent in any protest at the Negro's place at their table, Jeremiah drew a slow breath and nodded. Pearl hid her smile over that as well.

"So." Jeremiah took a spoon and smeared a dollop of blackberry jam over a slab of corn bread, took a bite, and promptly rolled his eyes in obvious delight. "Glory be, Pearl. I didn't think coming home could be improved upon, but—it is."

She dipped her head and avoided glancing toward Josh. But from the corner of her eye, she caught the grin he shot her way, regardless.

"I might as well tell you all I've seen," Jeremiah went on, once he'd chewed enough to speak. "Grant's trying to get pontoons built across the Tennessee. The Confederate boys up on Lookout Mountain are doing their best to see that don't happen. But"—he swallowed, wolfed down another bite—"Sherman's there now. Got there, they said, oh, a week ago."

Portius grunted. Josh and several of the others perked up.

Jeremiah gulped a few swallows of water. "Chattanooga and Lookout Valley are absolutely crawling with bluebellies."

Not a man in the room moved except Jeremiah.

Pearl saw all the convalescent Yankees sliding glances at each other. What would this mean for them? A hasty train ticket to Richmond? Or if they could hold out, possible freedom?

"Confederates hold Lookout Mountain," Jeremiah said. "And Missionary Ridge. They're pretty well dug in on Missionary Ridge, especially." He shook his head. "Federals might have supply lines open, and hold Chattanooga, but—"

He seemed to become aware of his full audience for the first time, and he shifted to look all around the room.

"I don't see how either side is gonna win this, easily," he said finally.

Easy had never entered into it. Josh knew it. Most of the other men in the room knew it as well, including Pearl's older brother.

They all exchanged glances. Resolve gleamed in the gazes of all but a few. Those who were even remotely recovered at this point were spoiling to get back into the action.

Josh hated that he felt even the slightest hesitation.

He considered the concern etched in Pearl's face and those of her family present. Thought of his own family—how Pa had shaken his hand like he'd never let go, tears standing in his dark eyes, and Mama had clung to him, weeping. "Come back to us," she'd whispered.

"Mama," he'd protested, but she'd only held on more tightly.

"I wish you wouldn't go."

"You'd be ashamed of me if I didn't," he'd popped back, and finally she too released him.

He'd already heard the conflicted feelings in Pearl at the circumstances of her brother's return. What were the others thinking? Clearly Lydia—usually so disaffected and self-possessed—had no issues with the situation. With supper finished, the children climbed into Jeremiah's lap, and old Mr. MacFarlane beamed at everyone in general, and Clem and Pearl looked happy enough as well.

Only Portius looked grim, and Jeremiah MacFarlane himself, though he exclaimed over the food and petted the children and looked longingly at the woman who'd given him those children.

And Josh was still not sure what he thought of that situation, though he'd received Pearl's explanation of it calmly enough. Just how far could a man justify going to be with the woman he loved? Or was it merely obtaining something to meet a baser need? Because that happened often enough—not that he doubted the intentions of someone Pearl regarded so highly, but one never knew.

Yet here was MacFarlane, after having walked his way back from Illinois, braving the wrath of family and community for how he'd been released instead of, say, going west, where no one knew him or what he'd been. Surely that counted for something.

"The children and I should move out of the attic for the night," Pearl said suddenly, then flushed crimson.

"We couldn't do that," Lydia protested, her own cheeks coloring, as Josh had never seen.

Both women just sat and looked at each other, while Jeremiah looked truly discomfited. "No need for that, Pearl. I'll just sleep in the barn."

She looked from one to the other, then suddenly rose, walked to the door, and went outside. Josh was halfway out of his chair, but Lydia put out a hand and bid him stay then followed her out.

MacFarlane gaped after the women before fixing narrowed eyes on Josh. After a moment, he shut his teeth on whatever it was he'd wanted to say.

"Mister Thorsson and I can vacate the downstairs bedroom," Josh said. "Surely we're recovered enough to sleep on a floor again."

"Downstairs bedroom? You mean—" It was Jeremiah MacFarlane's turn to flush, apparently. "You were sleeping in my sister's bedroom?"

Had he been? Josh's mind tripped into sudden awareness. The dim memory of a dress hanging where his own coat now hung, and a brush and jewelry sitting on a dressing table—

MacFarlane pushed to his feet, leaning across the table, but Portius and Josh rose as well.

"Just simmer down, now," Portius rumbled, while Josh hastened to explain.

"I confess, I did not know. We were all half-insensible when your cousin brought us, and that was—it was simply where we found ourselves."

"Honestly, Jer," Clem chimed in, "what are you gettin' all worked up over? Situation's no different here than for any of our neighbors. We had men dyin' here. I gave up my bed for Pearl, since she'd had to give up hers for Bernie, there."

MacFarlane's head snapped around to look at the Norwegian, who gave him an abashed smile and nod. Introductions had taken place when they'd all come back to the house for supper—names and regiments, at least—but Josh doubted that MacFarlane had retained much.

"So yes," Josh said, "we could give you the downstairs bedroom. It's only right, since you're family."

Thus, they were in the midst of clearing the room when the women returned. Pearl's look of surprise lasted but the barest instant before she nodded. "There are no fresh linens, of course."

"This will more than do," Lydia hastened to assure her.

It wrung an ache from her heart to watch her brother and Lydia stealing shy glances at each other, as if they were just now newly wedded.

Perhaps under the circumstances, it seemed to them as if they were.

Jeremiah tore himself away from Lydia long enough to corner Pearl in the kitchen, however, and seize her by the elbow. "What is that red-haired Yankee to you?"

She froze, meeting his gaze but feeling herself go hot. "Nothing, Jer. He's just another convalescent bluebelly."

Her brother did not budge. "He moved mighty fast when you got up to leave the room. Also was mighty quick to make sure you weren't discomfited tonight."

"He's a good man, one of several." She held firm, though his eyes were fierce. "There are some of those here. Some of course who weren't good men, but those are no longer present."

Jeremiah's expression went slack. "Have you been harmed? Or—Lydia?"

"No. But partly because of Mister Wheeler and others like him."

He seemed to chew on those words. "Why are they even still here? Didn't they ship all prisoners off to Richmond?"

"Travis has been busy," she murmured.

He sighed. "Likely not a bad thing, that." He released her arm and scrubbed a hand across his face. "I can't stay here, Pearl. Lydia and I will move back to the cabin in the morning."

Desperation flooded her. "Pa's not doing well. He's had a few more spells, just these past several weeks. I'm—I'm not ashamed to tell you I'm scared, Jer. I wish you and Lydia would stay."

His brows knitted. "Not with the Yankees here, Pearl. They ain't gonna tolerate Lydia and me living as man and wife any more than the rest of our community. Bluebellies don't care for Negroes more than anyone else, I've seen. So many of 'em afraid they'll move up North and take their jobs."

"I've seen that too." Pearl reached up and smoothed Jeremiah's beard. "Mister Wheeler, though, he's trustworthy. Mister Thorsson as well. Maybe it's just that I've known them longer—"

Jeremiah's hand covered hers, his gaze softening. "Do you love him, then?"

The stabbing in her heart returned in a rush. "How could you suggest such a thing?"

She tried to snatch her hand back, but he held it fast. A bitter smile curved his mouth. "We MacFarlanes can't be happy with the easy road, can we? But if he's as good as you say. . .maybe it's worth it."

All she could do was stare at him, mouth open, for what seemed like the hundredth time that day. Finally he tugged her toward him, and she flung her arms around him. "I'm so glad you're not killed," she murmured.

"Me too," he said gruffly into her hair, and gave her a hard squeeze. "I think."

That drew the chuckle she was sure he'd intended.

# Chapter 29

"The question is," Tattersall said, his voice nearly a whisper as the others huddled around him, "do we wait here for the Federals to break through, or risk the possibility of Bledsoe or someone else remembering that we're here and then hauling us off?"

The MacFarlanes had all gone to bed, Pearl upstairs, Clem in his pa's room, and the married couple in the other downstairs bedroom—Josh refused to think of them as anything else—and Portius had slipped away, likely for the very purpose of finding Bledsoe. Josh himself lay stretched on the floor, eyes closed but listening to the other men discuss their options. Most of them were in favor of attempted escape rather than wait around to see what would become of them during the inevitable, impending clash between Federal and Confederate.

Josh knew what the eventual decision had to be. Most of them were able enough to travel at this point. To even think of not attempting it was cowardly.

Except—except there was now Pearl for him to think about. And the sure knowledge that too many Federal soldiers did not regard any sort of law of chivalry or compassion, especially in the heat of battle.

Simply pondering it made him feel sick.

Someone tapped his foot. "What are your thoughts about it all?" The whisper sounded like Johnson. "You've more interest here than we do."

"Think you can tear yourself away from your Rebel girl?" Tattersall quipped.

Josh stifled a sigh. The tapping on his foot continued, and after a moment, he pushed upward to sit, swiping his hand through his hair.

"Not that any of us blame you for not wanting to," someone else muttered. Josh aimed a glare in that direction. Low laughter rippled across the group.

"I think we have as reasonable a chance of making it to Chattanooga as anything else," he said.

His heart sank even as he said the words. But it was their duty to try to rejoin their regiments.

They all nodded, their gazes eager even in the dimness.

"I do hate to just leave without even a word of thanks," he said, though the admission felt too revealing.

Another round of chuckles rumbled around the room. "Leave a note," someone said. "Better your sweetheart's broken heart than us dead because she gave us away."

"She wouldn't give us away," Josh said, very low.

"Maybe not," Tattersall said, "but we shouldn't chance it either."

He combed his fingers through his beard for a minute. "How do you propose we find our way through Rebel lines?"

Tattersall grunted. "That one's more difficult."

"I'm betting Clem would aid us."

"The boy would talk."

"He wouldn't. That one holds his secrets like the grave."

"Are we all going," another voice said, "or could a couple of us stay behind?"

Josh met Tattersall's gaze across the room, both of them grim. "Only should an unforeseen situation demand it, should anyone stay behind," Tattersall said. "And you risk being sent off to Richmond."

"The rain's going to make it miserable."

"It would be miserable anyway."

"Death if we stay, death if we go."

"Pretty much."

Josh felt flattened by the impossibility of the task. Dragging ten men out into the wet, expecting that they'd get away without detection or being tracked, or that someone would not catch their death in the damp and cold…

Of course, none of them had enlisted for anything but the adventure of it all. And none of them were now raw recruits. They knew hardship well.

"We should go tonight," Tattersall said. "Right now."

"I'm not going blindly into the dark," Josh said.

"Well, we certainly can't wait for that darky to come back—"

"Then you leave," Josh said. "Either we get Clem to guide us, or—"

The door at the top of the stairs opened, and soft, descending footsteps made them all quickly lie flat and pretend to be sleeping or trying to. Josh watched as Pearl came down, hesitated at the bottom, then continued on to the kitchen, where she poured a cup of water.

This time she didn't angle toward the stairs. "Y'all are a noisy bunch, for supposedly going to bed."

Josh held his breath then sat back up. Pearl eyed him, then the others who did likewise.

"What is it?" she said, at last.

"Miss MacFarlane, we are most regretful that we can no longer accept your hospitality," Tattersall said gravely.

Josh was already climbing to his feet and saw the cup when it started to slip from her hands. He lunged and caught it neatly, hardly spilling a drop, and at her yelp, he offered it back to her. Eyes wide, face pale even in the gloom, she stared at him, unmoving. "Come," he whispered, and gestured back toward the kitchen with the cup.

She turned, stiffly, and he trailed her as she made her way around the table and into the shadows near the back door. A low whistle followed them from the other side of the house, but Josh ignored it.

"You are leaving?" she breathed.

"Tattersall is a fool," he whispered. "That isn't how I'd have chosen to tell you."

He could make out the opening and closing of her mouth in the dark, the wideness of her eyes. She gulped a breath. "I—should have expected it. Y'all—"

As she glanced this way and that, he held out the cup of water until her hands came back up to take it. Once she had a grasp on it, he took advantage of the moment to cup his hand around hers. She went suddenly still. Her breath lurched then released in a long sigh.

"It's the best way," Josh said. "Leave tonight while Portius is gone. None of us wish to risk a train ride to Richmond. Better that we leave under cover of night and try to find the Union lines."

"You—" Another gulp of breath. "Jeremiah said the Confederate lines between here and there are too tight. You'd have to go too far around."

"I don't think the others are willing to wait, regardless."

She leaned toward him a little, her gaze searching his face even in the darkness. "What about yourself?"

He released a sigh. "I should do all I can to rejoin my regiment. It is, after all, what I signed up for."

Her head bobbed, but then she looked up at him again. "You could—stay."

The suggestion seared through him. "What do you mean?"

"As in. . ." She eased closer, tried to speak, but the words would not come out. "Simply—stay," she said finally. "At least until we see what happens with Chattanooga. But maybe. . .longer."

The word slid over him like a caress.

*Oh Lord. . .*

Would that he could.

"Pearl," he said, when he could speak. "You know I cannot. I have an obligation that sooner or later I must fulfill. Whether or not I can actually carry a rifle and fight again. I belong to the Union army until such time as they release me."

She did not move, except for the rising and falling of her breast beneath her shawl.

"Besides," he murmured, making sure this at least fell only on her ears. "You—you deserve so much more than half a man."

Her breathing quickened but nothing else changed. "Do you think me so empty headed? Have I given you any indication that such a thing would trouble me?"

"No, but—"

"But nothing, Yankee." Her eyes fairly flashed in the darkness, though her voice was still barely above a whisper. "Better a whole heart with a maimed limb than—than half a heart with a whole body, or no heart at all."

She was—so brave. So unspeakably darling. So everything he'd wish for in a woman, if he were free to choose.

And here he was preparing to leave her to whatever depredations were yet to come at the hands of either army. Didn't that make him worse than the ones he'd once tried to defend her against?

At his continued silence, her shoulders sagged, and she released another sigh. "I never asked whether or not you left a sweetheart behind. Or even—a wife."

"No. I was as you described your brothers once, too wild to settle." And it had to stay that way, because he sure as anything was not what she needed. No matter what she said.

She regarded him for a moment, head tilted, then swiftly swung away, setting her cup down on a nearby table, then back. Both of her hands came up to frame his face.

When she leaned up to kiss him, he met her halfway.

He couldn't do this. . .shouldn't.

As their kiss deepened, one of her arms went around his neck, the other around his shoulder, and for a few sweet moments, in her embrace, there was no North or South, no Union or Confederacy, just the two of them. Only Pearl and the shadows, and the heady taste of possibility.

And there in her arms, for those few moments, he felt whole again—just as he had up on that windy mountainside.

He broke the kiss at last but could not let her go—and she likewise clung to him. "I wouldn't go if I didn't have to," he whispered, cheek pressed to hers.

"I know," she breathed, warm against his skin.

She started to withdraw, but he held her close. "Could I—would I," he fumbled, "if I were to somehow make it back here—"

She swallowed hard. "You will always be welcome here, Yankee." She shuddered against him—was she weeping?—but then disentangled herself and stepped back, appearing composed.

He smoothed a strand of hair next to her face. "Thank you most kindly. Secesh."

A smile flickered and was gone. She cleared her throat. "Now. How on earth do you hope to get through to Chattanooga?"

She would not think about the implications of helping Federal prisoners escape. She would not. Especially convalescent ones, on a wet night, where every move would give them away and the mad errand was sure to end in them getting shot by those she'd given her own allegiance to.

But she'd not see them running willy-nilly out into the dark, either, without so much as a guide. And so she found herself tiptoeing into Pa's room, waking Clem, and insisting he get up and dressed.

She didn't give herself time for wonder that her younger brother offered not even a word of argument once she explained what was needed, but popped right up and plunged into the task.

Their guests, so to speak, were ready in a matter of minutes. They'd little enough to prepare, after all, and she supposed that after a couple of years' service on the march in all conditions, they were well enough used to packing on a moment's notice.

*"If I were to somehow make it back. . ."*

She'd not think about that either. Because even if he managed to avoid being captured again, or killed, there was no guarantee he'd return. And she wasn't sure what was worse—the possibility that he never would, or the hope that he could, and would, and all that might mean—

They were ready now, with far less clink and clatter than she expected, though she was sure a couple of times that Jeremiah would rouse and come investigate. While the rest of the men went out to the well to fill their canteens, Clem lingered on the porch with Pearl. "So, Jeremiah giving an oath of allegiance and all his talk about the Confederacy being done—what does that mean for us, Pearl?"

She shook her head. "I don't rightly know. I just can't send these men to their deaths, if I can help it—not after caring for them these past weeks." She hugged him tightly for a moment, and he surprised her by leaning into the embrace. "You also take care, you hear? Come back in one piece."

He nodded stiffly and, after a quick kiss to her cheek, trotted out into the yard, where the others waited.

That was it, then. But suddenly Josh was there again, hovering at the bottom step, his face a pale blur beneath the brim of his Hardee hat.

There was nothing more either could say, nor any need for more kisses or embracing. But when Josh tugged her close one last time, she leaned in, fingers curling into that dark blue wool she'd once hated. Savored the warm pressure of his mouth on hers, one last time.

"God be with you, Rebel girl," he murmured, releasing her.

With that, he tramped away across the yard.

A long while after the sound of their passing had faded, she turned and reentered the house. The sitting room lay empty, oddly echoing her footsteps. She stopped in the middle of the floor.

Agony beat where her heart once had been. How was she to go on, not knowing what was to come, whether Josh was marching to his own death or whether, please God, those steps would bring him back to her?

She sank to her knees in the middle of the room as the first sob took her.

And she, a proud, proper daughter of the Confederacy—what shame that she'd fallen in love with a Yankee. A Federal soldier sworn to fight and die for the Union cause. Not just accepted his kiss but wantonly sought it and, at the last, clung to him like she herself were dying.

Because, yes, she would welcome him back. A hundred times over.

Facedown she went, right there on the floor, face pillowed on her arms.

"Oh Lord God," she wept. "Please, Lord, protect him. Keep him safe. And if it be possible, bring him back to me."

# CHAPTER 30

*Wee hours of the morning,*
*November 24*

They'd marched for less than an hour before voices, and firelight from a camp, drew them up short and drove them to shelter among a tangle of boulders, in what remained of a thicket. Grateful enough for the break, Josh sipped at the water in his canteen and peered into the gloom.

"I just...don't know." Clem crouched next to Josh, shaking his head. "That picket ain't where I thought it was. Or at least, where it was a few days ago. I think Bragg must have everyone on the move again."

Josh snorted, but quietly. "Still out ranging, aren't you?"

Clem held his silence for a moment. "Y'all didn't seem to need me so much, lately."

"No," Josh owned.

Beside him, Bernie Thorsson held his silence, looking pale in the darkness.

"Gonna make it?" Josh asked him.

The Norwegian nodded tightly.

Tattersall crawled closer. "So kid, you still think you can lead us through?"

"Do you want to go back?" Clem retorted.

Josh wished he could say yes.

Tattersall sucked his teeth a moment. "Naw, of course not."

"Well then." Clem nodded briskly. "There is another way, but y'all need to keep quiet."

He led them back up over the rise and roughly parallel to the camp and picket line, as they could see it. The distant firelight gave the fog an eerie glow but lent just enough illumination to keep them from stumbling overmuch. At some point, Josh realized it wasn't just fog, but snow falling around them.

Thorsson huffed and stumbled. Without a word, Josh came up beside him and, sliding a shoulder beneath his arm, helped him keep moving.

The ground beneath their boots turned wet and squishy. Clem hushed them, but there was no mistaking the sound of marching through swamp. The youth turned them, and presently they were at the banks of a creek. Motioning them on, Clem descended into the middle of the stream and turned yet again.

The water closed about Josh's feet and legs, bitterly cold. He gritted his teeth and suppressed a moan. Thorsson's intake of breath, and the muted groans from others, betrayed a similar shock at having to take to the creek.

"Not far now," Clem whispered, and they trudged on slowly, navigating submerged rocks and sudden drop-outs in the creek bottom. Tattersall fell but regained his footing quickly enough with the help of another, a low stream of muttered curses his only apparent concession to the inconvenience.

Just when Josh was sure he'd never feel his legs again, and his arm was beginning to burn from supporting Thorsson, Clem sloshed out upon a sandbar edging the bank and scampered up the incline. The rest of them followed suit, trying not to breathe too hard or give vent to more than soft grumblings at having to keep walking while soaked through. At least the water had never risen above their hips.

The Confederate campfires were more distant here, but Clem warned that this was the trickiest part—creeping through a break in the picket still surrounding Chattanooga. And reduced to creeping, they were, crawling in a line through what felt like blackberry bramble. Josh sent Thorsson ahead of him and went last.

Every beat of his heart hurt, and more so the farther they got from the MacFarlane place. The fire that had kindled in him at holding Pearl had long since faded—though each time she returned to mind, which was nearly continuously, the spark was there, ready to return to life.

*"It is a hard thing, to walk away from one's sweetheart,"* Thorsson had whispered to him shortly after embarking on their journey. *"But it is because of our sweethearts that we fight this fight, yes?"*

Josh supposed that was so, even when that sweetheart stood on the other side of a long war. Either way, at this point the only way back to Pearl lay ahead. And he'd gladly crawl miles through the blackberries if it meant even a shred of hope he'd hold her in his arms again.

*Please, gracious God, let there be a way for me to return to her.*

He didn't realize that, ahead of him, Thorsson had stopped until Josh ran into the soles of his boots. He waited then gave one foot a shake.

"I—cannot," came Thorsson's weary, ragged whisper.

Josh shook the man's foot again, more vigorously. "Your sweetheart," he murmured back. "Remember—her. Find strength—for her."

It was all he could think to say.

*Remember—Pearl. Find strength—for her.*

The sweet fire of her kiss. The softness of her cheek, against his.

The Norwegian expelled a heavy sigh then began to move again. Slowly, but it was movement nevertheless.

And then, after what might have been either half the night or half an eternity, with a rustle and scuffling, fresh air blew in Josh's face, and he emerged into open night. Torch and firelight lay before him, illuminating a breastworks, behind which he glimpsed the silhouette of a series of buildings.

Josh edged closer to Clem, as he and the rest of his company huddled at the edge of the blackberry thicket. "Have you ever been this far before?"

"I have not." The not-too-distant torchlight outlined the fear rimming Clem's eyes.

Josh sat, surveying the breastwork stretching away into darkness, on the other side of an empty field, with the Confederate entrenchment just as clear, a mile or more off to their left at the foot of Missionary Ridge. To be caught in the open like this, with the likelihood of being fired at by either side, but most likely by the Federals—

He sucked in a long, steadying breath, held it, and let it out, slowly.

*God. . .holy, gracious God. Have mercy on us.*

"I think," he murmured to Clem at last, "that we've no choice but to make a run for it."

A tiny gurgle came from Clem's throat.

"What is it?" Josh asked, very low.

The boy shook his head, slowly. "I'm a good Confederate. I shouldn't be doing this." His gaze met Josh's. "You understand why I did, though, right?"

"I do. And we're most indebted to you for it." He hesitated. "You aren't thinking of going the rest of the way with us, are you?"

Under their layer of grime, the boy's cheeks were even more pale than they had been. "Did you know my brother took an oath of allegiance?" he choked.

"I do," Josh answered evenly.

Clem shot him a shocked glance. "What am I supposed to do with that?"

"You go home and help take care of your sister and pa. Just as you were before."

The boy's jaw set stubbornly.

"Listen. You might think you want to see the elephant, so to speak. We all did. It turned out to be not what we thought it would be. I'm obligated here, but you aren't. What do you think you'll do if you go along with us?"

His mouth worked, but no words came this time, only a slow wag of his head. Josh gave his shoulder a companionable shake.

"Go home, Clem. We can make it the rest of the way without you."

Even in the dark, he could see the boy's expression harden. Those were entirely the wrong words to use, apparently. "I want," Clem said very quietly, "to come along."

Josh let out a long sigh. "You have to stay with me. And not say a word."

"I can do that."

"You'd better."

Scanning the field again, Josh chose the darkest area, and then after signaling the others, he led the dash across.

They were not quite halfway when the first bullets whizzed past them. In desperation, Josh cried out, "Hold your fire! We are not the enemy!"

Of course, that left it to the hearers to sort out exactly who they were, but the brief lull was all they needed to cross that field and throw themselves into the trench on the other side. The shooting started again just as they reached it, and all of them tumbled into the man-made ditch.

Josh lay there, just breathing for a moment. A pair of faces peered over the embankment above them. "Be you friend or foe?" one man asked, his accent very northern—likely Pennsylvania.

"Sergeant Joshua Wheeler of the First Ohio," Josh panted.

The others called out their names, ranks, and regiments as well.

"We are all convalescents who have been held at a local house," Josh supplied.

What an utterly unsatisfactory way to describe these past two months. . .

"Glory be," the guard exclaimed. "Come on down to the east a bit, and we'll get you through."

They all moved, but Thorsson. Josh crawled to his side. "I—I am hit," he gasped.

*Lord, no!* But the Almighty would take who He would. "Come on," Josh coaxed him. "We're nearly there. I'll help you."

He hauled the Norwegian up by sheer force of will and, with more bullets zinging about, ran huddled after the others.

They were ushered through an opening in the embankment, where once again they recited ranks and regiments, and Josh informed the sentry of Thorsson's wound. Now that they'd gotten this far, weariness dragged at his limbs and dulled his thoughts, so that he could scarce believe they'd truly done it.

"And what about that one?" the sentry asked, peering at Clem, who lingered behind Josh, doing his best to imitate a shadow while examining everything within sight.

"That one I'll take responsibility for," Josh said. "He and his family have extended us hospitality beyond the ordinary, and he guided us here."

The sentry looked at them all in frank disbelief. "Why on earth would you come here and not just head north and keep on going?"

" 'Cause that one got himself a sweetheart behind Rebel lines," Tattersall sniggered.

Josh kept his expression stern, though prickling heat coursed across his skin.

The sentry snorted. "Definitely shouldn't have come back, then."

In this moment, Josh was inclined to agree. "My companion here is wounded," he reminded the sentry. "Could you kindly show us to the nearest doctor?"

The sentry considered Thorsson's drooping form and waxen complexion and nodded. "I 'spect, being convalescent, you should all get looked at. Then—if you be well enough, maybe they'll let you out to the field to join the fun today."

"And what sort of fun do they have planned?" Tattersall asked.

The sentry grinned. "Why, after yesterday's demonstration on Orchard Knob, they's planning on taking Lookout today."

Josh cast a quick glance over his shoulder at the mountain looming across the river as it looped beyond the buildings that comprised Chattanooga. Scattered campfires and torches lit the craggy slopes, swathed in fog.

Grant really was weary of waiting, it seemed.

While leading them through the maze of entrenchments and breastworks, the sentry kept up a running narrative. "Chattanooga might be the most well-fortified town in the country."

Josh could well believe it.

They turned a corner of the street and drew up beside what looked to be a hotel, but emanating such odor that Josh knew it had to be a hospital, and probably for the entirety of the occupation.

Before long, they'd found someone moderately in charge, explained their situation, and were in the process of having Thorsson's wound tended and their former wounds examined. With Clem still beside him, Josh took his blanket and stretched out on the floor near Thorsson. He was so weary, the room seemed to swim around him, but he took one last, long look around. A pair of nurses worked nearby, one bending over a man who cried out in his sleep, the other helping with Thorsson. Their sober gowns, well-used aprons, and plain white haircloths somehow reminded him of Pearl, if only by contrast.

She seemed so far away, and the past weeks, so long ago.

Pearl hardly slept. After finding herself dozing while still lying facedown in the sitting room in prayer, she retired upstairs, but curling up in her bed led only to more thoughts of the mostly empty house below, and more tears than she thought herself capable of shedding after all that had befallen them.

'Long about daybreak, the sound of guns came rolling from over across Missionary Ridge. Pearl bolted out of bed and opened one of the attic windows, then simply stood there for a long time, listening and praying.

She hadn't known she had so many prayers stored up inside, either.

"*Pearl!*"

The bellow fairly shook the floorboards, and startled the children awake. Running across the room, Pearl shushed them then flung open the door to downstairs.

Jeremiah stood at the bottom of the steps, wild eyed and wild haired, fists on his hips. "Where is everyone?"

"Doggone it, Jer, you woke the babies." Pearl came down the stairs, more slowly.

Behind her brother, Lydia emerged from the bedroom, hair in a mussed braid, a blanket about her shoulders. Her gaze swept the empty sitting room, and she pushed past Jeremiah. "I'll tend 'em."

Pearl let her by then descended the rest of the way. Jeremiah's gaze lingered on her face, no doubt noting her reddened and shadowed eyes.

"They left, didn't they?" he said quietly.

She could only nod.

He swore bitterly, surveying the room again. "Clem go too?"

"Yes."

Another string of invectives. "Well," he said at last, "I suppose Lydia and I won't be departing this morning, after all."

"Thank you," she murmured.

He shot her another sharp glance. "I'm not so unfeeling as to leave you to fend for yourself, with fighting going on just over the ridge." He twitched his head in that general direction. "Or contend with Pa being as he is."

So weary she was, she could only stand there, hands knotted in her skirts, and breathe out her gratitude in silent prayer.

# CHAPTER 31

The cold fog and the sound of guns like distant thunder lingered all day. Pearl slept much of the morning and woke to the smell of johnnycakes and bacon. Lydia had obviously dipped into the secret stores.

Downstairs, Pa sat at the table, his hair and beard not quite as tidy as she might have gotten them, but dressed and offering her a slight smile. Beside him, Jeremiah looked less than welcoming. Pearl guessed that Pa had given him a fit, getting him that way.

Head aching, Pearl accepted the cup of chicory Lydia handed her and sat across the table from Pa and Jeremiah. She sipped—the brew was too weak, but what had not been these past months, and the aroma still comforted—and eyed her brother.

She'd never noticed how much he looked like Pa. "I still can't believe you're really here."

Little Sally came scampering from the other side of the room and climbed up in Pearl's lap. "Mornin', Auntie Pearl," she lisped.

Pearl snugged her close. "Mornin', sweetie."

Jem also hugged her, then trotted around the table and climbed up on Jeremiah. The boy likewise looked the perfect combination of her brother and Lydia.

"Clem isn't back yet?" Pearl asked. "Nor Portius?"

Both Lydia and Jeremiah shook their heads, looking grim. "I don't rightly expect him to," Jeremiah said, "not with all that going on out there."

"No, I reckon not. Portius, anyway, but Clem. . ." She shot her brother another look. "Do you wish you were out there, with them?"

He stared back at her then glanced at Lydia, the children, and Pa in turn. "A man was made for fightin' for those he loves," he muttered, at last.

"A man is also made for caring for those he loves," Pearl said. "Which means sometimes staying put." At the spark in his eyes, she went on, "And sometimes staying put is the harder work."

"Sometimes," he snapped back, "a man hasn't any choice."

The echo of Josh's words from the night before whispered through her. *"I wouldn't go if I didn't have to."*

She rose from her chair, gave Sally a last squeeze and kiss, then set the child down in her own place. There was nothing to hold her in the house today. No one to tell her she couldn't wander alone, were she careful.

"Where are you going?" Jeremiah asked.

"Out. Probably to Mama's grave. I'll be back."

With her shawl wrapped about her head and neck, Pa's overcoat around her shoulders, and one of the revolvers in her pocket, she escaped out into the misty cold.

Her steps took her, as before, over the pasture and up the rough slope of the ridge. With all the leaves fallen, there was less cover than that day she had last been here. The day she'd been caught unawares by a Union soldier.

No, two. Because Josh had taken her as unaware, even more fully than that rascal who'd meant her harm.

The thunder of distant battle grew stronger. At times, the very ground beneath her feet trembled with it. Carefully, making sure she stayed alert to anyone following her—although who was there to do so now?—she picked her way up the path to her favorite lookout point. Climbed the rocks, until she stood at the top.

Scattered clouds and fog obscured most of the valley beyond, but she had a decent view of Missionary Ridge. Smoke rose from here and there—houses in between and beyond the edges of the camps. If she had a spyglass, she could see more.

And somewhere, there off to the right, beyond the point of Missionary Ridge, lay Chattanooga. Had Josh and the others made it safely? Where was Clem in his journey back? Although her younger brother's continued absence was worrisome, she felt a curious lack of the urgency which had infused her earlier prayers.

Maybe—just maybe—that was a good sign.

A day had never dragged on so.

Josh should have been grateful to be back behind Federal lines. Glad he was provided food, and with more abundance than they'd sometimes enjoyed these past weeks. Thankful to see Thorsson's wound dressed and the man resting comfortably.

But it all seemed cold, impersonal, unreal even, compared to being served supper and tended in the warm lamplight of the MacFarlane house, under the brisk ministrations of Pearl and Portius.

Clem stuck to him like a burr, hardly saying a word, the blue eyes overlarge but not missing a thing.

Most of the men remaining behind the fortifications in Chattanooga wanted to be out of doors, staring off at the mist-shrouded hulk of Lookout Mountain, where flashes of light punctuated the gloom and the roar of guns rolled across the river like thunder, and had since daylight. Josh felt equally restless but for different reasons.

An attending doctor finally found time to examine the stump of his forearm. Pronounced it "healing well enough," though he gave but a grunt at Josh's admittedly shortened account of the scrap where three fellow Federals helpfully stomped it and added cracked ribs to Josh's list of things to contend with. "Once the Rebels are dealt with," the doctor said, "we'll see about finding you a wooden hand. And either a clerk position, or something similar."

"I could still hold and load a rifle," Josh said. "And nothing wrong with my ability to sight and fire. Or lead others into battle, if necessary."

Another grunt. The doctor scrubbed thoughtfully at his bearded cheek. "Might be so, but any regiment commander would have my hide for letting you back out there today, unproven."

Josh clenched his teeth on a curse. This was the very thing he'd feared, being dismissed as useless and relegated to the rear with those too scared to be out on the front lines. And he'd already not admitted how much his ribs ached today after the exertion of getting here and having to help Thorsson.

The doctor rewrapped the stump, and as he moved on to other patients, Josh slipped his blouse back on, tucking the dangling sleeve up inside itself.

"Now what?" Clem asked, watching as he finished dressing.

"Well," Josh said, "I guess we go back outside and watch smoke rise on the mountain, like everyone else is doing."

They made their way back to the breastworks, though by this time almost all the best vantage points were taken. Clem stayed close at Josh's heels as he wandered the fortifications, and oddly enough, no one challenged him, after a glance at his shortened coat sleeve. Most met him with a nod, and the general mood was one of cheer and even in some cases, jubilation.

Josh did not share their mood.

At the moment, he didn't even care to try.

"Wheeler, is that you?"

Josh turned and, for an instant, wasn't sure he knew the face attached to the voice greeting him, but then recognition flared to life. "Elliot! Good to see you. What are you doing here rather than out there?"

Dark hair and beard, with brown eyes, the man shook Josh's hand and laughed. "Oh, trivial matter of a wound. You know how it is." He nodded toward Josh's left arm, chagrin suddenly clouding his gaze. "Don't look like you got off so lucky, though. Man, they told us you'd gone missing! We'd given you up for dead."

"I was taken prisoner and tended in a private house." Josh lifted the arm. "It's decently healed, but Doc still won't release me for duty."

"Well. Come over here and have some coffee, man. You can tell me what you've heard and I'll catch you up on the rest."

Josh and Clem trailed him to where a can hung suspended over a small fire, and Josh handed over his own cup to be filled then passed it to Clem. Elliot eyed the boy as he slurped the brew with obvious relish. "Somehow I'm guessing you're a new recruit. Or not a Federal at all."

Clem froze, eyes wide.

Elliot gestured with a second cup he'd filled, then handed it off to Josh. "You're enjoying that a little too much."

Josh chuckled and accepted the offering then inhaled deeply. It wasn't bad. Likely smelled better than it tasted, but he wouldn't complain. Not after two long months without any at all.

And it had been longer than that for the MacFarlanes, he was sure.

Clem had buried his nose in the cup again, his cheeks pink but otherwise making no comment. At least the boy was making good on his promise not to speak.

Josh sipped, let the bitter brew roll across his tongue. It tasted much better than he'd expected. "Mm. Definitely has been too long." He sighed and met Elliot's questioning gaze then nodded toward Clem. "His family cared for us. Showed a lot more kindness than one would expect from Rebs, and he's the one who guided us safely back. I told him to go home but—you know how it is. He wanted to see the elephant."

Elliot grunted and glanced away, eyes narrowing as he surveyed Lookout Mountain and the valley between it and Missionary Ridge, stretching away to the south and still occupied by Rebels. "Seems like there's just as much elephant to be seen by climbing the other hill and joining up with the Rebs. Never been a better time to be one, after Chickamauga."

"Maybe." Josh sipped again. "Were you as short rationed as was rumored?"

Elliot bobbed his head. "Yes and no. Some regiments suffered more than others, sure. We had a few uncertain weeks there before Grant arrived. But many would argue that Old Rosey was doing everything he could at the time, and forage wasn't too bad, at least at first."

They spent a companionable hour and more, discussing all that had taken place over the past couple of months, while the battle raged on. But Josh's gaze kept being drawn over to Missionary Ridge, and his thoughts to the small farm beyond that, sheltered by a smaller ridge, where he'd foolishly left his heart.

It felt like years ago, and a thousand miles away.

Sleep came but fitfully that night, despite the ranging Pearl had done for half the afternoon. And when it did come, it was with the most troubling of dreams.

She found herself walking through a field where every bush and tree stood at odd angles, stripped and shredded, and the shadows of rocky outcroppings lay interspersed with torn bodies of men and the bloated shapes of horses and mules.

And the blood. . .everywhere. The ground was dark with it.

Pearl could not look away. An unspoken need drove her as she went from body to body, examining the face of each man. Looking in particular at the color of the hair and beard, first for the browns of her brothers, but then as she went on, for something else—

Wait, she knew what she was searching for. And for whom.

She stopped and gazed across the field. So much blood. So much red. But none of it the particular fiery shade adorning a Yankee who had grown too dear for words.

She had to find him. He was here somewhere—and his life might depend upon her finding him in time. *"Some of these men have lain on the field all week,"* came the echo of Travis's voice. Could any of those in this vast field of slaughter even still live and breathe? Yet she had to search.

She tried to run, but puddles of red dragged at her feet. *"You—you are responsible for this horror,"* the blood itself seemed to say. *"Were it not for you, for the stubbornness of the Southern race, none of this would have been needed."*

"No!" she cried out, aloud. "This is my home! I had nothing to do with it—no decision was ever mine to make. It was the men who decided. Who said that they needed to go, regardless of what we womenfolk wanted."

She stared about, seeing now how blue and gray lay heaped together. The ruination of an entire nation riven in two. Not a breath of life stirred, and she could find no shred of anyone she knew or loved.

"God—oh God, have mercy." She fell to her knees, sobbing, as the crimson flood soaked into her skirts.

A hand, small but strong, settled on her shoulder. "Pearl Katherine. Get up, right now."

Pearl choked back her weeping. "Mama?"

Her mother stood there, clad in Pearl's best dress, clean and blue, with dark hair immaculately arranged and the cameo brooch at her throat. Matching blue eyes shone, more vivid than Pearl had ever seen them in life, then crinkled with her mama's lovely smile. "Get up, Pearl. This is not the end."

She could only gape, the aching in her breast still dug in deep.

"I know you feel like it is. But what our Lord has for you lies out there"—Mama leaned close, pointing past Pearl, and a gust of wind, sweet as honeysuckle, blew away the stench of death—"through this field, and beyond."

"But Mama—so much hurt, so much loss—"

Mama's hand slid over Pearl's head and cupped her cheek. "I know, darling. But over yonder, it'll all make sense. Our Lord is too good not to fix it all. . .when the time's ripe for it."

Pearl could only weep, again. "Mama. . ."

"Shh, now. Get up and go. It'll all be worth the journey—and the fight. I promise."

Then she was gone, leaving Pearl alone in the field of horror once more. A wail tore itself from her lips.

She awakened into the silent darkness, lungs heaving and face wet with her tears.

# CHAPTER 32

*November 25*

I ain't never seen anything like it," Clem breathed in tones of awe from his place beside Josh at the fortifications, for their second day in a row. "Look at that—all that blue arrayed for battle. Man alive! If I were born a Unionist, I'd be glad to be out there amongst 'em."

Josh nudged him. "Watch how much you admit, even here," he murmured.

"Oh." The youth went crimson. "I forget."

The irony of it, the Rebel boy longing to be out there with Federals, while Josh wanted nothing more than to be back enjoying the hospitality of said boy's Confederate family.

But especially the company of a particular Rebel girl.

*"Please. . .stay."*

Could such a thing even be possible? Could a son of the Union and a daughter of the Confederacy find common ground enough—peace enough—to make a union of their own? The question had circled endlessly in his thoughts through the past day and two nights.

The outcome of the fight brewing there before them would decide it, no doubt.

*Most gracious God, please answer us in this. You know how I long to hold Pearl again. I know it was no chance circumstance that put the two of us together. But You—You must be the One who makes a way for it to come of anything. I am completely powerless here.*

Perhaps. . .perhaps that was precisely where the Almighty wanted him.

He'd thought the day before had worn away without end. Today was even worse. As the sound of battle echoed across from Missionary Ridge to Lookout Mountain and back again, the troops arrayed in the valley between grew more restless, even to Josh's unaided eye.

Out on the field, the Fourteenth Corps were given the order to move ahead—take the trenches rimming the lower edge of the ridge. Josh leaned out over the log-lined edge of the breastworks, though he knew he should stay down. Thomas's men were a sight to see—and well he remembered their valiant stand just two months past.

Beside him, Clem hung over the top of the fortification as well. "So that's—"

"Old Pap Thomas. The one you heard the others tell how he held Missionary Ridge during the Battle of Chickamauga back in September."

Josh pointed out the others as he recognized their flags. Another man came up and filled the gaps where he needed them.

While they were explaining, and discussing the lines, something almost beyond credibility happened. The forward line of Federals not only broke through the entrenchments at the foot of the ridge, but in ones, in twos and threes, in clusters of men, they began pushing farther up the ridge.

A great collective gasp and outcry went up from not only the men watching at the breastworks but all around the rim of the valley.

"Who did that?" someone exclaimed.

"I dunno! I never saw any signal go out from Grant, across the valley, for them to take more than the entrenchment!"

But the blue, in wave after wave, pushed straight up Mission Ridge. Gray and brown began to break and run in the face of that relentless tide.

Clem tipped his head and scanned the ridge above, tears welling in his eyes. "I can't believe it," he muttered. "Does this mean the Confederacy is done for, Josh?"

"It's too early to say for sure," Josh murmured soberly.

He put his good arm around Clem's shoulders and held on as, amid cheers and shouts and the silent weeping of one Confederate youth, the Federals gained the ridge and swept the Rebels away.

"Pearl. Read to me, Pearl."

Pa's fretful, childish voice called out from his bedroom and tugged her from her reverie. She'd kept busy all day, stripping beds, washing linens, sweeping the entire house. The thunder of battle rumbled closer than ever and seemed to grow nearer as the afternoon wore on.

Lydia had taken the children and gone to fetch some things from her house, and Jeremiah likewise slipped away to see if he could find Clem, or at least spy out what was happening on the Confederate lines, so Pearl thought to steal a few moments to sit and do some mending.

Heaven knew there was always something in need of it.

"Pearl?"

"Coming, Pa."

Despite Jeremiah's effort to see Pa up and about yesterday, Pearl had returned from her ranging to find Pa sagging and exhausted. She'd helped Jeremiah get Pa to bed, then sometime about supper found that he'd soiled his linens. With a long, mournful look between them—it was a last, terrible indignity that they'd always hoped to avoid—they plunged into the task of cleaning and changing him. However matter-of-factly they'd been able to carry it out, Pearl had gone out back afterward, alone, and wept bitterly.

This morning, Pa had been unable to get out of bed. He'd slept most of the morning while she worked but now, obviously, wished for diversion.

She stepped into the bedroom, relieved to find the room absent of malodors. "I want to read Psalms," Pa said. "Where is that young man with the red hair who used to read for me?"

Pearl's knees nearly buckled, right then and there. "Oh Pa."

"He had a fine voice. A mighty fine voice."

She released a long breath. "Yes, he did."

"Reckon he'll be back to read for me?"

"I don't know, Pa. But I'm here. I'll read for you. Just let me fetch the Bible."

Pa snorted. "I don't know about that. You'll take hours before you come back."

She stifled another sigh. "I'm right here, Pa, getting it now," she called, dashing across the sitting room for the tome.

Settling in the chair beside his bed, she opened to the middle. "Which psalm would you like, Pa?"

"Thirty-seven," he said, eyes tightly closed.

She found the page and began to read. " 'Fret not thyself because of evildoers, neither be thou envious against the workers of iniquity. For they shall soon be cut down like the grass, and wither as the green herb. Trust in the Lord, and do good; so shalt thou dwell in the land, and verily thou shalt be fed. Delight thyself also in the Lord: and he shall give thee the desires of thine heart.' "

She stopped, the words clogging her throat. Or was it, for the hundredth time that week, more tears?

"Read," Pa said.

"How can that be?" She shouldn't question scripture, but the inquiry pushed its way out of her. "How can He promise us this?"

" 'Delight thyself also in the Lord,' " Pa said.

She almost couldn't breathe. "I—am trying, Pa."

He reached over without looking and patted her hand. "Just read, my Pearl."

" 'Commit thy way unto the Lord,' " she pushed on, " 'trust also in him; and he shall bring it to pass. And he shall bring forth thy righteousness as the light, and thy judgment as the noonday. Rest in the Lord, and wait patiently for him: fret not thyself because of him who prospereth in his way, because of the man who bringeth wicked devices to pass. Cease from anger, and forsake wrath: fret not thyself in any wise to do evil. For evildoers shall be cut off: but those that wait upon the Lord, they shall inherit the earth. For yet a little while, and the wicked shall not be: yea, thou shalt diligently consider his place, and it shall not be. But the meek shall inherit the earth; and shall delight themselves in the abundance of peace.' "

She spread her hands over the page and straightened. "Pa."

"Yes, Pearl?"

"Who is the wicked in this terrible war? Is it the Yankees? Or is it us?"

Pa sighed. "Oh, my dear daughter."

It wasn't fair of her to ask him these things, not with his mind so unclear. But again, she couldn't seem to hold back the question. Especially since Clem had voiced it as well.

Just when she was about to give up and begin reading again, Pa spoke. " 'There is none righteous, no, not one.' " He looked at her and added, " 'All our righteousnesses are as filthy rags.' "

"You should have been a preacher, Pa," Pearl said softly.

"He made us all preachers, Pearl. Even the heavens declare the glory of God."

Her fingers smoothed across the pages. She was not nearly diligent enough in her study of holy scripture. She could recognize when Pa quoted something from the words of this Book, but couldn't nearly draw that much of it from her own memory.

She should do better about that, henceforth.

"If we have not the comfort of knowing our Savior, Pearl, and doing our best each day to serve and follow Him, what do we have? Are not all equally lost, whether North or South, white or black, without knowledge of Him? We must seek to know God, and Him only. 'I determined not to know any thing among you, save Jesus Christ, and him crucified.' "

Her vision blurred with sudden tears, and she blinked them away. "So—it does not matter whether we defend our country? Whether we hold fast against the depredations of those who claim they only have our best interests at heart?"

His hand reached to hold hers again. " 'The thief cometh not, but for to steal, and to kill, and to destroy.' But you, dear Pearl"—he shook her hand for emphasis—"you 'cease from anger, and forsake wrath.' 'If thine enemy hunger—' "

" 'Feed him; if he thirst, give him drink.' " She huffed. "I did that, Pa. Faithfully."

"Then trust that your Father in heaven will reward you for it, darling one." His grip on her hand tightened for a moment, and then it loosened and he withdrew his hand. "Now. Keep reading. But this time, Psalm 27."

She turned back a few pages, cleared her throat a couple of times, and blinked so she could see. " 'The Lord is my light and my salvation; whom shall I fear? the Lord is the strength of my life; of whom shall I be afraid? When the wicked, even mine enemies and my foes, came upon me to eat up my flesh, they stumbled and fell. Though an host should encamp against me, my heart shall not fear: though war should rise against me, in this will I be confident.'"

"See? And have we not been blessed?" Pa asked. "Has the good Lord not taken care of us?"

Her throat burned. "Yes, Pa."

How had he known this would fit their situation so well? It was true, even at their hardest, whether the last several weeks or before, they'd been preserved from harm.

She went on, with more confidence. " 'One thing have I desired of the Lord, that will I seek after; that I may dwell in the house of the Lord all the days of my life, to behold the beauty of the Lord, and to enquire in his temple. For in the time of trouble he shall hide me in his pavilion: in the secret of his tabernacle shall he hide me; he shall set me up upon a rock. And now shall mine head be lifted up above mine enemies round about me: therefore will I offer in his tabernacle sacrifices of joy; I will sing, yea, I will sing praises unto the Lord. Hear, O Lord, when I cry with my voice: have mercy also upon me, and answer me. When thou saidst, Seek ye my face; my heart said unto thee, Thy face, Lord, will I seek. Hide not thy face far from me; put not thy servant away in anger: thou hast been my help; leave me not, neither forsake me, O God of my salvation. When my father and my mother forsake me, then the Lord will take me up. Teach me thy way, O Lord, and lead me in a plain path, because of mine enemies. Deliver me not over unto the will of mine enemies: for false witnesses are risen up against me, and such as breathe out cruelty. I had fainted, unless I had believed to see the goodness of the Lord in the land of the living. Wait on the Lord: be of good courage, and he shall strengthen thine heart: wait, I say, on the Lord.'"

"Wait on Him, my Pearl of great price," Pa whispered.

# CHAPTER 33

The tumult was tremendous. No other word to describe it. Josh stood at the fortifications for what must have been upward of half an hour, watching his fellow bluecoats tuck in under an increasingly uneven rain of fire and sweep up the ridge, while everyone around him cheered and hollered.

Everyone but Clem, who still leaned into Josh's side, shaking. All thought of joining the spectacle was now gone from the boy's mind, he was sure.

Crumbling Confederate ranks broke as the Federals kept going—and going. The spectacle was too incredible nearly to be believed, were they not witnessing it for themselves.

And at the top of the ridge, the blue tide did not stop.

"Bragg's headquarters is up there," Clem muttered. "Is that where they're going?"

"Most likely," Josh said, then chewed his cheek. If the Rebels retreated completely and the Federals pushed even farther. . .

A coldness gathered in the pit of his stomach. He could hardly breathe.

"Josh?"

In the blink of an eye, his decision was made. "Come on—we have to get back."

"What—how're we gonna do that?"

Josh weaved his way back through the press of soldiers, and to Clem's credit, he stayed right at Josh's heels.

"Borrow a horse, a mule, anything."

"They're all out there pulling wagons and artillery!"

"There has to be one horse somewhere in Chattanooga," Josh gritted out. "Just one."

All he could think about was getting to Pearl—before any of that battle-mad mob.

" 'And I will dwell in the house of the Lord for ever.' "

Pa was asleep again. Pearl closed the Bible, softly, and looked at him. He appeared so gray, so weary, but at peace.

Pearl wished she could likewise lie down and sleep.

She rose and set the Bible in the seat of the chair, then stretched to ease the aches across her shoulders and hips. The linens hanging outside should be dry by now, and if not, they'd still need to be brought in and hung in the attic.

Taking her basket from the kitchen worktable, she went outside. The linens were dry enough, but she was halfway through folding the second sheet before she realized that the thundering sounds of battle coming from over the ridge the past three days had largely stilled.

She stopped, clutching the sheet to her middle. The hush over the farm, over the entire hollow in the shadow of the ridge, seemed portentous. Pearl felt suddenly alone under the leaden sky.

But she was never alone. Scripture promised that. She tipped her face to the clouds then closed her eyes. *I know You see me, Lord. I know You're here, with me. Will You not yet show me good in this life? Help me to trust You with all that is to come.*

*And yes—protect Josh. And Clem, and the others.*

With a sigh, she opened her eyes and went back to folding.

"Pearl!"

She looked up, alarm bolting through her at the sight of Jeremiah running across the field—and the urgency in his tone. "What is it?"

Halfway across the yard, he stopped, leaning over with hands on his knees for breath. "Where's—Lydia and the children?"

She hadn't seen them in a few hours. "She had to fetch a few things from y'all's house."

Her brother's eyes were rimmed with white. "The—Yankees broke through Confederate lines. Our gray boys have scattered every which way, and Bragg is pulling back, toward Georgia. Yankees are in pursuit—all of 'em." He gasped a few more breaths. "Just—be ready."

As he trotted off again, she called after him. "Where are you going?"

"To find Lydia and the little ones."

She supposed it was his due to look after his own children and wife, but—to leave her here alone?

*"Though an host should encamp against me. . ."*

*Oh Lord—protect me as well!*

Snatching the rest of the linens off the line, she shoved them into the basket and lugged it back into the house. Quiet still lay thick over everything, so Pa must yet be sleeping. Pearl ran up the stairs to the attic and, from Clem's clothes chest, drew out the three revolvers she and Clem had reloaded and hidden there. One for each pocket, and one for her hands.

She came back downstairs and stood in the middle of the sitting room. *Lord. . .oh Lord.* She could find no other words.

Trembling, she went to the table and laid down the revolver then returned to the task of folding linens. Upon second thought, she stowed the revolver in the bottom of the basket.

Folding done, she set the basket in the corner of the kitchen and went to stir the pot of beans Lydia had set to simmering at the back of the stove. It wasn't as much as she'd been in the habit of cooking for the last several weeks, but it was more than she and Pa, and Jeremiah and Lydia and the children, certainly needed.

She'd just stirred and set the spoon aside when a pounding came at the door. Heart thumping in echo, she clutched her shawl around her with one hand, her skirts over a pocket with the other, and went to the door.

*"Be of good courage."*

She took a breath and opened the door. A man in a tattered butternut uniform stood there, rumpled and wild eyed. "Can you help me, ma'am?

Hide me from the Yankees, or at least give me something to eat?"

An odd calm settled over her. She should not allow the man entrance to her home, however, if she could help it. "Sit yourself down out here," she told him.

He looked uncertain until she pointed to one of the chairs still adorning the porch, then nodded. She dashed back inside the house, dished up a bowl of beans, and brought it to him.

"Thank you most kindly, ma'am," he said, finally dropping into a chair and making quick work of the beans.

While he sat there, yet another gray-clad soldier made his approach, and before half an hour had passed, she'd fed half a dozen such refugees.

It was the oddest thing, feeding Confederate troops this time, and not the Yankees she'd grown accustomed to these past weeks. It felt almost— wrong. Yet very right.

*"If thine enemy hunger. . ."*

*Well, Lord, thank You that I have the wherewithal to do so. You surely prepare a table before me in the presence of my enemies.*

"Do any of you know a Travis Bledsoe?" she suddenly thought to ask. "Sergeant of the Fifth Tennessee Cavalry?"

Most of the men shook their heads, but one looked thoughtful. "He was over away to the side of me, not too far. I didn't, however, see where he went when the Yankees took the ridge."

All looked slightly abashed at that.

"So the Confederate line was overrun?" Pearl asked.

"It was, miss. They had orders just to take the trenches at the foot of Missionary Ridge, but—they pushed all the way up to the top. We all took off. Ain't proud of it, miss, but—they's a mad lot right now. Screaming 'Chickamauga' with 'most every breath. Determined to beat it out of us that they lost two months back."

Pearl wrapped her shawl more tightly about her. Where were her former guests in all this? More specifically, Clem and Josh?

"Dear Lordy, take cover!" came the cry from one of the Confederates. "There's Yankees comin'!"

Over on the road, a handful of Yankee soldiers galloped into view, and the lingering Confederate boys scattered. For the barest moment, Pearl's heart leaped—but there were no familiar faces among the blue-coated soldiers.

*Oh Josh. . .*

But she couldn't think about that in this moment. Half the Yankees gave chase, while one—she supposed a captain or some such—dismounted and approached the porch where she stood. "Ma'am. I very much regret to inform you that we're going to burn your house."

Pearl sank into a chair. "What? Why?"

The Yankee's gaze remained stern. "For harboring Rebels, ma'am."

"But—" Neither her mind, nor her tongue, wished to cooperate for the moment. "I feed whoever comes to my door, sir! For two long months it was Yankees I cared for, in this very house—wounded men that I labored over, day and night, to preserve their lives."

The man scrubbed a hand across his unshaven jaw.

"Or do you mean to tell me you find it acceptable to repay my hospitality in this manner?"

"Ma'am," he said, "you are the enemy, plain and simple. And we have our orders."

Beckoning to one of the other men, he strode past her into the house before she could say him nay. She started to go after him, but another one of the men held her back. "My father's in there," she protested, "unwell and asleep."

Anything he would have said was preempted by one of the men inside calling out, "Captain? This man in here's dead."

It was as if the floor dropped out from under her. Pearl found herself screaming and shoving toward the door, kicking and cuffing her self-appointed guard.

"Let her go," the captain said.

She ran, scrambling, inside to Pa's bedside, where she fell to her knees. And surely enough—there was no more breath in the form that had been her father.

*"I will dwell in the house of the Lord for ever."*

# CHAPTER 34

J osh had tried not to push his poor, spavined mount any harder than he absolutely had to—it was only by severest necessity, driven by his need to get to Pearl, that he'd taken the obviously ailing wagon horse, but it was the best of the handful he'd found that had been passed over as wagon or artillery animals. And he felt guilty, riding it double with Clem on behind. When they turned the last bend before the MacFarlane house, however, and he caught sight of the cavalry mounts there in the yard and soldiers in blue in possession of those in gray, he set his heels to the horse's side and forced it to a canter.

A scream tore from the house, turning his blood to ice. Josh was off and running almost before the horse rattled to a stop in the barnyard, and though he could feel the men's stares, none moved to stop him. "Pearl!"

"*Out!*" came a shriek. "Get out of my house!"

Two blue-coated officers backed out onto the porch, followed by a feminine form wielding not one but two revolvers.

Everyone froze, as the two officers continued their retreat.

Pearl came to stand at the top of the stairs, face tearstained and flushed, hair disheveled. Her hem quivered with the tremors of her body, but both hands were absolutely steady, holding the revolvers.

*Dear Lord. . .no.*

She'd used deadly force before, without hesitation. Would Josh be able to persuade her away from it, this time?

"Pearl." He made sure to say her name clearly before edging his way through the crowd. "What's happened, Pearl?"

The captain in charge peered at him in surprise. "Do you know this woman?"

"Indeed I do. She nursed myself and several others back to health after Chickamauga."

Pearl only stood for a moment, staring at him with barely a shred of recognition in her eyes.

"Please do not fire, Pearl. It's me—Josh."

Her lips parted, breast rising and falling, but she kept the weapons trained on them all. "Josh?"

"Yes, sweetheart." He edged toward the steps. "Will you put the revolvers down? I'm sure whatever's happened, we can sort it out."

Fresh tears flooded her eyes. "Oh Josh. Pa has flown away to heaven."

An answering ache bloomed in his own chest at the news, but in the next moment, her arms sagged, and recognizing that her body was about to follow, he dived toward her, catching her in his arms.

Just like up on the ridge, that blustery day so many weeks ago.

And just like before, she fell against him, sobbing.

The revolvers clattered to the porch floor, and he kicked them out of the way, then gave his whole attention to gathering Pearl more fully against him. "I'm so sorry about your pa."

Her arms wrapped him about and tightened. "Oh Josh. You're here. You're truly here."

"I am. And I'm sorry it wasn't sooner."

She burrowed her face into his shoulder, still weeping. He glanced back at the others and found half the company, blue and gray alike, staring at them, openmouthed.

"Well." The captain looked thoroughly disgruntled. "Not just your nurse, but your sweetheart too, by the looks of it."

"She'll be my wife, if she'll have me," Josh said.

Behind them all, Clem smirked and looked away.

Pearl gave no response, but neither did she remove herself from his embrace. He smiled a little. Perhaps she simply hadn't registered the statement.

The captain sighed noisily. "She was sheltering Rebels. And we have orders to burn all houses and barns hereabouts if they aren't in use to support the Union cause."

"So, use this one to support the Union cause. I can attest that she'd already been doing so, however unwillingly at the time. Besides, wasn't there already such an arrangement with a prominent citizen over by Ross-ville, who agreed to tend Federal wounded in exchange for her house being left unmolested?"

The captain pulled off his hat and raked a hand through his hair, squinting at Josh. "Who are you?"

"Sergeant Joshua Wheeler of the First Ohio, sir. Taken prisoner of the Army of Tennessee after Chickamauga and had my wounds tended by a Reb sawbones." He lifted the partial limb and was satisfied to see respect and not a little regret in the officer's gaze. "The night before the Federals retook Lookout Mountain, a company of us made our escape, helped by Miss MacFarlane here, and her brother." He nodded toward Clem. "So I most respectfully request, sir, that you show this family all deference for their grace and hospitality." He hesitated. "Despite the fact that they've family members fighting on the Confederate side."

The officer shook his head then regarded the others thoughtfully. "We'll escort these men back as prisoners, and I'll get authorization to use this house for—well, more Federal wounded, I suppose." He eyed Pearl, still nestled in Josh's arms, but quiet now and obviously listening. "Would that be acceptable to you, Miss—did you say MacFarlane?"

After a moment's hesitation, she nodded, then lifted her head, swiping at her cheeks. "It would, sir. Thank you."

"And—my condolences on the passing of your father, miss."

She sniffled but held steady. "Thank you for that as well."

As the Federal cavalrymen rounded up the Rebels, Clem came closer. "Is it true, Pearl? About Pa?"

She nodded, shuddering against Josh. "It is." She struggled with her next words but choked out, "Could—could you go fetch Jeremiah and Lydia? I think they returned home this afternoon."

Clem nodded, his own face tight with the threat of weeping, and mounted the horse they'd ridden in on.

With a long sigh, Pearl took Josh by the hand and tugged him inside the house. "Come."

He let her lead him through the sitting room, empty and clean save for the beds still standing along the wall, and to her pa's bedroom. There, the elder Mr. MacFarlane lay, pale and gaunt but with an expression that spoke of near happiness.

"Do you see?" Pearl breathed, her voice trembling again. "The last words he heard from me were Psalm 23. 'I will dwell in the house of the Lord for ever.' He's at peace. After all he's suffered."

For lack of anything better to say, he drew her back into his arms. The weeping returned, but not with the storm of earlier.

"He asked after you," she murmured after a moment. "He wanted to know whether 'that red-haired Yankee' would return to read to him."

"Oh Pearl."

"He. . .approved of you," she went on, "or would have, if there had been time and opportunity—and understanding on his part." She swallowed. "He. . .faded so much these past few days. But today, he wanted me to read psalms to him. So I did."

Josh tucked her closer. "Is there anyone I should speak to about asking for your hand in marriage?"

She gave a little hiccup, which sounded suspiciously like a laugh. "My older brother, I suppose. But—perhaps you might start with—me."

A grin pulled at his mouth as he drew back to look at her. Remembered abruptly to pull off his hat and comb at his hair, likely a futile effort.

Pearl's eyes brimmed with mingled hope and apprehension. Her lips trembled.

"Pearl MacFarlane," he said. "Oh, Pearl of great price. Would you—"

To his acute distress, she dissolved again into tears.

"What is it, sweetheart?"

"He—Pa—" She gulped, trying to get the words out. "That was Pa's pet name for me."

A soundless *oh* escaped him, but she put a hand out and clutched his sleeve.

"No, it's. . .all right. I don't mind. It's just. . ."

He relaxed, this time reaching to smooth back a few loose strands of her hair. "I'm glad. Because you are of very great worth to me, Rebel girl." When she regained some semblance of control, he went on. "Will you, then, do me the very great honor of becoming my own Rebel bride?"

At that, she did laugh through the tears, then leaned her forehead on his shoulder.

He realized she was slowly shaking her head, back and forth.

"How?" she said. "How can we make this work, Josh? I am—well, you know what I am. My allegiance to the Confederacy has not changed one whit, except that I long even more for all true Christian men to cease taking up arms against their brothers. But—where will we live? If the Union prevails, Southern sentiment will die hard here in Tennessee. In Georgia too, I reckon. None here would easily accept my marrying one that they consider an invader of our country. But. . .I'm afraid to come North. Would your family accept a Secessionist? Especially if your mother had her heart set on you marrying a cousin as well."

Fair questions, all. Most echoed his own thoughts. But the only reply he could summon in the moment was to tip her face up toward his and to claim those sweet lips.

The fact that she responded as if already pledged to him helped not a bit.

"You can't kiss me that way and not say yes," he said at last, his own breathing ragged.

"I know," she said mournfully.

"Can we at least agree to trust, if this is right and ordained of God Himself, that He'll make a way?"

Pearl sighed, her fingers twining through his hair and beard. Leaned her forehead against his shoulder again. She had to trust. What other choice was there? But she just couldn't say the words. Not yet.

Josh let out a long, uneven breath, and his arms loosened around her. "I'm sorry. It's all too much right now, isn't it?"

She couldn't speak, couldn't breathe. *Don't leave me,* she wanted to plead.

All she could do was take Josh's hand and lead him this time out to the kitchen, where she pulled two chairs close together and gestured for him to take one.

They sat, side to side, and once more his arms came around her. She sank against him, breathing in the scent of woodsmoke and the outdoors, and something else that was uniquely Josh. Soon enough the others would be back, and the rush of life would pick them up and fling them downstream. All she wanted was to savor the moment.

"I still can't believe you're here," she said, at last.

His lips moved against her temple. "I am."

"I suppose you have to go, soon."

A tiny shake of his head. "No. A doctor examined me but refused to put me back on duty. So there's nowhere I have to be right now, other than here. Unless—unless you want me to leave."

The terrible tightness in her breast began to ease. "No. I—" Her breath caught. "I want to trust, Josh. I do."

"God will make a way," he whispered.

She leaned closer. "I pray so."

Could that be enough for them, for now?

He pressed another kiss to her forehead. "Would you have shot me, earlier?" his voice rumbled, under her ear.

Tilting her head, she peeked up at him. "You? Never. The others? Possibly."

He laughed and shook his head. "I should not find that so amusing, but I do."

An answering smile came to her own lips, in spite of herself. "I have a great-aunt who fed her future husband at gunpoint, the first time they met."

Josh straightened enough to look at her. "What?"

"Yes. It's true."

Another laugh. "Mm, so I should expect more of this sort of behavior from you?"

"Likely so. I am not, after all, a lady of genteel breeding. I'm told my grandparents were quite wild, as well, having both suffered captivity with the Shawnee."

She loved the sound of his chuckle, under her cheek.

"Well," he said, "I suppose that's some proof that we should suit very well. Our family is fond of whispering about how my grandpa Sam, during his wagonmaster days before the American Revolution, doubled as a masked vigilante—with a whip. My grandma fell in love with him before she found out he was someone she already knew."

It was Pearl's turn to sit up and stare. "A *whip*?"

"Yes, a long bullwhip. He died when I was very young, but I remember how good he was with it, right up until the end. I used to practice for hours and never could match what I saw him do." Josh smiled. "I should probably give it another try." His gaze fell. "Once I get back home. If I get back home."

A shadow crossed his face. Pearl reached up to touch his cheek again, and his eyes came back to hers.

"Pearl. Please—I want only you—"

She put her lips to his for a moment to silence him. That dratted tightness had returned to her throat, but saying the words at last felt right. "You'll get back home," she whispered. "And I would be honored to go with you, when that time comes, if God makes a way."

The dark eyes widened, his lips parting a moment before he swooped in and kissed her, at once tender and desperate.

Mercy, but right or wrong, hopeless or not, she did want to be his wife.

And she wasn't sure she could get enough of his kisses.

# EPILOGUE

*Two months later*

Pearl smoothed out the skirts of the blue dress, held wide by her corded petticoat, and adjusted the cameo and collar at her throat. After all this time, she could not help but think of Mama and that dream.

*"What our Lord has for you lies out there."*

She smiled, closed her eyes for a moment, then met her own gaze in the oak-framed glass hanging on the wall.

The Lord had made a way so far, after all.

Jeremiah, Lydia, and the children had returned to the house and helped wash and dress Pa's body, and they'd all seen to his burying. Reverend Mason had conducted the burial—a simple, private affair, with the entire countryside in mourning over Chattanooga's final fall to the Union, as the entire Confederate army retreated into Georgia. Josh stayed long enough to stand by Pearl's side through all of it, and then, having if not Jeremiah's express permission to marry Pearl, at least without her brother forbidding it, he returned to the Federal camps to see what could be arranged. And to Pearl's astonishment, Josh had been granted a transfer to a regiment delegated to stay and keep the garrison at Chattanooga, at least through the winter, with promise of a month-long leave beginning in January. They would use that time to travel to Ohio as man and wife, for Pearl to meet his family.

Jeremiah had questioned Pearl hard about it, despite his former encouragement. "And what about Travis's proposal?" he'd finished.

That had given Pearl pause. "I refused him once already," she said. But nevertheless, when Portius returned with the distressing news that Travis had been taken prisoner and shipped out to some Yankee prison to the north but that Portius intended to find him and see to his welfare, Pearl sent along the message that she wished him well and would pray daily for his health and safety, but her heart had found its true home in a certain fiery-haired Yankee.

Because for better or worse—as she was about to vow, in spoken words—she knew that wherever Josh was, that was where she wanted to be, whether North or South or, as they'd been discussing more recently, out West once the war came to a close.

Or sooner, if the opportunity arose.

She and Clem and Jeremiah were still discussing what best to do with the farm, whether to sell or have Clem stay to work it. Jeremiah and Lydia were feeling the tug west as well. Pearl was inclined to recommend that they do whatever was necessary for them to live peaceably as man and wife in truth.

And that likely would never happen, here in southern Tennessee. Although Pearl had done her best to see that they were given at least a beginning.

A knock came on the door of what was once more her own bedroom. Lydia slipped inside and gave Pearl an approving smile. "It's time."

Pearl caught her breath, trying vainly to steady her suddenly racing pulse. *What our Lord has for you lies out there.* Or more properly, who the Lord had for her, and doubtless he was not only standing, but pacing.

"Come now," Lydia said, her voice cajoling. "No more delay. Belonging to one man can be a very sweet thing." Her teeth flashed white, the golden eyes sparkling.

"Even when that one man is my most difficult brother?" Pearl teased in return, despite her furious blush.

But Lydia just grinned all the more and held the door for Pearl.

She stepped through to the sitting room, hands knotted in her shawl, that beautiful Oriental piece Pa had paid a dear sum for years ago for Mama. And across the room, Josh turned, his neatly combed hair and beard so vivid in the gray of the misty day that he seemed to light the entire room on his own. Warm brown eyes met hers, widening, then crinkling in his own grin. He reached out his hand, and she crossed to him.

"Well then." Reverend Mason cleared his throat. "Shall we begin?"

Jeremiah and Lydia stepped up beside her, similarly clasping hands. Pearl had bargained with the minister—threatened, more like—for his grudging agreement to read the marriage vows over her brother and Lydia at the same time he performed the service for her and Josh. To say the man was not happy about any of it was a sore understatement. But he also knew their family well enough to see that neither she nor Jeremiah would be swayed, and the prospect of Pearl traveling with a man not yet her husband and thus living in apparent sin, as he considered her brother had these past years, was enough to sway him. Not that Pearl would have necessarily followed through, although their status among neighbors had suffered enough already, she wasn't sure she'd have minded.

And all she wanted, at this point, was to follow Josh wherever he might lead—and someday to where North and South did not matter.

# Historical Note

I've often commented that history itself is too complex, too nuanced, for a novelist to do more than offer a snapshot, or maybe a series of snapshots, of any particular time period. The body of information available on the American Civil War is so vast that even if I'd been able to research nonstop from the moment I first learned I'd likely be writing this story, I wouldn't have covered it all, much less absorbed everything needed to make every detail correct. I often feel crushed under the burden of my own craving for historical accuracy. Human experience being what it is, however, perfection is, in a word, impossible.

Also, war is terrible, the Civil War particularly so in many aspects.

The statistics alone are staggering. Losses from both sides total well over 600,000, perhaps as much as 750,000, more than the number killed in all America's other wars combined. The dead and wounded in individual battles (which sometimes stretched over several days) numbered in the tens of thousands. The challenge of drawing a single story from the battles themselves, or from the overwhelming chaos and need afterward, felt so far beyond me, I despaired at times of even completing this work.

The story opens during and after the Battle of Chickamauga, which took place September 18–20, 1863, and is named for Chickamauga Creek ("River of Death" in the Cherokee tongue), flowing through the hills of northern Georgia up into the Tennessee River near Chattanooga, Tennessee. I chose this conflict because first, it garners little enough attention in works of fiction, and second, an interesting historical contradiction exists in the question of who won or who lost. It has been said that the Confederates won but thought they lost, while the Federals lost but thought they won. General Rosecrans of the Union forces had it in mind to take and hold Chattanooga, which he did (and initially without firing a shot). What he tried to do, however, was push the Confederate army, led by Braxton Bragg, southward into Georgia, only to find himself pushed back. The two armies stood at an impasse (really, a siege) for two long months, while Rosecrans was removed and General Grant put in his place. Another tactical push on the part of the Federals, referred to now as the Battles for Chattanooga, took place November 23–25, and what Rosecrans had initially attempted was actually accomplished by Grant, when Bragg withdrew his troops into Georgia.

For those interested in reading more, many excellent works are available. I would especially recommend those of David A. Powell, who has spent twenty years and more studying this particular set of battles. I wish I had discovered his work sooner! Among other things he addresses is something he refers to as the Myth of the "Cracker Line," which basically deals with the assertion that Federal troops were starving during the Siege of Chattanooga and that relief came only with Grant's arrival. Confederates had succeeded in cutting off Federal supply lines, naturally crucial for armies of any time but especially of that size, but Powell points out that even primary sources offer conflicting accounts of how dire was the situation behind Federal lines and that reports of need and starvation might have been exaggerated to add urgency to pleas for aid. I chose to be deliberately vague about this.

The situation of prisoners of war and whether exchanges and paroles were still commonly practiced at this time is also somewhat ambiguous. I learned that parole was simply a soldier being released with the promise that he would not return to fighting until being informed that he'd been formally exchanged as a prisoner. What this actually meant—whether soldiers went home or were still held elsewhere with a relative degree of liberty—is unclear. (It did seem to be halfway common for men to take advantage of parole and simply go home because they were weary of the fight, anyway.) My research tells me that most prisoner exchanges had been halted by this time because of the South's refusal to treat Negro prisoners as anything but escaped slaves, but David A. Powell documents that several groups of wounded were exchanged in the days immediately after Chickamauga. We also know that in addition to the establishment of several temporary field hospitals (usually large tents capable of holding up to a hundred men, but often nothing so grand), public buildings and private residences alike were conscripted for use as hospitals. This was provenance enough for my situation of Pearl's family being asked to host wounded prisoners, although in all honesty, the reality was far worse than I describe here. Perhaps Pearl and her family lived far enough out from everything going on to avoid the worst of it.

By all accounts, however, Confederates were still transferring Federal prisoners of war at this time to North Carolina and Virginia. Libby Prison in Richmond housed officers, while enlisted were placed in Belle Isle on the James River. Confederate wounded were often taken south into Georgia, to hospitals in Dalton and Atlanta, but the infamous Andersonville Prison wasn't established until 1864.

One particular difficulty was choosing Josh's regiment, and those of other characters. Regimental histories are unbelievably detailed—and yet, not. Trying to match where he came from with a particular regiment was possible, but then finding a regiment present at Chickamauga with a history that lined up with other elements I needed to include, or fixing exactly where he could have been on any given day during a battle? Much more difficult. So to any Chickamauga historian reading this, please know that any errors on my part are either unintended or just a bit of literary license. Likewise with describing troop movements and other tactical events during this time. Regretfully, I am not Jeff Shaara, so I leave the very detailed descriptions of military matters to others.

A particular regiment of note, however, is the Fifteenth Wisconsin, which I found mentioned among the other participants of Chickamauga. It had the distinction of being comprised mostly of Norwegian immigrants (some estimate as much as 90 percent, with the rest being Swedish, Danish, and Dutch), which earned it the nickname of the Norwegian Regiment or Scandinavian Regiment. Many of these farmers and tradesmen from northern Wisconsin spoke very little English but were full of pride to be able to fight on behalf of their adopted country. My character of Berndt Thorsson is a tribute not only to these men but also to the many residents of my current home state, which is so strongly Norwegian you can still hear the Scandinavian lilt in the local accents of North Dakota and Minnesota.

One pre-reader asked about my mention of signals during the battles of Chattanooga. An entire chapter of *Hardtack and Coffee* by John D. Billings is devoted to describing the use of flags and torches to signal across distance during the Civil War. Both Federal and Confederate used a system developed by Albert J. Myer, who entered the army in 1854 as an assistant surgeon but became the first Chief Signal Officer. Later, the armies of both sides developed their own Signal Corps. I haven't, however, researched these methods of communication in any depth beyond being aware that they existed.

Amputations during the Civil War—yes, they seem just as bad as all the rumors say, although lack of anesthetic was possibly more the exception than is often portrayed. One source insists that anesthesia, usually chloroform, was used in every case possible, that the screams heard were more likely the soldier receiving the news that he was about to lose a member. Cases do exist of men forcibly extricating themselves from the surgery setting and doggedly treating the wound on their own—and saving said members. Having seen sketches of minié ball damage, however, I think I can safely say there would have been no saving Josh's hand.

And speaking of minié balls—Civil War weaponry is far more varied than that of the American Revolution but just as interesting, as the introduction of breech-loading rifles (as opposed to muzzleloaders) and repeaters and revolvers came into play. I hope I haven't unduly bored my readers by dipping into just a fraction of what I learned in that area. It is possible that, as a merchant's son, Josh could have afforded a Henry rifle and likely would have deeply mourned its loss.

My fictional MacFarlane family is of no relation to the real-life McFarlands of Rossville, Georgia, for whom a local mountain gap is named. Lucy Ann McFarland, wife of Xzanders G. McFarland, is the prominent citizen I refer to, who agreed to house and care for Federal wounded in exchange for the house remaining unburnt. My MacFarlanes first appeared in a Revolutionary War novel that is yet unpublished, and Pearl is their great-granddaughter, as well as the granddaughter of Kate and Thomas from *The Cumberland Bride*. If Josh's last name seems familiar, it is his grandfather and great-uncle who appear in my novellas *The*

*Highwayman* and *The Counterfeit Tory*.

I often draw, however, from real-life families for patterns of history in my stories, and the Bledsoe family of Tennessee, Kentucky, and later Missouri were indeed based in fact. Pearl and her brothers and cousin Travis are related fictionally to real-life Bledsoe brothers Anthony, Isaac, Abraham, and Loving—two of whom appear as characters in my novella *Defending Truth*. Yes, I may like borrowing from real history a little too liberally—but the name stood out to me as being in common with a fellow homeschooling family back in South Carolina—who also are likely related, although I haven't taken the time to trace the connections.

Another character inspired by real life is that of Johnny, for whom Pearl dictated a letter home. In *The Chickamauga Campaign: Barren Victory*, David A. Powell tells of a young soldier from Dekalb, Illinois, who died of wounds sustained in the Battle of Chickamauga, and of his letters home, expressing both sadness but hope of eternity. History is full of such nuggets of individual drama, and it is the personal stories such as these that push me to write as real and vividly as I possibly can.

My reader might ask if there's any provenance for the relationship between Jeremiah and Lydia. One Southern history source tells me it was unheard of for the son of a well-respected white family, in this region, at this time, to live openly with a woman of color, even or possibly especially a light-skinned one. I knew from my research that legal marriage would be impossible, no matter what people might wish, and that societal pressure (often in the form of acts of violence) would not allow a woman of color to live alone under such an arrangement, official or otherwise. I also know, however, of at least two cases where a white man honored a commitment to a black woman, spoken or not, by providing for her and her children and, in at least one of these cases, remaining faithful to that woman by never marrying anyone else. Of course, maybe only the rich and famous could get by with this—the first was a member of the wealthy Ball family, planters in the Charleston, South Carolina, area (*Slaves in the Family* by Edward Ball), and the second is Jubal Early, an officer of the Confederacy (drawn from a complaint within a letter from another Confederate officer to his wife—at the time of this writing I cannot find the source, having lost the bulk of my research links to a recent computer crash).

So, this is why Pearl offers the explanation of Lydia being Jeremiah's "Creole housekeeper." Could Jeremiah and Lydia have gotten by with being man and wife, if they kept things quiet? Possibly, but most likely not. And the relationship might seem too convenient for some, and too politically correct, but—in the context of this story, it felt right.

Likewise with Portius. Despite the debates, evidence exists of black men fighting in support of the South. Lee, in fact, argued for arming black men for the Confederacy in exchange for their freedom after the war, and this plan was finally agreed to in early 1865—but too late to make a difference for the Confederacy. A similar event occurred eighty-five years earlier when John Laurens begged South Carolina planters to arm their slaves in defense of Charleston—and then as the planters dragged their feet, British troops took the city and occupied it for a year and a half. The delay occurred because too many feared a repeat of the revolt in Haiti, where white men, women, and children were indiscriminately killed, no matter their support or lack thereof for abolition.

So why would a black man support the Confederacy? Or give his loyalty to a man from a slaveholding family? Many former slaves stayed on as hired labor for their former owners, depending upon what sort of relationship they had beforehand—and not every slaveholder abused his position, although it was arguably too easy to do so. Much abuse and ridicule, however, occurred at Yankee hands toward enslaved folk taking refuge with the Federal army and elsewhere. Many Federal soldiers made it clear that although they took up arms to preserve the Union, they really cared nothing for black people. Some were afraid of job scarcity. Some did believe that dark skin equated with inferiority in intellect or spiritual worth, which is the true definition of bigotry from any side. So it isn't at all implausible that Portius could have suffered at the hands of Federals, or that Travis intervened, and thus a strong mutual respect and loyalty was born as a result. People do tend to respond with respect and loyalty to someone who extends the same to them.

Lastly, was the Civil War about slavery? That seems to be the question on everyone's mind. My answer? Well, yes. Even the cry of "states' rights" seems, to our modern eye, to be mostly, "The right to do what? Spread slavery, of course." But did the people of that time perceive it as such? In many cases, no. In some cases, most emphatically no. The reasons are far too complex to properly explore in a novel, although I've tried to offer at least a glimpse, especially of things I have no memory of hearing before my research for this story. And 150 years later, the debates are still raging on....

Are moderns able to be objective about the issues of our own time? For the most part, certainly not.

I did find it fascinating that Lincoln is quoted in his early career as having said he felt the Negro race were inferior and would never be equal to whites. Many Southerners felt it was their Christian duty not to "lord over" the enslaved blacks but to care for them, as fellow eternal souls who found themselves in unfortunate circumstances. Some felt that God used the war to judge the South for its sin of white men continuing to hold their own flesh and blood in bondage (in the case of slave owners who had children with slave women). That was a view I hadn't encountered before. They also felt the Emancipation Proclamation was a cheap ploy to add numbers to the Federal army, since it was not enacted until midway through the war and did not completely free the slaves but essentially only gave them asylum wherever the Federals occupied, and then only in particular states. Tennessee history is particularly interesting where abolition is concerned, though, because on October 24, 1863, right in the middle of the events of this story, Governor Andrew Johnson decreed slavery at an end in the state—this after freeing his own slaves on August 8, 1863. No, I make no mention of this momentous occasion in my story because, well, there is only room for so much.

Whatever the reasons, I endeavor here to portray people in the context of their own society, and as they perceived their own times. That portrayal, I suspect, will not satisfy some of my readers. That I cannot help, because no single story will hit every reader's "sweet spot." Also, it is very difficult, if not impossible, to accurately portray beliefs and opinions of the time without seeming to condone them.

My heart aches, however, over the contradiction of Christian men on both sides—sometimes men of the same family—taking up arms against each other because they felt it violated their convictions to do otherwise, and meeting on the battlefield with the express purpose of taking each other's lives. Such a thing could have brought only grief from the heart of our Creator, could it not? Yet He, in His infinite love and power, promises to work "all things. . .together for good to them that love God, to them who are the called according to his purpose."

Even this.

# Acknowledgments

As with all stories, I could not have written this without the help of many. Thank you so much to—

Lee. . .for prayers, tears, and encouragement;

Jen. . .for your prayers, always, and strong exhortation even when I haven't always wanted to hear it;

Corrie. . .you literally kept me going! Thank you for being willing to discuss anything—even if we've already hashed it out a hundred times before;

Breanna. . .for the encouragement, for hours of heart-to-heart talks. . .and with apologies as well;

Kimberli. . .for your very kind words and encouraging comments;

Denise. . .for providing a much-needed historical and Southern perspective;

Michelle. . .a sharp eye on critique, as always, and so much more;

Ronie. . .a strong ally on the journey, regardless of where it has taken us;

Beth. . .darling friend, unfailing encourager;

Ian. . .second-born of the Barbarian Horde, for your willingness to side-track from almost anything in order to discuss history with your nerd mom;

Skyler. . .my brother, Lt. Col. USMC, Jarhead extraordinaire, for very thoughtful and informative conversation while this story was still barely an idea;

Becky and Becky. . .for making the whole publishing and editorial process a joy; and

Troy. . .for always coming back to me. ♥

Lastly, my gratitude for the work of David A. Powell, whose study of the past two decades I wish I had discovered earlier; for the online work of Richard "Shotgun" Weeks, with one of the most comprehensive online sites of all things Civil War, including very thoughtful and reasoned articles on the political history of the conflict; and the effort and expense of the many living historians and Civil War reenactors who brought the era to life for me—especially Lornia Winnen and family, and James Snow, a true Southern gentleman who many years ago gave my family a personal tour of the camps near Augusta on a cold February weekend. We have never forgotten your kindness!

# Bibliography

Abbazia, Patrick. *The Chickamauga Campaign, December 1862–November 1863*. Wieser & Wieser / Combined Books, 1988.

Price, William H. *Civil War Handbook*. L.B. Prince Co., Inc., 1961.

Billings, John D. *Hardtack and Coffee: Or the Unwritten Story of Army Life*. 1887.

Chadwick, Bruce, ed. *Brother Against Brother: The Lost Civil War Diary of Lt. Edmund Halsey*. New York: Citadel, 1997.

Civil War Times Illustrated. *Great Battles of the Civil War*. New York: Gallery Books, 1984.

Commager, Henry Steele, ed. *Illustrated History of the Civil War*. Victoria, Canada: Promontory Press, 1978.

Fain, John N., ed. *Sanctified Trial: The Diary of Eliza Rhea Anderson Fain, a Confederate Woman in East Tennessee*. Knoxville, TN: The University of Tennessee Press, 2004.

Foote, Shelby, ed. *Chickamauga and Other Civil War Stories*. New York: Dell Publishing, 1993.

Lawless, Chuck. *The Civil War Sourcebook: A Traveler's Guide*. New York: Harmony Books, 1991.

Lewis, John H. *A Rebel in Pickett's Charge, 1860 to 1865*. 1895. tenant, Confederacy, 1895, Reprint, Big Byte Books, 2016.

McPherson, James M. *For Cause & Comrades: Why Men Fought in the Civil War*. New York: Oxford University Press, 1997.

Muhlenfeld, Elisabeth. *Mary Boykin Chesnut: A Biography*. Baton Rouge, LA: Louisiana State University Press, 1981.

Potter, William. *Beloved Bride: The Letters of Stonewall Jackson to His*

*Wife*. San Antonio, TX: Vision Forum, 2002.

Powell, David A. *Battle above the Clouds: Lifting the Siege of Chattanooga and the Battle of Lookout Mountain, October 16–November 24, 1863.* El Dorado Hills, CA: Savas Beatie, 2017.

Powell, David A. *The Chickamauga Campaign: Barren Victory: The Retreat into Chattanooga, the Confederate Pursuit, and the Aftermath of the Battle, September 21 to October 20, 1863.* El Dorado Hills, CA: Savas Beatie, 2016.

Robertson, William Glenn. *River of Death: The Chickamauga Campaign.* Vol. 1, *The Fall of Chattanooga.* Chapel Hill, NC: The University of North Carolina Press, 2018.

Symonds, Craig L. *A Battlefield Atlas of the Civil War.* Mt. Pleasant, NC: The Nautical and Aviation Publishing Company of America, 1983.

Watkins, Sam R. *"Co. Aytch," Maury Grays, First Tennessee Regiment; or, A Side Show of the Big Show.* 1872.

Williams, George F. *Bullet and Shell: The Civil War as the Soldier Saw It.* New York: Smithmark Publishers, 2000.

Transplanted to North Dakota after more than two decades in Charleston, South Carolina, **Shannon McNear** loves losing herself in local history. She's a military wife, mom of eight, mother-in-law of three, grammie of three, and a member of ACFW and RWA. Her first novella, *Defending Truth* in *A Pioneer Christmas Collection*, was a 2014 RITA® finalist. When she's not sewing, researching, or leaking story from her fingertips, she enjoys being outdoors, basking in the beauty of the northern prairies. Connect with her at www.shannonmcnear.com, or on Facebook and Goodreads.

# NEXT IN THE SERIES...

*The Blizzard Bride* (coming February 2020!)

Abigail Bracey arrives in Nebraska in January 1888 to teach school...and to execute a task for the government: to identify a student as the hidden son of a murderous counterfeiter—the man who killed her father.

Agent Dashiell Lassiter doesn't want his childhood sweetheart Abby on this dangerous job, especially when he learns the counterfeiter is now searching for his son too, and he'll destroy anyone in his way. Now Dash must follow Abby to Nebraska to protect her...if she'll let him within two feet of her. She's still angry he didn't fight to marry her six years ago, and he never told her the real reason he left her.

All Dash wants is to protect Abby, but when a horrifying blizzard sweeps over them, can Abby and Dash set aside the pain from their pasts and work together to catch a counterfeiter and protect his son—if they survive the storm?

Paperback / 978-1-64352-293-7 / $12.99

## More in the **Daughters of the Mayflower** series:

See the Series Line-Up and get Bonus Content
at www.DaughtersOfTheMayflower.com
www.barbourbooks.com